THIN ICE

THIN ICE

A MYSTERY

PAIGE SHELTON

Minotaur Books
New York

First published in the United States by Minotaur Books,
an imprint of St. Martin's Publishing Group

THIN ICE. Copyright © 2019 by Paige Shelton-Ferrell. All rights reserved. Printed in the United
States of America. For information, address St. Martin's Publishing Group,
120 Broadway, New York, NY 10271.

www.minotaurbooks.com

The Library of Congress Cataloging-in-Publication Data
is available upon request.

ISBN 978-1-250-29521-7 (hardcover)
ISBN 978-1-250-29522-4 (ebook)

Our books may be purchased in bulk for promotional, educational, or business use. Please
contact your local bookseller or the Macmillan Corporate and Premium Sales Department at
1-800-221-7945, extension 5442, or by email at MacmillanSpecialMarkets@macmillan.com.

First Edition: December 2019

10 9 8 7 6 5 4 3 2 1

For the approximately five hundred residents of Gustavus, Alaska.

*Thank you for the tours, explanations, delicious food,
medical care, wildlife and weather warnings,
and generous friendship.*

See you all again next time.

Acknowledgments

My husband, Charlie, and I had so much fun when we visited Alaska to research details for this book. Though the town of Benedict is fictional, our time in Gustavus and Juneau will forever be fondly remembered.

Thank you to everyone at the Annie Mae Lodge who not only welcomed us but made us feel at home in their beautiful (but really primitive) world. We were fortunate to make some lovely friends while we were there.

Hello and thanks to Sarah and Andy Pernick. Ready to go back?

Thanks to author Kate Carlisle, who came to the rescue when I said I needed a really perfect title. And, it took her only seconds.

Thanks to my agent, Jessica Faust, who always works hard, but this time she took it to a whole new level. I am forever grateful for her patience and persistence.

Thanks to my editor, Hannah Braaten, for everything, but this time it's for believing in this one.

Thanks to editorial assistant extraordinaire Nettie Finn; copy editor Bill Warhop; cover designer Jonathan Bush; and everyone at Minotaur. You are all magical.

My family is the definition of supportive. Thank you, Charlie and Tyler. I'm so lucky to have you both.

THIN ICE

One

The good thing about being suddenly overcome with fresh terror is that you forget everything else you were afraid of. At least temporarily.

The pilot next to me in the two-seat prop plane angled his almost toothless grin my direction and said loudly, "A little bumpy today. You'll get used to it."

I doubted that, but I was too scared to respond. Besides, we had to yell to hear each other over the engine; the headsets we both wore were merely ear protection. I swallowed hard and nodded, sure my face had turned gray, my lips thin. At least, that's how I'd once described what a sense of terror looked like when it came over one of my characters. Somewhere in the back of my mind, I was pleased that I'd nailed the description. And then the plane dipped again, my stomach following closely behind. I forgot about everything, characters included, but our plummet toward earth.

"Oh," I said with a catching breath.

The pilot, his name was Hank, laughed and then scratched his chin. "This is nothing. Like I said, you'll get used to it."

Not riding in this sort of plane ever again might be a good reason to never leave my new home. Surely, Benedict, Alaska, would suit me just fine. Everything was going to be fine. I was going to be fine there, feet on the ground, all the time. Totally fine.

We moved through a layer of gray clouds that dissipated quickly and the world beneath became exposed. I gasped at the sight, but I was sure Hank didn't hear. I was on the way to a small village, but all I could see from above was landscape so beautiful and gigantic that it stretched the edges of my very soul. Mountains, ocean, tributaries, wilderness, big puzzle pieces of geography with long borders. The small plane and our small selves were mere specks in comparison. And that was exactly what I'd wanted, what I'd searched to find—I silently reminded myself. If this expansive place didn't swallow me whole, it would hide me well.

"What's that you got there?" Hank asked as he nodded at the item on my lap.

"It's a typewriter," I said loudly as I looked at him. If he didn't hear me, he could probably read my thinned lips.

"You're sure hanging on to it tight," he said.

I hadn't noticed, but I *was* holding on to the old Olympia's boxy clip-on case for dear life. If I died and it remained intact, at least it might make a good souvenir for my agent or editor.

"You write?" he asked.

"Sometimes," I lied. In fact, I wrote a lot. As a writer, I spent most of my time typing. At least I used to. I'd brought the Olympia with the hope that I would be able to work again. I still had deadlines. I just had to figure out if I could do what I needed to do to meet them. Write. Create. Come up with *fictional* stories, thrillers. "It's a family heirloom," I lied again.

I'd bought it myself twelve years ago in a pawnshop hidden in the Missouri Ozark woods. I'd written every one of my six bestselling novels on it, but I wouldn't tell Hank about those either.

"Yeah?"

I nodded.

"Okay. Cool," he said as his eyes flitted over the c-shaped scar on the side of my head.

I'd had to take off the cap I'd put on to cover the scar so the headset would fit. The staples were gone and the hair around the scar was already growing out from the surgical shave, but the cut line was still conspicuous, without the cap at least. It would probably always be somewhat noticeable, or so my neurosurgeon had said. She'd mentioned that part after telling me that my brain hadn't been damaged badly and would recover fully; relief had overridden any vanity, but Hank's searching eyes sent a self-conscious wave through me. I pushed it away.

"Why are you coming to Benedict?" Hank asked a moment later. He didn't ask about the scar.

"I'm moving there," I said.

"Why?" He gave me a full once-over with his eyes. There was nothing lascivious about the inspection, just curiosity.

"I wanted to get away for a while."

"Mission accomplished, little lady. It's a great place. You'll love it, and it's made for people who want to get away for a while. Or forever, I suppose."

I cringed inwardly at "little lady" but sent the man currently in control of my survival another understanding but forced smile.

"Where are you staying?" he asked.

"A room at Benedict House."

It had been the pictures I'd found on the hospital's Internet of the old hotel that ultimately sold me on Benedict, Alaska. A timeworn, two-story building on the corner of the quaint, minuscule downtown, its Russian architecture was interesting; white with blue trim and topped by a golden dome. It was somehow both welcoming and regal, invulnerable, maybe fortress-like. Via Dr. Genero's computer—so no one could trace the search to me—I'd also looked at pictures of the nearby Glacier Bay and the surrounding mountains and glaciers, which had seemed big but not as big as they looked in person. However, it had been that old hotel, a place that seemed to promise safety and security, that had made my decision. As it was, I hadn't had much time to consider many options. I'd sneaked into the office with only a fifteen-minute or so window to use the computer unnoticed. I'd left the office just as a nurse walked around the corner. She'd smiled at me, her eyes flitting over the scar, which had been even more obvious two weeks ago, but she hadn't seemed curious as to why I was in that hallway, a wing with only doctors' offices, in my hospital gown and sweatpants.

"Oh, I see. What did you do to get put into Benedict House?" Hank asked.

"I don't know what you mean," I said after a pause.

He looked at me with furrowed eyebrows and a mouth agape. He said, "What do you know about Benedict House?"

"It's a Russian Orthodox Church building that was converted to a hotel, and had a room available?"

"Huh. Interesting."

I looked at him. "What's wrong with the Benedict House?"

"I didn't know they were open to *renting* out rooms." He rubbed his hand over his chin again.

"A hotel not open to renting out rooms?"

"Well." He shook his head at himself. "Not important. Hang on, we're almost there."

The plane dipped and tipped, and I held on to the typewriter even more tightly. I wished for the mysterious conversation about the Benedict House to continue if only to distract me from the impending crash.

I looked out at the landscape again and tried to breathe evenly. A couple of hours ago, I'd stepped off a bigger, normal-sized plane in Juneau and had been greeted by a cool, rainy day. However, my glimpse out of the bigger plane's window of the coastal city made me wonder if I should have chosen it over Benedict. Juneau wasn't big, but it was civilized. The flight in the smaller plane had taken us through lots of clouds, but now that we were well underneath them, I could see very little civilization.

But, again, that had been what I'd wanted.

"Where there isn't ocean, there's so much green," I said. However, my eyes scanned the ocean for the shadow or tail of a whale. The water was so clear, but, though I saw a few boats, no whales were in sight.

"What's that?" Hank asked.

I looked at him again, sure I sounded stupid, but I'd had a picture in my mind. "More green trees than I expected. It's not all glaciers, snow, and ocean."

"It's June. There's still snow on the tops of the taller mountains, and the glaciers and ocean are still there, but mostly you'll find a forest. Sitka spruce and mountain hemlock. You might have seen the glacier by Juneau, but you won't see any where we're landing. You'll have to tour the bay. You can take a boat out to see them."

I hadn't seen the glacier outside Juneau, and I wondered how I'd missed it. Below us, a wide river suddenly became the focal point, teal-ish, foamy water moving toward the sea. The natural beauty was breathtaking, unreal really. It was also fierce. Here, Mother Nature always won.

"That's the airport over yonder." Hank nodded.

I hadn't seen an airport, so I followed his line of vision past the river. A paved strip bordered an edge made of forest. An industrial-type building, not big but not too small, sat on the other side of the strip. In between the building and the strip someone stood on a tower that resembled something I'd seen in the end zone at my friend's son's high school football game: a place where a kid with a camera stood above the crowd and filmed. In fact, that tower seemed sturdier than the one I was currently looking at. This one seemed to lean precariously.

"Is that a man in a lumberjack coat, holding binoculars up to his eyes?" I said.

"Sure, that's Francis. We're looking for a checkerboard flag. That means we're aimed the right way and clear to land. The radio doesn't always work."

Even though I knew nothing about air traffic control, I didn't think that checkerboard flags were part of any official regulation for aircraft. Nevertheless, I kept my eyes on Francis and hoped for the signal. A strange relief mixed with jubilation when I saw him raise his arm and wave the flag.

"We're cleared," I said.

"Excellent!" Hank said. "Hang on."

The plane seemed to speed up toward the landing strip. Not only did I hang on to the typewriter, I pressed my feet to the floor, as if I could assist with what was sure to be a rough landing.

I closed my eyes tightly just before the wheels hit. I expected to be bumped and jarred around in the tiny cockpit, but I wasn't. The landing was smooth and though there were strong g-forces, it wasn't jarring at all. I opened my eyes.

We came to a stop right at the building, only ten or so feet away from the thick woods on our other side. The pavement wasn't in the best shape, but it looked like Hank had missed the bigger potholes. I was momentarily impressed.

"There's Gladys." Hank nodded toward the trees.

Again, I followed his line of vision. It took me a second to see what he saw; the woods were thick, dark, and shadowed, and tiny raindrops spotted the windshield.

"It's a moose," I finally said as the creature stuck its gigantic head out in between some branches.

"Yep. Gladys likes to greet the planes. If you stick around, you'll get to know her. She's friendly, but she *is* a moose, so be careful."

"What other kind of wildlife will I find around here?"

"All of it." Hank shrugged.

Okay. I couldn't look away from the moose. I was fascinated by the way she seemed to watch us closely, looking directly at me with her big, brown, intelligent eyes. She looked at Hank, at me, and then at Hank before she pulled back and became hidden in the shadows.

I'd never seen a moose in person before. I didn't know what "all of the wildlife" meant, other than moose and bear hungry for salmon swimming upstream to spawn. I'd seen the pictures, of course. I'd only been here a few moments, but I already knew that pictures couldn't do this place justice: this land colored outside the lines of anything I'd ever known or imagined. I was ill prepared. This world was different than my world, very different. And once again I reminded myself: that's what I'd wanted. Mission accomplished, little lady. And, I wasn't as scared of Alaska as I was of the reason I'd run to it.

Hank drove the plane, steering it in a tight right turn, still missing the bigger ruts and cracks in the landing strip, and stopped not far from the tower as Francis climbed down it. The pilot helped me deplane with my typewriter, and the one backpack I'd brought. I grabbed the Cubs cap from my pack and put it on quickly. My knees were slightly wobbly, but they'd stabilize. I'd worn a thin windbreaker with only a T-shirt underneath. It was cool and windy, the rain light with the promise it could get heavier any minute. We'd landed under thin clouds but I could see darker ones headed our way.

"How were the winds?" Francis greeted us. He'd stuck the checkerboard flag into his back pocket.

"Not bad at all," Hank said.

I couldn't chime in with my less positive report even if I'd wanted to. I was struck momentarily silent and breathless—my throat tightened as my eyes landed on Francis's jacket. Lumberjack; red-and-black plaid. It was a common coat, particularly here, I'd bet. I'd seen Francis on the tower and hadn't made the connection, but now I did. Or something inside me did. The man who'd kidnapped me, Levi Brooks, had worn the same sort of coat. I could suddenly feel its rough texture as he'd grabbed me around my neck. Until that moment, I hadn't remembered him grabbing me that way. I could suddenly smell his sourness in my nose and at the back of my throat, the rank inside his van, putrid and raw. Inwardly, I shook myself and cleared my throat. The memories were coming back, bit by bit, but now wasn't the time. I had to stay in control.

"You guys are twins," I said after I blinked myself out of the strange, hopefully passing stupor and looked back and forth between them. They were probably in their late sixties with matching unruly gray hair and friendly brown eyes. One of them parted his hair on the right, the other on the left, and Francis had more teeth than his brother.

"Yes, ma'am, Francis Harvington." He extended his hand and his eyebrows came together over curious eyes.

I took the typewriter from Hank and balanced it on a hip as I extended a hand. "Beth Rivers. Pleased to meet you." My fingers had gone cold, but I hoped Francis would think it was the weather. Were my fingers trembling? I couldn't tell.

"Yeah, you too," Francis said, not letting go of my hand yet. "You okay?"

"Sure, just getting my land legs," I said with a too-tight smile.

He let go and he and Hank shared a quick look before he turned back to me. "All right. Well, welcome to Benedict. We've got someone coming to take you into town, but he's not here yet. Want to step inside and have a cup of coffee, dry off a little?" He nodded toward the building on the other side of the tower. It reminded me of a metallic, giant-sized backyard shed. There were no other planes in sight.

"Love to. Thanks," I said.

Though the journey had been fraught with and inaugurated by despair and fear, I was here. I'd made it to Alaska, a part that wasn't easy to get to. I was finally safe, or at least temporarily safer. The relief that suddenly washed through me was surprising and tears pushed at the back of my eyes. I blinked and sniffed and avoided eye contact for a moment while I gathered my scattered emotions. I was glad for the rain.

I knew I was keeping it together by only the thinnest of threads, but that was better than not keeping it together at all. One step at a time. One foot in front of the other. I could do this.

"Here, I got that." Francis took the typewriter and turned toward the building. He tried to take the backpack too, but I slung it over my shoulder as I looked away from his eyes and toward the forest, so dark and thick. I wondered how Gladys made her way through the tight maze of trees.

Hank and Francis shared another look before Hank excused himself to attend to the plane. I followed Francis and cleared away the tears. I took in the surrounding area as we made our way, but all I could see were the landing strip, the airport building, and the woods. No other people were boarding or deplaning—in fact, there were no other planes. The rainy weather was frigid like nothing I'd ever experienced in June before, but it was warm inside the building.

It wasn't fancy, with a baggage check counter to the right and a small lunch counter to the left, where several people sat around tables and looked at their laptops. Francis must have noticed my curiosity.

"The only places we have any good Internet are here and the library. The library closes at noon for an hour. Everyone clears out there and will head back over when they reopen. The bagel sandwiches here are good. Cheap too."

I nodded. Good Internet in only two spots? Benedict was getting better and better.

Francis led us past the luggage desk toward an office and what seemed to be a luggage storage as well as one of the largest freezers I'd ever seen. Either he noticed my curiosity again, or he was used to giving the tour.

"For the fish," he said. "We get lots of fisher folks here. They get their fish processed—you know, filleted and frozen—down with Pip, and then we hold the stuff in our freezer until they leave town."

Again, I nodded as I followed him into the office. He motioned for me to take a seat as he set the typewriter on the end of the tidy desk.

A potbellied stove took up the corner, its large round flue stuck up through the ceiling. One wall was made of bookshelves packed with what looked like official airport or flying notebooks.

He handed me a towel. "Donner, your ride, should be along shortly."

"Who scheduled my ride?" I asked as I used the towel on my hands and face. I hadn't had enough time to do more than call the hotel, reserve the room, and book my flight. "The hotel?"

Francis shrugged. "Guess I don't know the details." He sent me a quick smile as he crouched and opened the door to the stove. He poked at the burning wood pieces inside. "None of my business, of course."

"Thanks," I said, not quite understanding what he meant.

Francis closed the stove door, stood, and wiped his hands on his jeans before he moved to the coffeepot. "No other bags?"

"This is it," I said.

He looked at me expectantly, but I didn't say more. The backpack contained what I needed to work, a few toiletries, a couple of shirts, and five pairs of underwear, all of which I'd purchased with cash at the hospital gift store. My mom had gone to my house and gathered the typewriter, my laptop, and the portable scanner that put my typewriter-written words into a format my publisher preferred. Mom had brought the items to the hospital and hadn't asked me why I wanted them. She would have done whatever I'd asked, without needing to understand why. Millicent Rivers and I had lived that sort of life since I was seven years old—unpredictable and on the fly. Our mother/daughter silent communication was based on the simplest of simple: trust. I suddenly missed her. I would see her again. I wasn't hiding forever. Hopefully.

Francis turned and brought me a steaming mug decorated with a smiling frog. He sat down in the desk chair, but he didn't pour himself one.

"Are you from here?" I asked.

"Yep. We were born and raised. Our paps came to search for his fortune in gold. Didn't find any, but he was good with a plane. Now, Hank flies, and I'm air traffic control, as it is. We have other planes coming and going but not many."

"Bigger planes?" I asked.

Hank laughed. "Some a little bigger. Eight-seaters, but we have quite a few small in and out. Other than the ferry, and that only runs one day a week in the winter, three in the summer, there's no other way to get here."

"There's a way to get here by boat?" I hadn't managed to discover that in my hurried research.

"Sure, ferry from Juneau. Cruise ships pass by but they don't stop here. There's a lot of the year that no one comes or goes much. Can't because of the weather."

I was glad that access to the area was at least limited some of the year; okay, I'd done my speedy research fairly well, if not perfectly. "Good."

"You're used to living away from civilization, then?"

"No, I've lived in Denver, Colorado, all my life. This will be my first time . . . away." Another lie. In fact, I'd lived in Milton, a small Missouri Ozark town, and then St. Louis when my books began to sell, all my life; nothing like Denver, so all the better.

Francis's eyebrows came together and he bit his lip. "I see. Well, you'll get used to it here, and hopefully you won't have to stay long."

"I'm looking forward to being here."

He sent me a quick sympathetic smile. "Okay. Might as well have a good attitude, I guess." He leaned forward in the chair and put his elbows on his knees. "You kill someone or something?"

"No!" I said, wobbling the coffee inside the frog mug I'd balanced on my leg. "I just needed to get away from it all."

He nodded as if to tell me he knew better. "Well, you are going to Benedict House, though it's been some time since we had an accused killer in town, and that was for self-defense. Most of them are nonviolent offenders and most are from Anchorage. I just wondered."

"I . . . I guess I don't understand. Killers at Benedict House?"

Francis looked at me a long beat and then rubbed his chin just like his brother had. "Uh-oh. Damn that Viola, she didn't tell you, did she? She just took your money and didn't tell you anything. She's been told to shape up, but she's a greedy one, that woman. But . . . oh boy, I bet there's a big misunderstanding."

The pieces were there, but I hoped I was putting them together incorrectly. I needed to hear the words.

"Please tell me, what is Benedict House?" I said.

"It's a halfway house. For women only though."

"Not sure that makes it better." I thought a minute. "Actually, yeah, that does make it a little better. However, I'm not staying at a halfway house. I'll just go someplace else."

"You might be able to find a place. We have a few summer lodges and some cabins for rent, but it's June and most things are taken. The fishing is pretty good around here. Whale watching, river running, and Glacier Bay National Park right over there." He nodded. "I'm not sure you'll find anything quickly. Other folks not convicted of crimes have stayed at Benedict House without incident, though it's only been for a night or two, and when they were stuck here with no other options. How long did you reserve a room for?"

I swallowed hard the irony that I, victim in ways I couldn't have imagined before three weeks ago, had been mistaken for a criminal, even a nonviolent one. I thought about my friends and former co-workers at the Milton, Missouri, police department. Before my books took off, I'd been their secretary, their dispatch, and in an unlikely turn of events, their math whiz. They'd get a good country-police-force laugh at this one. There was also a time I would have been excited to immerse myself into some research for a book to be set at a halfway house. Not so much after the last three weeks, though. I held back a sardonic laugh. "I thought two months would be okay."

Francis smiled, with more pity this time. "Well, something might open up by then."

"Great."

The only person who knew where I'd gone was the lead investigator on my case. Detective Majors swore she would find Levi Brooks and put him behind bars, and she swore she would keep the place I was running away to a secret. She'd been the one to take me to the airport directly from the hospital, all the while noting she was against my self-discharge. She'd been surprised by everything I had planned while recovering from the brain surgery needed to clear a subdural hematoma and the various cuts, scrapes, and bruises that had come with me flinging myself out of Levi's van when the brief and fleeting opportunity had presented itself. At least that's how I sort of remembered it happening. I still wasn't one hundred percent clear on the sequence of events.

I *had* reserved a room with someone named Viola. Using a credit gift card I bought with cash at the gift shop, and calling the phone number using a hospital switchboard phone, from a room that wasn't mine. I hadn't had to use an alias. Even Levi thought my real name was Elizabeth Fairchild, not Beth Rivers. Credit for that went to my mom suggesting the idea of a pen name when I submitted my first book to publishers four years into my secretarial career, ten years ago. She thought it would give me some separation from my day job and any level of celebrity I might achieve. She'd predicted my writing would make me, or at least my books, famous. She'd been right.

But neither of us had predicted that someone like Levi Brooks would uproot my life.

Mom had wanted me to choose a pen name for another reason too. When my father disappeared when I was seven, my mother's life had turned upside down and inside out. Mine had too, but she'd become obsessed, still was. We still didn't know what had happened to my dad, but Mom had wanted the success she knew I was going to have to be separate from him, wherever he or his body was.

For now, I'd be me, just Beth Rivers, though no one in Benedict would ever know I was also Elizabeth Fairchild, the name even the media had used to tell my story.

And, I'd find another place to stay, eventually. Hopefully quickly. "You said nonviolent, right?"

"Yes, ma'am. Theft, mostly. Fraud. So, watch your stuff." He lifted his eyebrows.

"Right." I took a sip of the strong coffee.

The rumble of a loud engine reached us inside the small building.

"Sounds like Donner's truck," Francis said.

He stood and sent me a long look. He grabbed a piece of paper and a pen. "Here, here's my number. You don't know me or my brother, but if the Benedict House is just too much to deal with, we do have an extra room or two. Call me, or just tell someone to direct you to the Harvington place. You're welcome to stay there."

I took the note after too long a pause and said, "Thank you."

Before I'd been stalked and kidnapped, I would have thought the gesture kind, sweet. I remembered those sentiments, even as a reactive panic started to tighten my throat.

"Oh, please don't be worried," Francis said. "This is just the way we are. Friendships and trust are formed fast in Alaska. We have to. Mother Nature is brutal out here. It's okay though, I understand your concern. Ask around about us. We're harmless."

A thin layer of perspiration had broken out above my lip. "Thank you, Francis. That's extremely kind. I'm not worried at all. I'm touched. I'm a little thrown by the fact that I've reserved a room in a halfway house, but I'm truly honored by your invitation."

He inspected me a long moment. Clearly, he didn't believe that set of lies. Nevertheless, he nodded. "Alrighty. Let's get you to Donner's truck. He's an impatient one, and I'm afraid he wasn't expecting to drive anyone around today, at least according to the string of colorful words he used when he called me to let me know. Try to ignore his bad humor."

Francis grabbed the typewriter and moved to the door, stepping to the side for me to exit first.

I steeled myself for some bad humor and walked out to the small parking lot and back into the rain.

Two

Donner Montgomery was not in a good mood. That was easy to determine, even if all I could see of his face were his eyes. His eyebrows too, underneath the Chevy cap. His dark beard was so long and bushy that I couldn't see the frown that must have gone along with the perturbed green eyes. After Francis introduced us, Donner took the typewriter, hefting it like he was going to throw it carelessly into the space behind the passenger seat of his truck, which was a Ford, an interesting contradiction to the cap that I silently noted to myself.

"Uh, that's fragile," I said just as the Olympia was about to be flung.

His eyes transformed from perturbed to distinctly bothered before he carefully placed the Olympia in the spot behind the seat. He reached for the strap of my backpack.

"I got this," I said as I twisted my shoulder away from him.

"Hop in," he said as he turned and made his way around the back and to the driver's side.

I did as he commanded and buckled up, noticing the worn-thin fabric bench seat and the greasy stains along the gunmetal gray seat-belt strap. The inside of the truck reminded me of my grandfather's trucks when I was a little girl. Gramps had been Milton's police chief, my boss for a while, and his trucks had always been old and filled with stuff: stained, and smelling of that tinny oil scent that came more with a mechanic's life than a law enforcement officer's. Milton had seen some big crimes; it had almost become a thorough-fare for drug runners and human traffickers, but Gramps had saved the town from such a fate. He'd been a great lawman, and he'd been a tinkerer. When he wasn't saving Milton, he spent his free time in his barn, under one hood or another. I sniffed, enjoying the olfac-tory reminder.

Once he was in the truck too, Donner grumbled something in-coherent, and turned the key. The engine seemed almost as loud as the airplane's.

He wasn't friendly, but that was okay. I wasn't in the mood for small talk anyway. I took note of what he wore—a National Park Ranger jacket, faded jeans, and work boots. Was a ranger also a law enforcement officer? I thought so but didn't know for sure and I didn't want to ask. If he was a lawman I wondered if all small-town lawmen folk enjoyed tinkering under old trucks' hoods. As the heater vents sprung to life, I reminded myself that it was June in the rest of the world. A shiver moved through me and Donner angled his eyes my direction. I sat silently and hoped the ride would be brief.

"Where're you from?" he asked a few beats later as he slid an old lever that would make the warm air even warmer. At least, that was what it was supposed to do; it was hard to tell if it worked.

"Denver." I looked toward his profile. Even with the beard and the attitude, I had to admit it was an appealing profile. I forced my eyes away and wondered why I'd even noticed.

When I didn't continue, he did. "Wow. That's a long way away. What did you do to be carted to B. House?"

"Oh, no, I'm not going to Benedict House because of its . . . status. I just rented a room there. No one told me I couldn't."

He nodded and the attitude and irritation evaporated just like that. Maybe I hadn't needed to come up with a story, just let everyone assume that I was a criminal in need of rehabilitation. I wished I'd thought of it, wished I'd known what Benedict House was when I'd talked to Viola. There might have been a way to make that work.

"Dammit to hell, Viola. You just visiting, then?" he asked.

"No, I'm moving here for a year or so. I just reserved the room for a couple of months to see where to go from there. I'll have to see if I can figure out anything else sooner."

"Gril will take care of it," he said.

"Who's Gril?"

"The police chief. He's the one who sent me out to get you. He didn't explain that you . . . well, I thought I was picking up another felon."

"Police chief?" I said, red flags raising, warning bells going off in my head. "Why would he care about someone coming to town if I weren't a criminal?"

Donner thought a moment. "It's probably just that, then. Maybe Viola told him what was going on and he thought he should warn you. We don't even rank big enough to be a small town. Chief Gril knows everyone in and out of here. He didn't pass any other message on to me, but he couldn't come get you because he was called out to a crime scene."

I nodded, still wondering how Chief Gril knew about my arrival, and planning to find out as soon as possible. "What happened? What kind of crime scene?"

"One of our residents was found dead."

I swallowed hard as my heart rate sped up and sweat popped out above my lip again. The reactionary panic came on quick. Hang on. There was no reason to think a death in Benedict had anything to do with me or Levi Brooks. At least not yet, not before I even got there. Still, the panic blossomed and spread like spilled liquid.

"Murder?" I was impressed that I kept my tone even.

"Don't know the details yet, but Gril was busy."

"You have many murders in town?"

"Not many, but some. Old age, Mother Nature, and stupidity are our biggest killers. People get stupid sometimes. Bears get hungry sometimes."

"But that's not what happened this time?"

"I don't know. I'm probably speaking out of turn. Anyway, welcome to Benedict. I'm glad you're not a felon." He sent me an apologetic smile, via his eyes. Still couldn't see his mouth.

"Thanks." My gratitude was distracted.

We were silent again as he drove the truck between woods of tall spruces, and I told myself to calm down.

"We have about ten miles of paved roads," Donner said. "This one T's with one that leads down to the dock." He nodded as we came upon a couple of buildings in the trees to our right, one brick, one industrial. "Brick building is Pip's, the fish processing place. The other is the school."

"High school?"

"All the schools."

I glanced back at the building. "That's pretty small."

"Yes ma'am."

As we continued for a mile or so more, I was glad I hadn't tried to walk.

"We have some businesses downtown, but if you need a lot of groceries, you'll have to travel about a half a mile west. And when I mean a lot, I mean bulk. Suzanne Tosh opened Toshco's last year. She ferries into Juneau once a week, picks up stuff from Costco and resells it here. It's been good, but we've all been trying to figure out where to store all the paper towels."

"Never thought you'd need so many, huh?"

"Exactly."

"Are there cab services, Uber, in town?" I asked as we traveled in between more spruces, darkening the path ahead. The tunnel-like illusion made me squint.

"How much do you know about Benedict?"

I heard his question, but I couldn't respond when my eyes caught sight of something on the side of the road. After we passed it I whipped my head around to check if I'd really seen it. As I looked back over my shoulder, I couldn't spot the lone daisy I thought had been there. Had there really been a single flower by the side of the road, on the edge of the Alaska woods? Or was that just something else Levi Brooks had done to me? Was I going to see daisies where there weren't any? I gritted my teeth and turned back to face front.

"It's a small town," I said, an unwarranted determination to my words.

"Right," Donner said after a pause. "We have no cabs per se. The inns have shuttles, vans, for their guests. Not enough reliable phone or Internet access for Uber." He paused again, and I knew he sent me another glance, but I kept my eyes forward. "None of my business really, but you seem unprepared for this. No need to give me any details but I feel like I should let you know, if you don't already, this can be brutal country, a lonely place if you're used to lots of people. You have other luggage coming?"

"No. I thought I would buy what I need here."

"Okay. Town's population's about five hundred, unless it's summer, and we have visitors, tourists, but winters are long, dark, and isolated. Five hundred can feel like about five, or fewer, in the winter. You can go months without seeing neighbors, even the ones you might consider nearby."

"I understand." I knew my understanding was cursory though, made of things I'd read, movies I'd seen, bits of research I'd done. I'd never lived it. I couldn't explain how what he was describing was exactly what I wanted though, what I'd spent those precious fifteen minutes on Dr. Genero's computer looking to find. I knew I seemed unprepared. I was. But I would get up to speed.

"Keep this date in mind, August fifteenth. It can get tougher to get in and out of here after that. We call that day Freeze-Over."

"I will. Thank you."

"Not much for tourism, am I?" Donner said.

I sent him a quick smile. "I really do understand. I'll be okay."

"You're hiding from someone or something?"

"No," I said a beat too late to be the truth.

"Okay."

"What are *you* hiding from?" I asked, feeling patronized.

"Oh, I'm hiding, in a way. Most of us around here are. If we aren't hiding, we're searching, maybe just running away. You'll see."

I took in the sights again as I hugged the backpack closer but didn't ask for more details about what he was hiding from. I suddenly felt too exposed. As surreptitiously as possible I took a deep breath and tried again to calm down, make myself normal. How would I have reacted before Levi Brooks came into my life? I wouldn't have been frightened. I would have smiled, maybe laughed and told Donner that everything would be okay. I would be noticing everything around me and the way those things and people made me feel. It had become natural to be observant and acutely aware. Who knew what I might be able to add to a book someday. I liked to soak it all in. Used to, at least. I felt none of those things now. I was losing that old me, that carefree person, probably had lost her the second I opened the door and smiled at the bouquet of daisies Levi held.

"You write?" Donner changed the subject. "That's a typewriter behind the seat?"

"Letters. It's a family heirloom. I didn't want to risk shipping it."

"Smart move. Things don't travel here easily."

I cleared my throat. "I'll need to buy quite a few things, it sounds like."

Donner sent me the same up and down look Hank had. This one wasn't lascivious either, but it got under my skin more. "I'm not sure the mercantile will have the kinds of clothes you *like* to wear, but you'll need warm things and things to keep you dry. You won't be lower-forty-eight fashionable, but you can get lots of gear at the mercantile. Get in there before the last week of July though. Randy—the owner—places big orders for winter, but . . . well, the weather is unpredictable, but I'm repeating myself."

I'd never shopped for gear before. Or at a mercantile. "I can make that work."

"Has to if you don't have other things." He shrugged.

We came upon a more populated area. But only slightly more populated, and only if you included horses in the count. There were three of them, all untethered, unsaddled, and domesticated enough to ignore the truck as we approached. The woods had been mostly cleared away in the bowl-ish cut of land, but some trees, more of the same kind I'd already seen, remained. None of the pictures I'd ever looked at had done justice to size. Alaska's geography was so big that other things seemed smaller than they normally would, things like Hank's plane and Benedict's downtown.

Two streets, the one we were on and the only other paved one, I assumed, made the T; no, it was more just a corner. Benedict House took up most of the corner, but there was also a bar named "Saloon" and a restaurant named "Food" on one side of the corner. The other side held a "Mercantile" and a "Post Office." A statue of a friendly-looking bear stood in front of the whole setup.

"That's Ben the bear. He's a black bear. Brown bears, grizzlies, have humps on their backs at the shoulders. You might want to keep the difference in mind. Make noise and big movements with black bears, play dead with grizzlies."

I swallowed hard and nodded. "I thought there were a few more buildings. I looked at pictures."

"You saw old pictures, then, before the fire two years ago. Took out everything but the Benedict House. We've been rebuilding, but it's been slow. We have to barge all supplies in from Juneau, and the winter brings challenges."

"A fire? I didn't read anything about that."

Donner shrugged again. "Our news isn't front-page very often."

A surprising wave of relief rolled through me. Not front-page was ideal. "Perfect."

Donner laughed once. In my head I heard the words he didn't speak: *So, you* are *hiding.*

"I'll get you inside, but I'm sure Gril will be by later. You might as well rest in a room until then, unless you'd like to wait at Food or Saloon," he said with a wry smile to his voice.

I looked at the Benedict House. It stood out like the proverbial sore thumb, with its peeling painted white walls, blue trim, ornate metalwork around each window, and golden dome atop. The other buildings were smaller and newer, made only of straight wooden edges, reminding me of old Western storefronts more than actual stores. There was something about the Benedict House. I was drawn to it; however, I hadn't met any of its other residents.

"A room sounds great," I said.

"All right." Donner stopped the truck outside the Benedict House's front door and threw the vehicle into Park.

"Where do all the five hundred people live?" Other than the Benedict House, there were no other homes nearby; nothing that looked like apartments either.

"We live around. Lots of houses and cabins in the woods, some just on the edge of town. I have a cabin out there."

"Who do the horses belong to?"

"The Stimsons, but the horses just roam most of the time. They're friendly, and they like carrots. Brown one is Caramel, black one is Coffee, and the white one is called Cream."

"Should be easy to remember. What about the bears though? Are the horses safe?"

As if they knew I was talking about them, all three horses looked curiously our direction. Caramel lifted a top lip but then seemed to smile, Coffee snorted once, and Cream just stared at me. I wished I had a carrot to share.

"They're probably safer than the humans. They can smell a bear coming and run away before it gets there. But it's a risk. The price we all pay for living here."

He said the words as if living there was a privilege. Of course it was. You wouldn't live here unless you really wanted to, unless you thought it was the perfect place to be. Donner seemed to fit with the surroundings. He seemed so comfortable in his skin, fine with the barest of civilizations. Or was it just that it was all so new to me?

I looked to our left and was struck by a visual of a swath of ocean in between all the trees and an island on the horizon. "A beautiful view."

"It is. The Blue Spike River is over there too." He nodded to our right. "You probably saw it when you were flying in."

"I did."

"If you fish or hunt, you'll find things to do."

"I look forward to it." I'd never done either, but fishing didn't sound as awful as hunting. Maybe I'd give it a try.

"Let's get you inside, hopefully locked in a room before any of the criminals get you."

I blinked and looked at him. He didn't smile, at least not that I could see, but I wondered if he'd been joking. He was out of the truck too quickly for me to ask. I took a deep breath, got out too, and grabbed the typewriter.

Three

"You're Beth Rivers," the woman behind the counter said. She was probably in her seventies and wore no makeup, but the wrinkles that made up her face were so pleasant, it seemed like she'd put them there on purpose, drawn and shadowed them in. I couldn't see her hair. She wore an Indiana Jones hat that might have seen better days, a long time ago. I thought there might be a coffee stain on her denim jacket. Her bottom half was hidden by the counter, but I guessed she also wore jeans and boots.

"I am. Viola?"

"Yes, this is Viola." Donner looked at her sternly. "What happened to guests only in emergencies?"

She leaned forward on the counter. "It was an emergency, sweetheart. Ms. Rivers called just a few days ago. She wasn't going to find anything else on such short notice. We only have three girls right now, so that leaves six rooms open. I keep my girls on the top floor. Ms. Rivers can have this room right by the front door. She can escape easily if necessary."

My eyebrows came together.

They looked at me, and Donner shrugged yet again.

"Those are good points, Vi," he said. "But Gril won't be happy."

"Gril's never happy. It's in his job description. But he can be the one to tell our guest to leave town when she can't find anyplace else to stay. I," she stood up straight and slapped her hand to her chest, "am just being a good host."

Donner rolled his eyes as she frowned.

"You have great eyes, Donner, but I know I've told you that," Viola said.

I couldn't help but look. Had I not noticed his eyes? Oh, yes, they were green and had seemed bothered, were still bothered. Between my needing a ride and Viola's rationalizations, he was probably ready to get back to whatever he'd been doing before this errand the police chief named Gril had sent him on.

Viola looked at me, but I couldn't read her expression. Maybe curiosity, maybe she was just waiting for me to say something.

Donner said, "This room going to be okay for now, Ms. Rivers? I know Hank and Francis would be happy to have you stay with them."

"She doesn't want to stay with two old guys. Look at her. Pretty, young. Ish," Viola said.

"Perhaps two old guys would be better than criminals." Donner picked up the typewriter I'd sat on the floor.

"I've got three thieves, and none of them were armed. Shoplifters down from Anchorage, all of them. They won't even be here long, maybe gone before Freeze-Over. They're helping out around town and rehabilitating just fine." Viola looked at Donner.

The front door of the hotel slammed open and we all turned as a woman entered. She was barely five feet tall, skinny, and topped with short steely gray hair and black angry eyes. Her thick denim jacket was worn thin at the elbows and misbuttoned.

"Sorry to interrupt," she said before she turned toward one of the hallways. She hadn't meant it.

The lobby didn't disappoint. The front desk and the panels on the walls were made with cherrywood that, like Viola's hat, had seen better days, but was still beautiful and rich. The box panel behind the front desk held keys, mail, and a variety of personal items. The beige linoleum on the floor was dirty and peeled up at a few corners, but gave the place more an air of "loved well" than "worn out." A painting of two bears standing on their back legs and facing off had been hung on a side wall. I wondered if it was a paint-by-numbers creation and if it was something Viola had done.

She wasn't a small woman, but her bulk seemed strong, if not muscular. She stood even straighter as her eyes followed the other woman. I thought I glimpsed a gun holstered low at Viola's hip, mostly hidden by her jacket, as I also confirmed that she did wear jeans, but the counter was still in the way for me to get a full view.

"Willa," Viola said. "Where you been?"

Willa stopped and turned to look at Viola, her eyes now resentful but obedient. "I went for a walk. It's not check-in time yet and I didn't have to report at the park today."

Viola nodded. "But you've got dinner duty."

"I know. I'm back in time."

Viola made a big deal of looking at the watch on her wrist, despite the old windup clock perched on the counter next to her that seemed to be displaying the correct time. "So you are. Get cleaned up and get cooking."

"Yes ma'am," Willa said, the words tight and clipped. She turned and resumed her fast pace down the hallway.

Viola bit the inside of her cheek and watched the woman walk away. I watched Viola.

Body language, words spoken in certain tones—all these things meant something. I'd learned as much in that small-town police department, even as a secretary. I'd learned even more from the research for my books, but Gramps had always said there was no better way to learn something than taking a job doing it in a small town. It had been ten years since I'd worked in that office, ten years since research had taken over practical application, and my first book had hit big. And, twelve years since Gramps had died. Those voices from the past often spoke to me when I was researching or writing, loud and clear and confident in my fictional worlds, but this real-life application as I watched everybody was jarring. Willa wasn't scared of Viola, and Viola wasn't scared of anyone. Donner just wanted to be done with us all.

"She any trouble?" Donner asked Viola after Willa disappeared.

"They're all trouble at one time or another," Viola said. "But she makes me want to double-check my pocket for my wallet all the time."

Viola did exactly that, patted her back pocket. I had an illogical urge to check for mine but I didn't.

"Want me to tell Gril anything?" Donner asked.

Viola looked down the empty hallway. "Not yet. I'll let you know." She turned to me. "The stairway is at the end of that short hall. No elevator. You're welcome to join us for meals. Don't worry, I make the cooks test their food in front of us all to make sure it hasn't been poisoned."

I blinked, but, again, neither she nor Donner smiled.

"What do you think? Want to stay or go?" Donner asked.

"I'll stay. Thank you." I looked at Viola. "Key?"

"Yep. Right here. I suggest you keep your door locked at all times."

Seemed obvious. I nodded at her. I still didn't think I would be staying long. I'd find something else. Surely. I had plenty of money; didn't that usually solve these sorts of problems? Getting access to more than I'd hidden in the money belt around my waist was going to be a challenge, but I knew what to do. For now, though, I was in the middle of nowhere, living with felons, and I felt safer than I had in almost a month.

Donner sent both Viola and me hurried and distracted good-byes, and once I got Viola out of my room, I took off my cap and felt stress slither its way out of my muscles. It had been hard work, behaving normally around all those people.

My fingertips went to the side of my head and moved gently over the scar. I was behind a closed and locked door. I was far away from that other world, the place where Levi Brooks lived. Mountains, oceans, rivers, trees, bears, and a possibly armed woman were between him and me. He might find me, but not today, not right away. The death Donner spoke about didn't have anything to do with me, even if it turned out to be murder. I was safe.

Hopefully.

It was as if I could almost take a full breath, but only almost. The flashes of memory I'd been having set me on edge. Dr. Genero had mentioned that things might come back to me, but she'd never gone into much detail. Was I going to remember big things or only little things like a lumberjack coat and daisies? How distracted was I going to be? Had my rush to leave town delayed these memories, and now that I'd made my escape, what was going to happen?

I'd hope for the best, ask Dr. Genero at some point if I thought I needed to, but for now I'd have to find a way not to worry about it.

My room was a comfortable size, clean and tidy. I quickly decided that if the rest of the rooms were as nice as this one, the felons were all treated well. A brass headboard filled the space behind the full-sized bed. A colorful quilt and shams sat atop new cotton sheets and a down comforter. The wood floors weren't shiny; they were scuffed along the frequently traveled routes. A good-sized desk sat underneath a window with a view of the woods, unless I craned my neck to the right, where I could once again see that swath of ocean.

The bathroom was tiny but had a tub with a shower, a toilet, and a pedestal sink. Two wooden shelves were attached to the wall above the toilet and were the only places to store anything. Three clean towels and two new rolls of toilet paper sat on the bottom shelf. Though small, it was cozy, decorated with colorful wall tiles. Bears, moose, and puffins were painted on squares that were stuck intermittently throughout the rest of the off-white tiles. I'd have to ask but this must have been a legitimate inn at one time.

I glanced at my reflection in the old wood-framed mirror.

"Hello, stranger."

I was not yet acquainted with the person looking back. The haircut was my own, a hasty mess I'd created in the hospital bathroom, using scissors that were made for cutting off medical tape and casts. Because of the recent surgery, I couldn't put dye on my hair, but thanks to Levi Brooks, I got a color change anyway. Because of the terror he had executed so well during my kidnapping, my hair had turned white. The hospital staff had seen it happen before, but not as quickly as it had happened with me. I'd arrived at the hospital a beat-up brunette, but when I'd awakened after emergency surgery and twelve hours of drug-induced rest, something inside of me must have clicked, and caused the color to change. Dr. Genero, always trying to be positive, said that it was much more blond than old-age gray. I didn't know, and I didn't care. I looked nothing like Elizabeth Fairchild, and that was good. Beth Rivers had been born again, different than before she'd become famous.

Of course, the scar was both my most interesting and most horrific feature. It had been stapled together nicely, but Dr. Genero said the hair was sure to grow out funny around it. With her constant optimism, she'd said something like, "But cowlicks help with styling sometimes, don't they!" I hadn't responded, though I did appreciate her saving my life.

I moved out of the bathroom and grabbed my typewriter. I placed it on the desk and wished I'd brought more paper. Maybe the Mercantile carried some. I opened and turned on the laptop, and then switched on my own satellite hot spot; one that was untraceable and guaranteed to give me access to the Internet, even out in the wilds of Alaska, hopefully even under cloudy skies. It wouldn't be blazing fast, but it would be able to handle emails—without attachments, but that was okay. The hot spot had been an online purchase, something Dr. Genero hadn't even known she'd helped me with. Cash for the gift card in the gift shop and then a request to use her name for a delivery (because I would be harder to find in the hospital) got me the tech items I'd needed and the Chicago Cubs baseball cap. No one would expect someone from St. Louis to be wearing a Cubbies cap.

Once everything was fired up and running, I set up a new generic email. Only four people would know the address: Detective Majors, my agent, my editor, and my mom. I'd think about giving it to Dr. Genero. It wasn't that I didn't trust her. I did, but she was so exposed to the public that I didn't want to do anything to put her in potential harm's way. I sent similar emails to my agent and editor, keeping the notes simple. I wasn't in the hospital or in St. Louis anymore. I sent my agent, Naomi, our new code word, letting her know things were okay.

Naomi and I had come up with two code words, one to use to signify that everything was okay, one for when things looked to be headed or had already gone south.

I'd been on the phone with her when Levi Brooks had knocked on my door. She'd heard the ruckus of him taking me, and then she'd called 911. It was all too late. Levi had me gagged and in his van in what felt like seconds in my fuzzy memory, the bouquet of daisies a strange bread crumb–like trail from my door to the van, and a pattern I was remembering more and more. No wonder I thought I was seeing daisies by the side of a road in nowhere Alaska.

Naomi hadn't recovered either. She was nervous, and even though she'd said the right words to me when we'd talked last week, they'd been clipped and lined with trauma. I'd asked her if she was okay, and she'd sighed and said she would be eventually. I was glad she hadn't lied, told me she was already fine. She would be relieved I decided to hide away, disappear for a while. I could write anywhere if I could still write at all, and knowing Levi Brooks couldn't get at me easily would hopefully give us both more restful nights, and me more words.

It wasn't that I thought Levi could somehow read my emails, but I had become convinced that anything was possible, and it was always better to be careful, wary, even too much so. He'd stalked me for months, maybe years, leaving me strange gifts, appearing at places I ran errands, showing up at signings. I hadn't noticed most of those incidents as they'd happened, but I had noticed some of them, chalking them up to coincidences or the fact that we probably lived in the same neighborhood. Hindsight and the flashback memories helped me now see them for what they truly were—scenes of a stalker on the prowl.

I sent a quick note to Detective Majors, letting her know I was safe. Hopefully, she would have some good news regarding the police's search for Levi. I wasn't sure if she'd admit to her superiors that she took me to the airport or if she'd pretend she didn't know where I'd gone. She might be in trouble because of her assistance but when I'd asked her about it she'd said she'd be fine. As I sent the email, I hoped for a quick return. I could make my trip to Alaska a vacation instead of an escape if Levi was found quickly. I could be home long before Freeze-Over.

Finally, I wrote to my mom. Undeniably, her world had been rocked when I'd been so hurt and violated, but she was made of tough, steely stuff. She'd been glad I was going to be okay, but her life's motivation hadn't been altered much. Revenge and retribution had long been on her to-do list. A part of me had wondered if she'd now start looking for Levi more than trying to discover what might have happened to my father. Would Levi become her bigger obsession, or just an add-on?

My dad had disappeared, fallen off the face of the earth, it seemed, when I was seven years old. Since then Mom had been driven by one goal: find out what happened to him. I suspected he was dead. She'd come to hope he was dead; she couldn't face it if he'd chosen to leave us. Maybe it wasn't hope, maybe it was just a way to preserve her diminishing sanity.

He'd been a salesman, the kind that knocked on the doors of houses in small Missouri towns, selling cleaning supplies. Before he'd disappeared, we were just a small family living in a two-bedroom, post-WWII clapboard house in an Ozark town where my grandfather was the law. But after Dad disappeared, Mom became unhinged, according to Gramps, who raised me more than anyone else had.

I finished high school early, having skipped middle school altogether, so I'd graduated at sixteen and wanted a job. I hadn't been marked with the burden of being any sort of genius, but I'd managed school more quickly than my peers. With no desire for college and no one pushing me to make that choice, I'd happily become Gramps's secretary. I saw myself at that job forever, saw me working with Gramps and the other officers all my life. But when I was eighteen, Gramps died—his heart just stopped—ruining my forever plans. Writing took over, giving my head somewhere to go when all I kept noticing were the empty places he'd left behind. I'd worked with him for two wonderful years, and then I became a bestselling author, first book out of the chute had sold millions of copies. And the other five books since had only done better.

Mom and I had always gotten along, but ours was more a friendship, a partnership—sometimes just a trusty companionship, more than a mother-daughter loving bond. I didn't know any different, and I wasn't bothered by whatever we lacked. Gramps had more than made up for anything that might have been missing.

I didn't know quite what to say to her in an email though. I kept it simple for now.

I'm okay. I ran away, directly from the hospital. More to come. Email me if you need me. I'll text soon. Be safe.

I'd send her a text later, one that would get her to a phone she could use securely. I wasn't ready to talk to her yet. If Levi ever figured out my real name was Beth Rivers, he could track down my mother, but she'd already told me she wouldn't care.

Yeah, well, he knocks on my door I'll castrate the son of a bitch and then I'll kill him, so let's hope he finds me. Fucker'll get what he deserves.

As much as I believed her words and as much as I hoped he got what he deserved, I didn't want her to ever experience his evil. It wasn't something even the toughest person I'd ever known could handle. Some evil is otherworldly, incomprehensible, even to people who'd seen bad things. I didn't remember all the details of my time with him yet, but, yes, I remembered the pure evil of Levi Brooks. It was the only thing he was made of, and I still couldn't shake it all off me. I could still taste it in the back of my throat.

Mom had been with me every day at the hospital, until I'd discharged myself. I'd called her early and lied, telling her I was already on my way home and would call her when I got there. I hoped Detective Majors had somehow let her know I was okay.

I didn't write to anyone about the rest of it—that I was still in a daze made of leftover fear, hours of air travel, snow-covered peaks, a vast ocean, and a place so distant from the world I'd known that its downtown was made only of a corner. I didn't share how suspicious I was, how more things were coming back to me, or how relieved I felt to be so far away. I didn't mention the potential murder Donner had told me about. But these things were all running through my mind.

I really did hope I wouldn't have to hide for long.

I finished the emails and a gigantic wave of tired came over me. It was something I hadn't felt so completely for three weeks. It came with a sense that I might be able to close my eyes all the way, give in to a deep sleep without figuratively or literally keeping one eye open, or having nightmares. I turned off the equipment and crawled under the quilt. Then I got up and checked the lock and put the chair in front of the door before I returned to the bed. Then I got up one more time and packed the equipment back into the backpack. I brought the pack to the bed with me and got comfortable again.

It took less than another minute before I was out cold.

Four

hadn't meant to sneak up on them, but they were headed toward the dining room and I left my room just after they passed by.

"You are such an opportunist, Willa," a woman I hadn't met yet said. She wore clothes that didn't seem warm enough for the temperatures, but I still had only my T-shirt and windbreaker. What did I know?

"I'll tell her, Loretta," Willa said.

"If I don't give you money, you'll tell on me. Oooh, I'm so scared," the other woman, Loretta apparently, said.

"You should be. It's a parole violation," Willa said.

The two women stopped, and Loretta grabbed Willa's arm, none too gently. The kitchen was on the other side of the lobby, around a corner. They still didn't see me, I stepped backwards, hiding on the other side of the corner again, as I listened. I knew their conversation was none of my business, but I was curious, and I didn't want to let them know I was there.

"Listen to me, that's blackmail, extortion, plain and simple. Who's going to get in more trouble? Me for my petty parole violation or you, the blackmailer?" Loretta said.

A long moment later, Willa laughed. I was bothered by the confidence in that laugh.

"Chill, 'Retta. Chill," Willa said.

Loretta didn't answer, but made a sort of quick growl noise before they continued into the dining room.

I gave it another second before I moved to join them. Once around the corner, my foot kicked something that bounced off the baseboard next to the door. I crouched to gather it.

A tiger. A small plastic tiger. A kid's toy. I stood and turned around again. I hurried to the lobby and put the tiger on the corner of the front desk. I could have taken it into the dining room, but it didn't seem valuable, and I didn't want Willa and Loretta to think for a moment that I'd heard them.

Finally, I headed back to the dining room, now completely curious about my fellow Benedict Housemates.

"All right, Willa, have at it," Viola said.

She hadn't been joking, she really did have the cooks test the food first.

I did catch a look between Willa and Loretta when I came in, as if they wondered if they might have been overheard, but I acted like this was all new to me. Viola did some quick introductions and told me to sit down. I did.

I'd slept hard, dead to the world until Viola had pounded on my door announcing that breakfast was being served.

I'd sat up in the comfortable bed, confused and needing a moment to figure out where I was and how I got there. Had I really escaped to Alaska? It appeared I had. After throwing on my inadequate clothes and the baseball cap, I'd left my room to join my fellow housemates in the small dining room next to the small but modernly equipped kitchen.

There were three felons; all of them had not only come from Anchorage but they said they were originally from there too. Willa, Loretta, and Trinity. Willa now kept her words brief, and the sour expression on her face continual. She was the cook for the rest of the week and didn't have much to offer to the introductory conversation beyond yeps and nopes. Cooking duties were for breakfast and dinner. Everyone was on their own for lunch. The felons were required to attend the prepared meals, but I could make my own choices. Had Viola said I was required to be there, I would have obeyed. She was a force to be reckoned with, and another small part of me relaxed because of the power she exuded. So far, she was on my side. Something in me wanted someone else to be in charge of something; meals and a sense of protection were a good start.

I sat next to Loretta. For breakfast she had chosen the attire of a tank top and cutoff denims. It was summer after all, or so she'd stated when Viola questioned the outfit as the food was being served. She was either in her forties, or had had a rough run-up into her thirties. Lines around her pretty eyes and around her mouth were deeper than they seemed they should be. She'd put on more red lipstick for breakfast than I thought I'd worn in my entire thirty years. Her voice was big, but not quite as big as her chest. Behaving as if the contentious moment with Willa hadn't stayed with her, she'd licked her long-nail-adorned finger, given me a critical frown, and then tucked a stray piece of my hair back under the cap, ending her inspection with a smile and a hug. I liked her, even though I'd already witnessed a tougher side to her—or maybe because of it. However, I wondered if she would have taken my money if it had been in one of my pockets when she hugged me. As it was, I had to push away the urge to pat the money belt around my waist.

Trinity was the mousiest felon I'd ever seen, and I'd seen a few back in that Missouri police department. Tiny, with a sad smile that would melt even the hardest of hearts (probably not Viola's though) and small bony fingers that made me wonder how she could steal anything bigger than a stick of gum. Her skin showed signs of what

I thought was drug use, but it could just be that she had a bad complexion. She didn't behave as if she was under the influence of anything except anxiety; she seemed a little jumpy.

Willa, without the jacket she'd worn the day before, was even smaller than I'd thought. She was also in the best shape of the three parolees, with toned, muscled arms and what looked like a firm six-pack under her tight T-shirt. She had to be in her forties at least, but she must work out all the time for that shape.

She took a bite of the pancake Viola held on the plate, and then a bite from a slice of bacon. We all watched for signs of poison, though I watched everyone else too. They took this moment seriously, particularly Viola, who, in fact, did wear a gun holstered around her hips. I wondered if she'd ever had to use it.

A few moments after Willa's successful swallows, Viola startled me with a fist pound on the table and declared that it was time to eat.

The dining room was paneled in the same cherrywood as the lobby, the two round tables and four chairs institutional and stark compared to the rich walls. One chair was brought over from the other table so we all sat together, not overly crowded but with little elbow room. The pancakes and bacon were either the best I'd ever had or I was hungrier than I'd ever been. My stomach had turned into a never-ending pit.

"Take it," Viola said as she saw me eye the last pancake on the serving platter. "Willa made more. They're under the warming lamp in the kitchen, but we'll bring them over."

"It's the fresh air, sweetie pie," Loretta said. "And you slept good and hard. We knocked last night for dinner."

"You did?" I said with a mouth full of pancake. "I didn't hear a thing."

"We figured," Viola said. "Happens all the time. Not to worry."

"Yes, we did," Trinity said quietly. I had to strain, lean closer, to hear her. "You put a chair by your door. We thought you were either tired or had killed yourself."

I'd missed some excitement. "You tried to get into my room?"

"Yes," Viola said. "Just me."

The pancakes and bacon in my stomach moved to an uncomfortable position, but I told myself to remain calm. I didn't trust my reactions to know if being bothered by Viola checking if I was alive was appropriate or not.

"I understand. I'm sorry I didn't hear you knock. I was very tired," I said, too evenly, almost eerily.

Four pairs of eyes looked at me with furrowed eyebrows above. I strained a smile, but I probably just looked maniacal. I cleared my throat and took a sip of coffee, causing the others to resume eating.

"Viola told us you're from Denver. What do you do, Beth?" Loretta asked.

"I'm a consultant. I help businesses organize their file storage structures." After all, that had been my first victim's job. Fictionally speaking, of course. *37 Flights* had introduced Hailey Boston, who was attacked inside a corporate building where she was working one evening. The entire book had been one night of cat and mouse as she tried to get out of the building alive. Of course, the attack and subsequent chase had given her the chance to think about her jaded past and forgive herself for the mistakes she'd made, figure out ways to right the wrongs she'd done. If she could get free, she'd apologize to those she'd hurt, never regret anything, ever again, including the things she'd been forced to do that night.

"My goodness, that sounds boring," Loretta said.

"Loretta!" Viola rolled her eyes.

Willa and Trinity sent Loretta disapproving frowns.

"We should all be so boring," Willa added.

"It is methodical. I like tedious and methodical." I didn't mention that *Publishers Weekly* had loved the book, saying, "You'll hold your breath the whole way through."

My lies kept piling up, but they were necessary, and this one had been one I knew well. In my head, Hailey was a three-dimensional person. Taking on her career was like borrowing a sweater from a good friend. And, I wouldn't have to work too hard to remember the details.

"Whatever," Loretta said.

"You're doing that in Alaska?" Trinity asked.

"No, I do most things via email, Skype every now and then. I don't need to visit offices in person much. I've done this for so long that I can make the appropriate suggestions via a written report. Clients only have to pay for the consult, not get a personal visit from me unless they want one. They prefer it that way."

That had been poor Hailey's biggest mistake, visiting a client in person when they'd asked her to. It had been a bloody, hard-fought battle, but she'd come out alive, and mostly a better person. She'd still have some flaws to work through, but who didn't?

"Is that full-time?" Loretta asked.

I shook my head. "Not really. I can set my own hours. Sometimes I have a few customers, other times none. I've made it work and I live simply, don't need a constant income."

"Why are you here?" Willa asked. "How'd you get the scar on your head?"

I didn't know they'd seen it. I resisted an urge to rearrange the cap.

"I fell off a horse," I said. "No real brain damage but the doctors had to go in and get rid of some accumulating blood, a subdural hematoma. And I'm here because my apartment flooded." I shrugged. "I was completely displaced until the entire building is rebuilt. I read a book about Alaska not long ago, and I thought it would be fun to spend some time here. After the accident, bucket list things have become more important to me."

"Goodness, when it rains it pours." Viola's eyes held a suspicious squint. I ignored it.

"Until August?" Willa asked.

"Well, I heard I need to leave by August fifteenth if I don't want to risk getting stranded, but maybe a year here wouldn't be so bad."

"I don't want to be here a year," Loretta said. "But I don't get to decide. All of the three of us are in the same boat."

"I don't mind it," Willa said.

"I miss Anchorage, but I like the wilderness, even in the winter,"

Trinity said. Surely, she would blow away in a semi-strong winter wind.

I wanted to ask about their crimes, but not quite yet. Over some more un-poisoned meals as we all got to know each other better maybe, but not yet.

A familiar sense of camaraderie came over me. I didn't know these women and they were criminals, but I didn't immediately dislike any of them, even Willa. Until Levi Brooks, most of the criminals I'd met had had some redeeming qualities. They weren't all bad people; some just made bad choices, some were so pinned in one of life's corners that they couldn't see any other choices. I wasn't ever a cheerleader for a proven lawbreaker, but I'd always tried to understand them. Maybe that's why I could write the books I wrote.

Some criminals were bone-deep bad though. I shivered and hoped no one noticed. Maybe that's why I'd eavesdropped; it was good to get to know these criminals. Old habits, even those I'd learned by observing Gramps all those years ago, died hard.

Maybe there was a psychologist in town I could talk to.

The door to the dining room flew open and I wondered if the wind took all the doors, even the inside ones, or if forceful openings were just the way of Benedict folks.

He should have been carrying an ax—was my first thought when I saw him. Seemingly cut from the trunk of a large tree himself, his grizzled presence filled a space that hadn't seemed available before he stepped into it. He brought in scents of both summer and winter—strawberries and snow—and I wondered if he could actually see out of his grimy glasses. Like Viola, he had a gun holstered around his hip. He also wore jeans and boots, but his were much more worn than hers.

"Chief?" Viola said.

"Hey," Loretta said, sitting up straight and forcing a strained smile his direction, as if she was rehearsing for the role of teacher's pet. She wasn't going to get the part.

Willa looked down at her plate and Trinity seemed to become

more nervous, her small fingers twisting and twitching together on the table, next to her plate.

"Vi," the man said with a rich baritone. Like Donner, he had a beard, but his was gray, short, and not so thick as to cover his chapped lips. "I need to talk to our new resident."

Viola looked at me, sent me a glance like she'd been expecting this meeting, and nodded her head toward him. "Go on to my office."

The police chief seemed to know where we were supposed to go, so I just followed his wide body. He slipped off the hat he'd been wearing, exposing his short, unruly gray hair, a shade darker than his beard. Inside the office, he closed the door behind us and directed me to take one of the chairs. The room was messy with papers and notebooks everywhere. I wondered if Viola was also a writer; the mess reminded me of my own office back in St. Louis. There were only two chairs in the room. I took one and Gril sat in the one behind the desk.

I took a deep breath and let it out. I expected him to apologize for Viola's mistake of allowing me to book a room at the halfway house, and then maybe offering me help in finding another place to stay. In my mind I lined up all my lies and hoped I wouldn't have to tell him any new ones. Keep it simple, if possible.

"I'm Grilson, Gril, Samuels, Benedict police chief." He extended his hand over the desk.

"Beth Rivers." We shook.

Then he sat back and spoke quietly. "It's okay. I know who you are. I know what you've been through, Ms. Fairchild."

It wasn't my given name, but it's who I'd been for so long that it felt right to me, and fit better than Beth Rivers. I didn't know how the police chief knew who I was, or what he was going to do with that information, but it was in the next second that I became sure my reactions were off, my emotions still stirred up and going in the wrong directions because of Levi Brooks's violence.

After the chief revealed that my secrets weren't secret after all, I had a complete and uncontrollable emotional breakdown.

Five

He let me cry. I didn't wail, but I did some sobbing and sniffing. Messy stuff. But I couldn't have stopped myself if I'd wanted to. I'd cried—I'd freaked out—more than once since Levi took me, but there had always been something wary to the release, something reining it in. Yes, I'd let some of it out, but I always wondered—was Levi there watching me, peering around a tree, through a window, witnessing how deeply his damage had gone? Was I giving him more of what he wanted? Here, I felt like he hadn't caught up to me yet. I let it *all* out.

Of course, I was sure that later I would be embarrassed by my behavior in front of Gril, but for those minutes, it felt wonderful, cleansing, powerful even. Still.

"I'm sorry, Chief," I said as he handed me a tissue.

"It's okay. You've been through a lot. It's okay." His tone was matter-of-fact.

I blinked at him. If I'd made him uncomfortable, he didn't show it. He'd been stoic and still, watching me, but patiently looking away too. He'd taken off his glasses and wiped them on the flannel shirt he wore underneath his official coat, CHIEF embroidered over his heart. However, the "C" was frayed, making the word almost look like HIEF. Despite his efforts, the glasses were still grimy as they magnified his eyes.

"How did you know?" I finally asked after about ten long minutes.

"Detective Majors from St. Louis called. I thought you knew she was going to give me a heads-up."

"Oh." She hadn't mentioned to me that she was going to call anyone. She'd promised to keep my secret. Maybe she hadn't decided to make the call until after she'd dropped me off at the airport—thinking someone should know. "I . . . I'm just getting . . . If Detective Majors told me she was calling you, I didn't catch it."

"Call me Gril. Everyone does. You've been through a lot. Frankly, and in an ironic way I suppose, it's why I didn't protest when I heard you were staying at Benedict House. Viola is good with a gun, and the current residents are harmless." His eyebrow quirked, and he frowned. "I think. I would like to get you someplace else, but this is the only option. It's a good option. For now."

"Does Viola know who I am?"

"No, and I'm not telling anyone, including my small staff. It will just be you and me. And, you've done a good job. Using a pen name to write your books was wise, fortuitous probably, and you really look different than the picture on your website. Hank has already spread the news about the scar on your head, though, so what's going to be the story there?"

"Of course. Small town. I fell off a horse." My housemates hadn't *seen* the scar. They'd probably just heard about it.

While on a brief layover in Seattle, I'd seen my latest book as I'd walked past an airport gift shop, on a front display. Elizabeth Fairchild, and her long, smooth, and sophisticated brown hair, smiling back at me from the top of the display. Perfect eye makeup. Nice lip gloss. Even then, I hadn't recognized her, just as much as I hadn't recognized my reflection yesterday. She wasn't who I really was either, but now I wondered who I'd turn out to be.

"Got it." He looked at me a long moment. I had no sense that he was hesitant to ask any question he wanted to ask, but instead he paused because he didn't want me to feel interrogated. He was treading lightly. Lots of people had been doing that lately. I'd never experienced it before and it made me feel weak. I straightened my shoulders, hoping to override whatever pity I'd drawn from the crying. He finally continued. "The kidnapping and your escape were big news. After it was reported that you were going to recover, not much else was mentioned, but all the pictures they put out there . . . you still had brown hair."

I nodded. "Old publicity pictures." I hesitated and then took off the cap. "My natural color until this became my natural color. I was coherent enough to express how much I wanted to keep my condition somewhat mysterious. The police agreed. My publisher and everyone there tried to keep things quiet. In fact, we were all hoping that my optimistic diagnosis wouldn't be released to the press for a while, but it became apparent pretty quickly that I was going to recover. This color," I pointed at my head, "happened on its own. Trauma can do that sometimes, or so the doctors said."

"Huh. I guess I've heard of that. Hair going white. I didn't think it was a real thing though, just some urban myth or something. Yours looks blond, not gray."

"That's what my brain surgeon said; I thought she was only making me feel better. I don't know if it's a permanent change, but we'll see. The haircut is my own."

Gril's frown deepened. "Damn, that scar . . ."

"It's healing very well. No outside stitches. Staples removed. Everything else is on the inside. No permanent issues, though that's a complete miracle. I got surgery soon enough after the injury that I was saved from brain damage, and death, of course. A few headaches for a while." I shrugged. "But I should be fine in a month or so."

"Unbelievable. Detective Majors asked what sort of medical personnel you'd have access to. I'm afraid not much. You'll have to go to Juneau for anything extensive, or Anchorage maybe. We've got two folks in the area who might help a little, a real doctor who moved here a few years back, and a native Tlingit man who knows herbal and natural remedies. He knows his stuff, but it might not be the stuff you need. That's the best we'll be able to do for you. If you need to get to Juneau or Anchorage, you should go before winter sets in."

I put the cap back on. "I might try to get a CT scan in a month or so, but it's not required. We'll see how I feel. I might need help with someone prescribing the scan." Gril nodded as if he could get that done. "I've covered my tracks pretty well, I think, but the scar will probably always be obvious. The subdural hematoma was reported in the news, so there's a chance my kidnapper knows I had surgery on my head, but we can't be sure. I'll work on a better haircut, or a wig if necessary."

He shook his head slowly. "The news said you escaped on your own."

"I jumped out of the van . . . ," I began, but my throat tightened again. "I'm not sure how yet, or why I hadn't tried before three days into him having me. The memories of what happened, and the stalking beforehand, they're coming back but much still isn't clear. That sort of amnesia can happen with head injuries or psychological trauma. I got a twofer. I do remember a brown nineteen-seventies-ish van, but I don't remember what my kidnapper looked like. I remember his voice though, or I think I do. And, I think he'd been stalking me for years. But, I can't even be sure of that." I cleared my throat. "I also knew his name. When I became coherent, the name that came to me, without a doubt, was Levi Brooks. I've never been so sure of anything. That at least gave the police a starting point in searching for him. However, that information isn't being released either. Not yet, at least."

Gril leaned forward, his arms falling onto stacks of paper on the messy desk. "I'm so sorry."

I took a deep rattled breath and nodded.

"I think you were probably safe down there," he nodded south-ward, "and you would be protected by the police, but I understand the need to hide. You were smart to get here like you did. This is a good place to not be noticed, or maybe just to recover, give yourself some time."

"I was scared enough to try to think clearly. I covered my tracks using items in the hospital gift shop. I hope I've managed it."

"Research?" he said weakly. "I've read a couple of your books. You know a great deal about hiding and running from bad people, covering tracks. *37 Flights* scared me for days, in a good way, of course."

I was surprised the man who might have been cut from an Alas-kan spruce or maybe a glacier, instead of being born like a normal human, had read any of my books. Sure, men read my books, but this wasn't one I would picture. "Well, it's different in practice than in research, but we'll see, I guess. Frankly, Chief—Gril, I have no idea if I've done anything correctly. I just knew what I was com-pelled to do, and . . . here I am."

Gril leaned back in the chair again and inspected me another mo-ment. "Detective Majors said you're one of the smartest people she's ever met, that you have experience in law enforcement."

I laughed once. "She was trying to make me sound much better than I am. I was a secretary for my grandfather and his staff back in a small town, Milton, Missouri. Gramps was the town police chief. I was good with numbers and crime scene measurements. I was able to help with some of that is all. I didn't go to college. I'm a good secretary though, and I suppose my typing skills have helped with my writing."

"I suppose. And, well, college does not a smart person always make." Gril smiled, still with sympathy.

I cleared my throat again and sat up even straighter. "When you talked to Detective Majors, did she have any new information about the case?" My hands became icy. I was afraid of the answer to that question every time I asked it, and it always left me cold with anticipation.

The irony that I'd run to Alaska, a town in the shadow of glaciers, wasn't lost on me.

"I'm afraid there was nothing new to report. I did ask."

I nodded. Still cold.

"I'm glad you're safe, and I have an idea. Do you feel like you could come with me?" Gril asked.

"Sure," I said after I hesitated. I had a genuine fear of going with someone to a place I didn't know, even if that someone was a police officer and a decent guy who'd let me cry in front of him. I didn't think I would ever get over my new reflexive fear of strangers, but maybe that was a good thing.

"It's all right. I think you'll like it," he said.

"Where are we going?"

"Not far."

I didn't have to explain my puffy eyes and red nose to anyone. Gril and I left Viola's office and then Benedict House, stepping out into bright sunshine and cool, on the verge of cold, air without seeing anyone else. Gril handed me some sunglasses when we were inside his truck.

"It's bright right now, but it'll rain soon."

"It doesn't look like rain." I took the glasses and put them on. The inside of the truck was similar to Donner's and I was once again taken back in time. I suddenly wanted my own old truck. Or my grandfather's.

"It always rains. You can count on it. Did the sun keep you up late?"

I had to think a moment. I'd forgotten that the sun set late this time of year in this part of the world, around ten o'clock. "I was so tired. A spotlight might not have kept me up."

"Glad you got some rest." Gril pulled the truck away from the muddy curb, the engine growling like it was happy to be on its way.

I nodded. "Can I ask you a question?"

"Sure."

"The man who gave me a ride yesterday mentioned . . . was there a murder?" I said as Gril took a quick turn onto one of the unpaved roads that led toward the woods. It looked smoother than it rode. I had to brace myself for bumps. Like Hank with the plane, though, Gril seemed to instinctively know how to miss the biggest potholes.

"Oh. There was a death. Maybe suicide, maybe murder. We're investigating." He looked at me. "No, trust me, it has nothing to do with you. I didn't even connect the timing with your arrival. I'm sure there's no correlation."

"What happened?"

"One of our residents was found dead inside her cabin. It was . . . we thought maybe a suicide, but we're not so sure."

"What was the COD? I'm sorry." I shook my head. The official terminology sounded oddly phony from me. "What happened?"

"No problem. GSW, gunshot wound." He sent me a knowing lift of an eyebrow. "We're bringing in a medical examiner from Juneau. She'll be here later today. Feel like polishing off those crime writer and secretarial skills and helping out?"

The first words that came to me were: *It would take a lot of polish.* I didn't say them aloud though, even if they were true. It *had* been a while. But I quickly came to the conclusion that being in the middle of the investigation of something that kept setting off alarm bells inside my head might be a good way to silence some of them.

Did I really think this . . . whatever it turned out to be might have something to do with me or Levi Brooks? I couldn't give myself an unequivocal "no," even if a part of me knew that was irrational. Alarm bells were alarm bells and they usually rang the loudest when you thought they shouldn't be ringing at all.

I'd spent a long time not paying attention to those bells. I was never doing that again.

"I'm still good with numbers if you need me for any of that.

I'm also a good sounding board, my grandfather always said so. If you're serious, sure, let me know how I can help."

"I am serious, and I will let you know," Gril said. He sent me a quick look. "I'm not too proud to admit that I'm a small-town lawman with few resources, Ms. Rivers. I'm happy to have another resource in town, a consultant, if you will. I also hope it gets figured out quickly and no real investigation is necessary, but still."

"Yeah. But still," I said.

"So, since you were a secretary and all, do you use shorthand to write your books?" Gril asked, changing the subject.

"Nope. I never used it as a secretary. For my books, I write on my typewriter and then scan in the pages and edit from there."

"Seems tedious."

"It's how I started, and I can't seem to do it any other way."

Gril nodded. "Good with both numbers and words. That's a rare combination."

"That's what my grandfather always said." I smiled sadly but kept my attention out the windshield.

Gril took another right onto a road that was even rougher than the one we'd been on. It might not have been considered a road. It was wet from an earlier rain, though there was enough brush on the ground to keep it from being too muddy. There were no flowers out here, daisies or otherwise, but thick trees that seemed deep, dark, and unfriendly. It would be difficult to run through these woods, which also meant it would be difficult to chase someone through them.

"Why is it unclear? Murder or suicide?" I asked.

Gril just shook his head and didn't look at me. "Hard to pinpoint it, but it's just . . . something."

"Hmm," I said. I'd heard that sort of thing before. Gramps had done a lot of investigating just because something sat funny with him. Instinct, gut feeling, whatever it was, Gramps thought it was important to listen to it. It looked like Gril thought so too.

"We're spread out here," Gril continued. "We used to have a slightly larger downtown but there was a fire. We have other places of business throughout the woods. We're a small community, only about five hundred full-time residents, but we still need things. One thing we used to have was a newspaper, not much in the way of delivery people, but folks could stop by and pick up a paper copy if they wanted to, and a bunch of copies were always left downtown for pickup there too."

I didn't mention that Donner had given me many of the same tour highlights.

Gril parked the truck directly outside a double-wide tin shack put together with four old and uneven sides. Its weathered gray walls were topped by a green peaked tin roof, and the entire structure leaned a little to the right. A hand-painted sign was nailed atop the door. BENEDICT PETITION.

"How has that building survived? Surely it snows like crazy around here," I said.

Gril half-smiled. "Well, so far so good, but reinforcements have been made. It's an old hunting shed. What do you think?"

"You want me to hunt something or work at a paper?"

"I want you to *be* the paper. Well, only if you want to. Old Bobby Reardon started it and did it for years. There's no rent on the building, and there's no charge for subscriptions. We couldn't pay you, but Detective Majors said you don't need money."

"I have book deadlines." I didn't add *if I ever write again*, but the words echoed in my mind. They wouldn't go away.

"Oh, this wouldn't interfere with those. Not much news up here. Mostly, you would note event times and places, things like potlucks and Girl Scout meetings. It's pretty easy. We don't have enough Internet access throughout town to make a website or anything, but if you lean over that way, you'll see another building."

I leaned to the left and saw a small brick building about half a football field into the woods.

Gril continued, "It's the library. Most times, the library's Internet access works okay from the *Petition*'s building, but it's not a far walk to the library if need be. You'd write the paper, print copies, and drop some off at the Mercantile where people can pick them up. Once a week. Bobby died almost a year ago. We've missed him and the paper. You could work from here. Ride a bike from the Benedict House for now. Winter comes and you're still here, we'd have to come up with other transportation. I think it would make a good cover for you. You could work, write your books in there, and no one would know the difference."

"I told Viola and the others that I was a consultant."

"For what?"

"Office organization."

His eyebrows came together as he looked at me. "Like Hailey from *37 Flights*? Do you think they believed you?"

"I don't know."

Gril shrugged. "I think you could make it work here. And I've saved the best part for last. We have a very spotty cell phone signal around here, but for a reason we never could understand, it's good here."

I nodded. That part did sound appealing. "How would we justify me being *the* paper? I mean, we can't tell anyone I'm a writer."

"Bobby didn't have any writing experience. We'd've given the non-paying job to someone else if they wanted it, but no one else did or does. No experience necessary. Grammar and punctuation aren't all that important either; you'll see. We'll just tell everyone you wanted something more to do while you're visiting, and this was my first idea. It'll be good to have it back, no matter how temporary."

"Can I think about it for a day?" I said, only because it seemed like the right thing to say. I didn't want to commit to anything and, given a day, maybe I could find a better way to say no.

"I think it would be better if you just did it for a day. Come on, I'll let you in, show you around the place, and you can have some time to get acquainted with our *Petition*. I think you're going to like it."

Gril agilely moved his burly body out of the truck. I had no idea if he was a good police officer, but I appreciated his efforts to help me, a stranger to his world. I was already beginning to feel the embarrassment from my earlier breakdown, but I had no doubt that he'd never bring it up again, and would shrug it off if I did.

I got out of the truck and made my way inside to the official and leaning offices of the *Benedict Petition*.

Six

ere's the key. There's everything else. I can get you a new computer, and the printer is good, almost brand-new. Look around. Get a feel."

That had been the extent of the tour. There'd been a bicycle with two flat tires sitting in the middle of the space. Gril offered to take the bike while I got acquainted with the shed-turned-newspaper-office. He said he'd get the tires taken care of and return it. I could either walk back to the hotel or wait for him to bring it back. He said he wouldn't be gone long.

The newspaper office was made up of two messy desks, two messy tables against walls, a nice printer-copier, a watercooler that Gril said he would replenish, and four file cabinets that overflowed with papers I didn't think could possibly all be necessary for a newspaper the size of the *Petition*. Everything was old, about circa last mid-century if I knew my office equipment, and I wasn't so sure I did. A chalkboard, dusty with old chalk, had been nailed to one of the walls. Whatever had been written on it had been erased, but the board hadn't been cleaned in a long time. A hula girl lamp sat on one desk, a lamp made with a football base on the other.

The small space with only one window felt like something out of an old black-and-white movie, like the ones I used to watch at my grandfather's house late at night on channels that only antennas could find, films with actors like Humphrey Bogart and Lauren Bacall. In fact, there was even an old *Casablanca* poster on the wall, faded and frayed around the edges.

I blinked back a wave of more nostalgic tears when I saw the large, clunky typewriters on each desk, one an Underwood, the other a Royal. I'd always wanted to type on a Royal. I needed to limit myself to one emotional breakdown a day though, so I swallowed the tears. There was something about those old machines. Sometimes I wondered if I'd wanted to be a writer because of the stories in my head or the joy my fingers took in the process of creating them. I sniffed and told myself to shape up.

I sat at a desk, my finger absently pushing lightly on the Royal's "B" key, and envisioned myself working there. I looked out the side window. The view of the woods was similar to the view out of my home office in Missouri, but these woods were darker and more unsettling, jammed with more trees. Also, more protective. I'd already determined that these trees could keep out Levi Brooks much better than the trees back home. I leaned backwards, looked out the window, and spotted the library. A brick building that looked like it should be a library, it seemed older but in great shape. Several cars and trucks were parked along one side. It wasn't too far away. I watched as a young woman and a little boy came out of the doors, each of them carrying a stack of books. The little boy dropped a book, but just as I was about to go outside and call over to let them know, he ran back and got it. The two of them and their books piled into a small car and drove away.

I turned back to the desk. My Olympia would fit with the other two typewriters, as well as any computer I might get from Gril. I'd hidden some burner phones in my backpack, but one was deep in my pocket. I hoped the cell reception was as good as Gril had claimed, but I'd try it later.

I was under the impression that I could make the *Petition* whatever I wanted to make it, but I didn't know where to begin. Did that matter? I had never studied journalism. I concluded that even if the job was simple, it just wasn't something I could commit to, even in a small way. It wasn't me.

However, just as I made the decision, more thoughts took shape. The building *would* give me a place to go. I could work and no one would be bothered by my noisy typewriter keys. Working at the *Petition might* be the perfect cover. And, I reminded myself, I'd never studied creative writing either. I'd just done it.

I hoped that Levi Brooks would be caught soon, that I wouldn't have to hide for long. But whatever my tasks here would be, they could be just as easily abandoned by me as they had been by Bobby Reardon. If I said I'd do it, Gril wouldn't need two weeks' notice when I left.

I didn't know if Gril was serious when he asked if I wanted to polish up my old skills; maybe he was just working hard to give me something to do. But I *was* curious. No, something a little more than curious, something that could maybe turn into an obsession if I wasn't careful. It pulled at me, this mysterious local death that *might* be a murder. Was it simply pure coincidence that Benedict, Alaska, had potentially seen a murder during the same time I was making my way to the small village—a place that didn't see many murders other than those committed by Mother Nature? Probably. But I couldn't stop wondering.

Working at the *Petition* might also give me a way to gain a quicker understanding of what had happened and if, long shot that it was, it had anything to do with me or Levi. I knew I was overreacting, being paranoid, but it was something I couldn't seem to ignore.

Yeah, I wasn't ever going to ignore those alarm bells again, no matter how loud or quietly they rang.

As I thought about what I was going to do and the decisions

I'd made to get there, to this tiny outbuilding in Alaska, the door opened again, moving gently, but startling me nonetheless. I swallowed a gasp.

"Tires should be fine," Gril said as he wheeled the bike in. "At least you'll have something. I'll get the watercooler taken care of this evening."

"I could buy a truck."

"Sure, if you want. But you might want to make sure you're staying before you do that."

I nodded. "Chief, I have some questions for you regarding the alleged murder we spoke briefly about. Could I get some answers, on the record?"

He looked perturbed and confused at the same time. "That's not really what I had in mind, either with the job at the *Petition,* or helping me."

"Well, that's what I want to make it. I'd love to help you out in any way I can, and if you're okay with that, I'll also take this non-paying job and do my best with it."

A variety of expressions continued to move over and around the shaggy beard and grimy glasses, but ultimately he said, "All right. I have a few more minutes. Let's talk."

Gril didn't think I'd really write an article about the recent death, I could tell. He probably thought I was just being writer curious, researching, gathering information. He might have been correct, but as we talked, I wasn't sure what I was going to do with the information. I just knew I needed to have it.

The name of the deceased was Linda Rafferty. She and her husband, George, had moved to Benedict three years earlier. They'd come from South Carolina, crossing the globe to get away. Having lost a teenage child to a car accident, their grief had been their compelling force. They'd purchased a home in what Gril called the West coordinate. Though not a part of any official map, Benedict was spread out in sections, four directionally named, square-ish vast plots of land. It proved an efficient way to give directions.

Quiet folks who mostly kept to themselves, from the moment they'd arrived in Alaska, George and Linda had devoted themselves to the Glacier Bay National Park, working some paying jobs but also volunteering in any way that was required.

"What ways are required?" I asked Gril. "What do people who work at a park made of glaciers do?"

"Boat tours, kayak tours, set up camping, look after the visitors' center, café, and there's a lodge there too. All of us help out if we need to, you'll see, but I know that both of them worked house-keeping for a while. Linda had been working in the café recently. And . . . I was . . ." He stopped abruptly.

"What?"

"Nothing."

"You're going over to check out a lead or something?"

He looked at me a long moment, and his eyes changed, hardened. Only a short time ago he was speaking to a new resident, someone frightened and emotional, and now, for all intents and purposes, I was asking questions as a member of the press, one that he'd hired. This was a quickly transforming acquaintanceship, and probably not exactly what he had in mind.

"Look," he said as he stood, "get acclimated. I'm glad you want to do this, but I'm not sure it's what you think it is. Look over old copies, old files, whatever is in here. You'll see that you have time to write your books and work on the *Petition*—in its original incarnation. Feel free to call me if the bike doesn't work. There's a good cell signal here. And, I'll call if I have anything I'd like to run by you. You said you're good with numbers, crime scene measurements?"

"Yes."

He placed a business card on the desk. "Good to know. And, call me if you need anything at all. I know it's been rough."

"Thank you," I said.

"You're welcome."

The space was compact so he didn't have to take many steps to get to the door. Once there he hesitated and turned to face me again.

He sent me a small smile, one that came with duty and obligation. "Welcome to Benedict, Beth. We're glad to have you here. I know you've been through a lot, but I really do believe you are safe. I will receive manifests of all visitors coming over via ferry, and Francis keeps track of everyone flying in. I check with him all the time, will do so even more now. I hope you can enjoy your time and relax."

"I feel safe," I said. "I feel a little like I've traveled to another planet, but I think that's good. Thank you for everything."

In fact, I felt *safer,* but not completely safe. Maybe I just needed some time, maybe it was normal, considering what I'd been through, that all my senses were still on high alert, that I wasn't ready to relax. After hearing about Linda Rafferty, there didn't seem to be any way at all that her death had anything to do with me, but my deep curiosity hadn't abated.

Gril nodded, and then turned to leave, closing the door just as gently as he'd opened it a few minutes earlier.

I looked around the shack some more. It was a complete mess, and I did need to get acclimated to Benedict, Alaska.

Gramps's words rang in my mind. "No better way to learn how to do something than in a small-town job."

I got to work.

Seven

I'd just finished clearing off the top of one of the desks when a knock sounded on the door. I froze in place and the silence that followed grew big in my ears.

I gritted my teeth and held my breath. I understood my post-traumatic reaction, and I also understood it was uncalled for. It was as if I was operating in two different but parallel realms. I knew normal, remembered it, could see it there next to me. But I was in that other realm, where the monsters lived.

The knocks came again. "Hey, Beth."

I deflated with relief at the female voice. I was pretty sure it was Viola. I'd taken off my cap, but I put it back on and then stepped over a couple of piles of paper to get to the door.

"Hey, Viola." I unlocked and then opened the door wide.

"Hey, yourself." She squinted. "I brought some of my world famous—not exaggerating there—chicken soup in a thermos, but we need to talk. Gril told me you'd be here."

"Come in."

She stepped over the threshold. "Love what you've done with the place."

I couldn't help but smile. "Well, I'm just getting started. Did Gril tell you what I'm doing?"

"He said you were the new Bobby. Don't know about that though. Bobby's mud boots will be pretty hard to fill. You got what it takes?"

I shrugged. "I don't know, but I'm willing to try. For free, even."

"Maybe you should get yourself some of your own mud boots first."

"Not a bad idea."

She nodded and pursed her lips as she looked around the small space, this time with a deeper curiosity. She was looking for something.

"What?" I asked.

Her wandering eyes stopped on me. "Nothing, just getting a feel. I like to see what people do with their places around them. It's a curious thing, you know, how people decorate places. Tells you— well, me, tells *me* a lot."

"All I'm doing right now is straightening up and filing. It's a losing battle, so far."

"See, that's exactly what I mean. Are you filing, say like a person who tells other people the best ways to file things, or are you a willy-nilly sort of girl who doesn't, in fact, tell other people how to file things at all? Because, I gotta tell you, that was one of the worst lies I've ever heard." She made a quick, incredulous noise that was peppered with a little anger. "And I hear more than my fair share of lies."

The gun was holstered at her waist and I was suddenly surprised that she didn't look like a cartoon character. My mom had a gun but she never wore it on her hip; usually it was in a holster at her ankle, well hidden by her jeans. The old hat on Viola's head might have its own stories to tell, but even that didn't seem inauthentic. She was real, three-dimensional, and not just in my fictional frame of mind.

I wouldn't say I felt threatened by her. I didn't sense that she was about to draw and fire if I didn't tell her the truth. I did sense that she was a person I wanted on my side though.

"I found a bottle of whiskey in a bottom drawer. Can I interest you in a drink over some conversation?" It worked in the Ozarks; perhaps it was a universal way to begin a friendship.

"Yes ma'am. Would be impolite to turn down such an offer. You can save the chicken soup for later."

I cleared off two chairs and grabbed two shot glasses and the bottle. I placed them on the desk that now held only one of the typewriters. I'd moved one to the other desk. The motions of hospitality gave me time to work on formulating a story, something I could tell Viola that would sound closer to the truth than my earlier lies.

And, I came up with nothing.

"Any special toasts around here?" I poured the amber liquid into the two shot glasses. There was no date on the dusty bottle and I'd never heard of the brand, but the smell that wafted up to my nostrils left me confident and hopeful, if trying hard not to cough. I watched Viola as I finished pouring; her eyes told me she enjoyed whiskey.

She took the glass I handed her. "Today, we're going to toast to truth. It sets you free, you know."

"I used to think that." I lifted my shot glass and we clinked.

The whiskey burned going down, but landed softly. I couldn't remember the last time I'd had a shot of whiskey. "And to Bobby Reardon." I glanced upward. "I hope to fill his mud boots at least partway, and I thank him for the drink."

"Right. To Bobby," Viola said sadly.

"He was a friend?"

"Sure. We're all friends around here, even if we don't like you. We have to be. Small place. Rough weather. Mean weather. We have to take care of each other, so even if we don't like you, we have to know we can at least trust you. For example, Gril seems to think you're a good egg. I'm not saying you're a bad one, but your story doesn't jibe. I wouldn't care, mind you, if you were just visiting.

I wouldn't even care if you were one of my girls—they lie all the time—because I'm in control of them, even if they don't rightly recognize it. Here's the deal, you don't have to tell me your truth, but I gotta hear something so's I know I can trust you. Tell me something good."

I looked at her a long time. She looked back, and neither of us seemed in a hurry.

"My name really is Beth Rivers. I'm running away from something and I need to hide for a while, hopefully not for a long time, but I don't know. I don't want to tell you any more than that because I'm afraid. I'm not dangerous, but I don't know how to prove to you that I'm not out to harm anyone here."

Viola nodded and poured herself another shot. I shook my head when she held the bottle my direction. "Could you take off your cap?"

I did. If Hank had told everyone, it seemed silly to hide it anyway.

Viola sucked in air through clenched teeth. "That's ugly."

"Yes."

"Does it hurt?"

"No. I'm okay."

She nodded and downed the shot. She licked her lips and I could envision her drinking with Bobby, though as faceless in my mind as Levi Brooks was, I could imagine a friendly guy welcoming all visitors. Did the *Petition* see a lot of company? Would I need to restock when this bottle was done? Was I going to have to keep the door unlocked?

"You should wear a cap that doesn't look like you purchased it in an airport gift shop on the way here," Viola said.

I smiled. "How about one like yours?"

"This?" She thumbed the brim. "No ma'am, this is one of a kind, and I'm the only one who gets to wear it."

"That's the answer I expected."

She sighed big. "Thing is, I know you, Beth Rivers. I don't know why or how, but I do. You're familiar."

My cheeks burned. Short of plastic surgery, there wasn't much more I could do to disguise myself. I didn't recognize any of the versions of me. I didn't think I looked a thing like Elizabeth Fairchild. Maybe I looked like someone else Viola knew. What were the chances she, or someone else, could figure it out? I previously had no distinguishing feature—no mole, no dimples. I was of average height, currently a little thinner than normal because of everything, but not even close to skeletal. My features were rather ordinary, except for the scar and the shock of white hair. I looked good in my author picture, but that was more about makeup, lighting, and a little help from Photoshop. I opened my mouth to say something, maybe protest, but nothing came out.

"Right," Viola said. "I appreciate why you don't want to tell me, but if you really are in hiding, you might not be hiding as well as you think. Tell you what, if I figure out who you are, you have to tell me I'm right, okay? I'm eons smarter than pretty much everyone, so no one will figure it out before I do. When I do, you'll have some time to figure something else out, maybe another place to run to before whoever you're running from figures it out too, but you have to agree to tell me honestly if I pinpoint it. 'Kay?"

I nodded, still searching for words. She had a good point. If she could recognize me, how far behind her were all the mere mortals? I didn't think I was recognizable though.

A jolt of pain suddenly seared through my right temple, making even the side of my nose hurt. I tried not to show the pain, but my eyes closed reflexively as tears squeezed out and slid down my cheek.

"Beth?" Viola said, from some faraway place.

In a disjointed way, I felt her touch my arm and, through the pain, I wondered if she had come around the desk or reached over it. But I couldn't open my eyes to get the answer.

I gurgled a watery noise, and then, just when I thought I might pass out, the pain subsided, like it rolled out with a quick tide. Relief blossomed as I was able to open my eyes.

"I'm okay. It passed quickly," I said.

She'd come around the desk and was crouching beside me. Concern pulled at her eyes under the brim of the hat. "What passed quickly? Are you sure you're okay?"

"Yes."

She squinted at me just long enough to be impolite and then stood and went back to the chair on the other side. The chair squeaked as she sat. "Darlin', whatever that was, it wasn't good, and it might need to be looked at."

I shook my head lightly, careful to see if the movement brought another nail to my brain. It didn't. "I'm okay. My doctor said this would happen."

Sort of. Dr. Genero had said that I might experience some headaches, but she'd never discussed the level of pain or any sort of sudden onset. I was fine now, but if I had many more of those, I would agree with Viola and plan a trip to Juneau or Anchorage for a CT scan. The random memories were better than the headaches. For now, I didn't want Viola to know the episode had bothered me.

I might have thought I was looking at Indiana Jones's mother. The eyes she now gave me under the brim of the old hat reminded me so much of those movies that I felt an involuntary smile tug at the corner of my mouth.

"All right," she said. "Well, I hope you let your doctor know about it. I watched for one side of your face to sag or something but I didn't see that at all."

"That's good news."

Viola scowled. "Look, you escaped from something, I get that, but you might have taken off out of wherever too soon. And you chose this place to hide, I get that too, but maybe you should spend some time in a bigger city, closer to real medical care. A few weeks."

I shook my head, again slowly. I would be looking over my shoulder enough. Here, when I did, figuratively and literally, mostly I would see woods and maybe glacier. In a city, any city, I was sure I'd sense Levi everywhere, hear his voice rise above crowds. I'd rather have the headaches and the memories.

I needed a change of subject. "I put something on the front counter this morning. A toy. A tiger. Hopefully it made it to its owner."

"Yeah? I didn't see it. After breakfast?"

"No, right before."

Viola's eyebrows came together. "I didn't see it. I don't know who it belongs to, but maybe one of the girls claimed it, or swiped it."

"It didn't seem worth much of anything."

"Well, they like to take things, no matter the value sometimes. Where did you find it?"

"On the floor. I kicked it accidentally."

"Why didn't you bring it into the dining room?"

I shrugged. "Not sure. Just seemed like putting it on the counter was appropriate."

"Hmm. Well, I don't know."

"Probably no big deal."

"Probably."

Viola fell into thought. I'd only brought up the toy to change the subject, but something about what I'd said had given her pause. Maybe she had her own set of alarm bells.

"What are you thinking about?" I asked.

"Nothing." She poured herself another shot.

"Hey, Viola, what can you tell me about Linda Rafferty and her husband, George?" I asked.

"What? Why?"

"Have you heard what happened?"

"Of course I have. Linda Rafferty might have killed herself. Why are you curious about them?"

"Gril wonders if it wasn't suicide, if it was murder."

"I'm not surprised." Viola chewed on her bottom lip as she fell into thought.

"Why aren't you surprised?"

"I don't know . . . It's just that Linda didn't seem like . . . Well, I know it's hard to always know, but Linda didn't ever seem like she'd kill, or hurt, herself."

"She was happy, content?"

Viola had fallen back into thought.

"Viola?" I said.

Her attention swung back to me. "No, I didn't know." She stood. "I need to go." She put her hand on the gun as she turned to make her way to the door.

"What's up? What did I say?"

"I gotta go, that's all."

"Can I go with you?" I stood too. The pain was still there, though muted and a good wavery distance away. I hoped it wouldn't come back full force as I tried to keep my face normal.

"Hell no." Viola pointed at me. "You stay here, Missy. Eat that soup. You hear?"

"Sure." I'd wait until a better time to remind her that I wasn't one of her felons.

Her eyes pinched as her tone softened. "Just . . . I'm sorry, I have to go."

"See you at dinner?"

"Yeah, see you then. Eat that soup, I mean it. It will make you feel better. It cures all ails."

Viola left. The door shut with such force that my eyes went up to the ceiling. Should I brace myself for the building coming down around me?

The walls remained upright, and I sat back onto the chair. My head was clear with only a small promise of returning pain, but new anxiety rattled me. Was I going to have to deal with flash headaches *and* flash memories? Is that what Dr. Genero meant?

Also, what had set Viola off? What did it mean to Linda Rafferty's death?

"I didn't even know Linda Rafferty," I mumbled to myself.

But even posthumously, there was a way to get to know people.

As I swiveled the chair so I could reach for a computer keyboard, I realized there wasn't one there. Even if I could grab some of the library's Internet, I had no way to access it. I hadn't brought either my laptop or my satellite phone. With my research thwarted, I decided to use the burner phone. It wouldn't hurt to talk to Dr. Genero about the headache.

I pulled it out of my pocket and powered it on. Gril had been correct, the bars were all lit. I didn't have this good of reception in my St. Louis home office. A red light was also blinking, as if to tell me I had a message. I didn't remember giving the number of any of the burner phones to anyone, but maybe I had.

I hit the call button and was immediately connected to a computerized voice.

"You have one new message. To hear the message, press 1."

I did as instructed.

"Hey, hey, hey," was all the message said.

In a male voice. A voice tinged with an Ozark-like accent. A voice that sounded a lot like Levi Brooks's.

At once, my hands iced and shook, my breath caught, and my stomach plummeted. I listened to the phone's instructions and played the message again, focusing extra hard, paying attention to the fact that if I didn't do everything correctly, I would accidentally erase it, erase something that might be evidence, erase it so I would wonder if I'd really heard it at all.

"No! Not possible!" I said as I played it again, and again.

Finally, I flipped the phone closed and threw it onto the desk.

"No!"

Eight

eth?" Detective Majors said, her voice a high point amid surrounding chaos.

I didn't know if the background noises were because of where she was or because my heartbeat was still booming in my ears.

"Yes, it's me. Can you talk?"

"One second."

The noises disappeared after what sounded like the shutting of a door. I couldn't envision the room Detective Majors had moved into. I'd only met with her at the hospital. I imagined a typical police precinct interview room.

"Beth, where are you? Are you . . . there?" she asked.

"I'm there. Listen, did I give you this number? Did you give anyone else this number?"

"No, you didn't give it to me. I would never have shared it if you had. What's going on?" Her voice was tight and charged, like an electrical wire.

"Something . . . happened."

"Are you hurt? Are you okay?"

"I'm fine." I took a deep breath and tried to calm down. It didn't work.

"Go on."

"I got a call . . . a message. It was . . . it might have been Levi. I can't be sure, but it sounded like him. I think."

"What? On a burner phone?"

"Yes."

"That doesn't sound like something that could happen, Beth. I mean, there's no way it could have been Levi. No way."

We both knew that it was improbable, but not impossible. Nothing was impossible. Not anymore.

"Is there anything you can do? Can you trace the call, or check on it? The number it came from is marked private," I said.

"I'll try."

I imagined her reaching into the pocket on her shirt for the small notebook and the pen she carried. When I'd first met her, I'd commented on how short she was. It had been a thoughtless remark, impolite, immature even. The comment hadn't bothered her. It hadn't bothered me at the time, but it had later, along with other thoughtless things I'd said. When I'd mentioned my concerns about my impulsive words to Dr. Genero, she'd told me that head injuries could cause personality changes, though for me they were probably temporary. Since I'd later regretted the remarks, I hoped the changes were resolving.

Detective Majors was also young, particularly for a detective. She was maybe almost thirty, but I hadn't asked. She wore her dark hair pulled back in a short, tight ponytail, and she never smiled. Even when she was being friendly or sympathetic, her mouth remained in a straight, grim line. She was smart, and I did trust her—to investigate the crimes done against me, not to protect me. I didn't trust anyone but myself to do that.

"All right," she said. "Tell me all about the phone. I might need more than the number."

I gave her the details, the brand, even the serial number, but I could hear doubt in her voice. Nothing was completely secure, but burner phones were named as such because of their somewhat off-the-grid nature; use and burn them up, so to speak. It was getting harder and harder to be off the grid though. I knew that. I sensed that her tracing the call was a long shot, but she would exhaust her options.

"Have you talked to the local police chief? I let him know you were coming. I felt it necessary," she said after I gave her the phone details. "But I didn't think about it until after I'd dropped you off. There was no way to let you know. Sorry."

"It's okay. I have met him. He's . . . being helpful."

"Good."

I felt the back of my neck bristle. I turned to look behind me, but I was alone in the tin building and no one was looking in through the window. "Detective Majors, do you have anything new?"

She sighed. "No, not really, Beth."

"What does that mean?"

"It means I'm looking at every little thing that might have something to do with Levi Brooks. I'm hitting lots of dead ends, but that's not a surprise. I won't stop looking. I won't give up. You should know that by now. I—"

"You have *something*. I can hear it in your voice." It might have been wishful thinking, but I didn't think so.

"Someone called in yesterday about a van; a woman near Weyford. Someone else called about the same van, we think, close to the same location, near the cemetery out there, about thirty minutes later. I checked it out, but there was no van."

"What did you find?"

"There were some good tire tracks in the mud across the old two-lane highway from the farmhouse that might match the ones by where . . . where you escaped. We're testing everything and talking to everyone. Do you know a Geneva Spooner?"

"I don't think so. Doesn't sound familiar. Why?"

"She's one of the people who called in. She lives in the farmhouse, an old widow by herself. The other person who called claimed to work at the cemetery, but no one got his name. I'm not concerned about them, I just wondered if you knew her."

"I don't know anyone named Geneva."

"Okay . . ."

"What?"

"Well, I told your mother about the sightings."

"You did what?"

"Yeah, I told her. She's so . . . so."

"Such a pain in the ass?"

"That's not what I was going to say."

"She's obsessive, Detective Majors. My father used to be her only obsession. Now, she has two. I have no doubt that she will hunt down Levi Brooks." I paused. It wasn't the worst thing that could happen, but I didn't want her to get hurt or pay too high a price for her vengeance.

I'm going to find your daddy, young lady, you don't ever need to doubt that. I'll find out what happened to him. I won't give up until I do.

Is that why I have to live with Grandpa?

We are both living with him, Bethie. He's just watching over us for a while. Just for a while.

"Beth?" Detective Majors said.

"I'm here. I wouldn't tell her anything else if I were you, not even in passing. She'll get in the way. I'd like Levi Brooks gone from this world, but she'll kill him, Detective, and I don't want her paying for a murder rap. I'm alive, and I'm going to get better."

"All right. Too late to do anything about what I've already told her, but I'll keep anything else to myself."

"Did she do something in Weyford?"

"I think she went to talk to Geneva Spooner, but I can't be sure yet. I'll find out."

"If she did talk to Geneva, she might have scared that poor woman to death. I don't know. People can go either way with Mom, but she usually ultimately ends up making friends—for the purposes of using them for information though. It's just her way."

"I'll talk to Geneva again. I'll make sure she's okay."

"Good idea." I sighed. "All right, so we're talking Weyford?"

"Yes."

"Not far from Milton?"

"Not too far."

"That's . . . worrisome."

"Not really. No need to think he's figured out you're from there. He's a Missouri guy, we think. He's bound to be near Milton sometimes."

I wasn't so sure. "Right."

When I first became published another one of my mother's suggestions had been to create a fake biography. That was more about my dad than my anonymity. She wasn't going to ever give up hunting for him. If he'd run away on his own, she didn't want him contacting me because he'd read on some website a paragraph or two that mentioned where I'd been born and grown up. Elizabeth Fairchild was "a Missouri girl" all her life, but that was about as specific as my biographies ever got.

I didn't have pain like earlier, but I suddenly felt heavy-headed. My eyes closed reflexively, and my mind focused in on a memory. It was of a passing road sign. WELCOME TO ILLINOIS, LAND OF LINCOLN.

But I'd jumped out of the van outside St. Louis. I'd been found in Missouri, not on the Illinois side.

"Beth?"

"He took me to Illinois," I said. "At some point he took me there. I remember the road sign now, but I can't see anything else, just a 'Welcome to Illinois' sign."

"Are you sure?" she asked. "I mean, you might have seen that sign at some other time too."

Detective Majors had asked me many times to name the places Levi had taken me. Many police officers had. One of their specific questions had been if Levi taken me over the state line. They hadn't hidden their hope that he had. Crossing state lines would give them more things to put him away for. I thought he'd done more than enough to be put away for good, but I understood why they wanted to pile on as much as they could.

"I am sure," I said. I was pretty sure.

"Can you give me any more? Can you describe anything else you're remembering, the kinds of trees, the weather, other traffic? What about something on the dashboard? Can you see anything?"

My eyes were still closed. "No . . . no, wait, there was a hole in the top right corner of the sign. Not a bullet hole, something bigger, but it was round, definitely round. Detective Majors, it was a 'Welcome to Illinois' sign with a hole through the top right corner. Find that sign and you'll find where we were." I shook my head. "I can't see any more than that. I don't know where we had been before or where we went afterwards, but I'm pretty sure we crossed over into Illinois."

"Okay. All right."

Like a switch had been flipped, the memory was over. I immediately wondered if it had been real, but I didn't say that out loud. I didn't want to waste Detective Majors's time, but I had to believe my brain wasn't so far off its rails that it would make up something as vivid as what I'd just envisioned.

I cleared my throat. "How long before you know about the tire tracks?"

"Today."

When I'd jumped out of the van, it was speculated that Levi had slammed on the brakes and swerved over to the side of the road. He'd left tracks in the gravel and summer dry dirt there. Or another vehicle had left those tracks. The police were hoping the tracks came from Levi's van, but unless I could remember those moments clearly—had a swerve like that occurred?—no one would know for sure.

My patchy memory *had* managed to dredge up the facts that Levi's van was brown and either said Chevy, Chevrolet, or had a Chevrolet emblem somewhere on it.

I closed my eyes and heard Detective Majors call my name yet again. Something else was there, on the edge of the memory.

I said, "I remembered that he wore a black and red lumberjack coat. Do you know the kind I'm talking about?"

"I think so."

"For some reason, I'm remembering it clearly right now. None of that helps much, I know."

"Hey, Beth, like I told you, everything helps. And we never know what might lead to a big break."

"Uh-huh."

"I wish you'd come home. You need medical attention, and Dr. Genero is the best doctor for you. Rethink your plan."

"I'm fine. I'll take it easy. I feel good."

"Sure." She paused. "You can trust the police chief. I believe he's a good man. I checked."

"All right," I said, but the urge to end the call was stronger, the tingle on the back of my neck, prickled again. "I'll call you tomorrow. It might be from a different number."

"All right. I'll answer all calls just to make sure I don't miss you. Take care of yourself."

I made a noise that could be mistaken for agreement. And then I flipped the phone closed. I needed to destroy it, but not before I could record the message somewhere else.

I stood from the chair and went to peer out the window. There was no one in sight. Just trees and the library and more vehicles parked outside it. Dark clouds were moving in quickly and the sun was suddenly hidden. I shook off the feeling of being watched. At least I tried to shake it off.

I turned back to the desk and started opening drawers and looking through stacks.

"Come on, Bobby Reardon, don't fail me now. Any good reporter would have a recorder."

If I were to find one, I expected it to be one that used cassette tapes, either full sized or small. I could have recorded the message on my laptop if I had it.

My search was finally rewarded. I found a small digital recorder in the bottom of a file drawer that was otherwise filled with notes about kayaking. I pressed play.

Bobby, I assumed, came alive digitally.

"Testing, testing." His voice was deep and phlegmy, but strong.

I made a mental note to research him more closely at some point. For now, I stopped the playback and set up the phone and the recorder and managed to get the message saved. The second after I confirmed that my efforts were successful, I put the phone on the floor and stomped it to pieces.

I probably overdid it, but it felt good. When I was done, little bits of the phone were all over the place. I'd started to clean up my mess when an unfamiliar boom shook my world.

Nine

'd probably heard rain on a tin roof before, but I didn't remember when. I know I'd never heard thunder like the rumble that shook the *Petition*'s walls. It seemed so close, and the booming beats were like almost everything else in the forty-ninth state, big. Once I pinpointed that I was hearing thunder as well as rain, I opened the door and watched. The real storm was in the distance out over the woods. I could see the demarcation, the sunny trees in one part, the dark, foreboding ones in another, the line in between moving closer to the shack. Things were going to get bigger and louder.

I didn't want to be under the old roof during a heavy storm. I took a few long seconds to calculate if the bike and I could beat the rain back to the Benedict House. I sensed I took too long to consider my options.

In a flurry of movement, I put the hat back on, gathered the bike, and headed outside. I locked the door and set out. It didn't take long for me to not only regret my decision but to regret many of my decisions. One of them being the fact that I wasn't wearing any sort of "gear" yet. I'd need some soon, if I didn't die of hypothermia first.

The rain was heavy and cold, the air turning more frigid as each second passed. I wore only my jeans, shirt, and flimsy jacket, but under normal circumstances (riding my bike in a St. Louis storm), I would have been fine. Back there in Missouri, I would ride on designated bike paths or on the sides of roads, and even if the air was cold I would have known I could make the few miles trip and make it home and get warm quickly.

In Alaska, there was no real road under my wheels, nothing paved, just a foliage littered path that became quickly muddy. The cold wasn't like the cold I was used to either, something gradual that nudged at you with the temperature change. As I trudged my bike over the muddy ground, the cold hit me ferociously, and packed a debilitating punch of wind with it.

Before the full brunt of the storm even made it to me, the rain began to fall unreasonably hard. Between the wind and the water rolling down my face and into my mouth and nose, I kept losing my breath. I was losing everything—my balance, my energy, my warmth, my sense of direction.

I stopped and tried to get my bearings. I knew which direction I was supposed to have gone; how had I gotten lost? Was I lost? For a long few moments, I felt so helpless that I understood how people just gave up. But then I snapped out of it. Levi Brooks hadn't gotten the best of me, this storm wouldn't either. I pedaled forward again, through the mud and now blinding rain. I lost where I was but figured that if I fell into the ocean I'd know to turn around and go back the other direction.

The sludge I pedaled through seemed to grow deeper. I was sure it was worse than pedaling through sand, though I was cognizant enough to wish for a beach instead of where I was. I pedaled so hard that my foot slipped, and in a combination of clumsy moves, I ended up on my side, on the ground, the bike landing hard on the inside of one of my legs. It hurt but other things seemed more important. I felt myself sinking into the mud, and I wondered if it was quicksand and if the bike would disappear with my body. Strangely, I didn't panic, and was still aware enough to realize I hadn't hit my head and that was the good thing amid all the bad things that were happening.

Then, as abruptly as it had hit, the storm was gone, the darker clouds moving away. A ray of sunshine shone on me and I was grateful for even that small patch of warmth. I was shivering hard, but the sun would bring me back quickly. I wasn't sinking any deeper, so at least it wasn't quicksand. I was stuck, the mud keeping a good grip on my side, but there was a chance I could wedge myself out.

I pushed away the bike and with side leverage I'd never used before, unstuck myself with a slurping noise. Once I'd done that, I got up easily.

I looked around. I'd gone the right direction. I was on the path Gril had brought me down, but I was only about twenty yards away from the *Petition*'s building; a building that was still standing, sure and solid. I sensed it mocking me.

The library was out of my line of sight now, but even if I'd gone that direction, twenty yards wouldn't have gotten me there. I had traveled a very short distance.

I gathered the bike—it wasn't damaged, just as muddy as I was. It would be easier to walk through the rest of the mud than pedal. I sent the building one last look and shook my head.

"I'm an idiot," I muttered. It agreed.

I pushed forward.

A couple of long miles later, I was still muddy and drenched but warmer as I came upon Benedict's downtown. Clouds had come back but for the moment they were less threatening. The two intersecting roads were spotted with parked trucks, cars, and an old station wagon with a scratched wood panel down the side. All of the vehicles glimmered as the sun shone on the leftover rain spots.

I recognized one of the trucks as the one that had brought me into town the day before. I hoped Donner wasn't inside the Benedict

House. I didn't want him to see me like this. I was irritated at myself for caring. I told myself not to care.

It didn't matter anyway. Donner wasn't inside the Benedict House. He'd been inside the Mercantile and walked out just as I was approaching.

In auto mode, he first sent me a quick smile, did a double take, and then stopped in his tracks as he tucked the bag he was carrying under his arm.

"What the hell happened to you?" His tone was critical, his smile gone.

"Got caught in the rain."

"In those clothes? On a bike?"

"Evidently." I pushed the bike forward and wished he'd just go away.

"Ah, I see. You have a death wish. You've come to Alaska to kill yourself."

I sent him a look and then continued toward the Benedict House.

Out of the corner of my eye, I saw him hesitate before he put the bag into the back of his truck.

"Look," he said. "Go dry off and I'll take you shopping. It seems your host doesn't care about your safety. I'm happy to show you what you need."

I kept pushing forward.

"And you will need stuff," he added.

He was correct. I would need stuff.

"I'll be right back out," I said over my shoulder.

"I'll be right here."

I left the bike by the front door and went inside.

"Oh, sorry," I said as I came upon Willa, looking at a piece of paper.

She turned to look at me, her eyes red-rimmed and puffy. She sent me some indifference before she turned to face the paper again. She put her hand over a full key ring sitting on the counter, gathered it in a fist, and put it in her pocket. Did she think I was going to take her keys? What did she have keys for anyway?

I hesitated too long.

"Can I help you?" she asked, her tone not helpful at all.

"No, thanks. Sorry to interrupt."

She folded the paper and looked at me. "Who are you?"

I shook my head. "Just heading to my room." I started walking again.

I thought she might try to stop me, say something else, but she didn't. As I made my way to my room, however, I noted that she was looking at a tri-folded piece of paper. A letter.

Parolee letter? I wondered, but I didn't say anything. Oddly, her attitude didn't bother me as much as all the other weird things had bothered me today. She reminded me of some of Milton's small-time criminals. I knew that attitude. Tough girl. But not really. I wasn't here to help her though, and I wasn't going to let her, or any of my housemates, get under my skin. Other than Viola, of course.

Inside my room, I took off the cap and rubbed a towel through my hair before I put the drenched cap back on. I had nothing other than the extra underwear I'd brought. I'd have to go shopping as I was. I pulled some cash from the money belt still around my waist and placed it into my damp pocket. I dug into the secret pocket on my backpack and found another burner phone. I didn't turn it on, but slipped it into my other damp pocket. No one was in the lobby as I left again.

Donner was leaning against his truck, his arms crossed in front of himself, his attention toward the three horses that were galloping down the street. Just galloping, seemingly for fun.

"They're beautiful," I said.

"They are," Donner said.

For a moment, I glimpsed his soft spot. He might love Benedict, Alaska, but he really, really loved animals. After the horses were out of sight, he looked at me. Again, his expression turned into something that told me he couldn't quite believe what he was seeing. I was a mess, but I didn't want to dwell on it.

"Just the Mercantile, right?" I asked.

"Yeah. That's all we've got for what you'll need."

"I can just go by myself," I said, sensing way too much scrutiny.

"No, I'll come with you this time. Randy can help, but he might forget something. I'll make sure you have the right stuff. Did you honestly come to Alaska with only that?"

I nodded once.

He shook his head. "All right. Let's go."

As we made our way, it was as if we stepped back in time, back to when horses ruled the roads, not just as wild creatures but as modes of transportation too, and women wore only skirts. The merchandise inside was modernized, even if the ways it was displayed were from a bygone time. The shop smelled of the plain wood it had been recently built with, outdoorsy and clean. Shelves lined the walls; chunky tables and barrels packed with so many things took up the rest of the space.

"How much money do you have?" Donner asked.

"Enough."

"If you don't, Randy will set you up an account. Don't worry about it."

"Thanks."

"Hey there, Donner, this our visitor who fell off the horse? The one with the"—he pointed to his head, almost right where the scar was located—"scar?"

"Didn't hear about the scar." Donner looked at me.

I took off the cap. My hair was pasted to my head. I looked about as bad as I could possibly look.

"Holy . . . that's wicked," Donner said.

"Whoa, doggies. That's worse than I'd heard." Randy whistled.

"It's not as bad as it looks." I ruffled my hair. "I'm fine."

Randy frowned but nodded approvingly. "Welcome to Alaska,

darlin'. My place is your place, and if you don't have the money, I can set you up an account. But I do make you pay eventually."

"I appreciate that." It was also a business practice that couldn't possibly be profitable, but I didn't say that out loud.

"You fell off a horse?" Donner interjected.

"I did. In Denver." I cleared my throat. "So, what do I need?"

The list was manageable. In fact, I did have enough money to cover everything but as I was behind the curtain of the small dressing room, trying on some of the sturdiest jeans I'd ever worn, I decided to behave as if I needed an account. It wasn't that I didn't want to pay, I just didn't want rumors about all my cash to spread as quickly as the news about the scar had.

"Hey, Donner," I said from behind the curtain. "Did you know Linda Rafferty?"

"Of course. Tragic."

"Right." I pushed open the curtain.

Donner had been looking through a barrel full of thick socks. He'd placed a couple pairs over his arm as he turned and looked at me.

It was strange, him helping me shop. It wasn't intimate at all. It was all business, and very important, according to his and Randy's back-and-forth discussion.

She'll need some rain boots too, Donner. Not just winter boots. We got these newfangled things here.

Randy, are you getting more hand warmers in soon?

Not just britches, make sure you get her a full Carhartt. (He referred to an orange, padded onesie, by the way. I got one, for those occasions when I'd be riding on a snowmobile, or perhaps behind a pack of dogs.)

"Now, those look like the right length. Comfortable enough?" Donner asked me about the jeans.

"Umm, well, for what they are, I suppose."

"They'll soften up a little, but you need warm."

"Right. So, Donner, have you heard about me working at the *Petition*?"

"Bobby's paper?"

"Yeah."

"No, I hadn't. That's good. We could use someone there. It was a good way to know what was going on."

It seemed Donner was the last to pick up on the gossip.

"Even I'd heard about that." Randy was ringing up a customer, but the place was small enough that nothing could be missed.

The customer wore a John Deere cap, but I did a double take when he turned his head and smiled in my direction. He looked just like Willie Nelson. Maybe a younger version, but the long, gray braids were there. He caught my eye and after he took his change from Randy, walked my direction.

"I thought I saw someone out there today," he said as he approached. He extended his hand. "Orin Capshaw."

"Beth Rivers." I shook.

I didn't know if it was my imagination or if Orin moved in a cloud that smelled distinctly of weed.

Donner came up next to him. "Orin is our resident computer genius and librarian. He spends most of his time at the library, but sometimes helps out at the airport. If you need anything found on the www, he's your man."

When Donner didn't continue, Orin looked at him and said, "Dude?"

Donner looked back at him and then nodded. "Right. Orin has done work for the FBI, the CIA, and even some for National Geographic. You'll see the Nat Geo ships out there in the water. Even they need some computer help sometimes."

"Wow, that's impressive," I said.

"That's better, Donner man." He looked at me. "I saw you in the *Petition* building. Glad someone'll be putting that together again. Bobby used me a lot. I'm free for residents of Benedict. I hear you're going to be here awhile, that your apartment building in Denver is being rebuilt."

"That's correct. I'm impressed."

"Shoot, that's just the gossip. I haven't pulled you up on the old," he tapped Donner's arm with the back of his hand, "www just yet."

I smiled. Orin was immediately likable. "Let me know what you find."

"Oh, I will. Nice to meet you," he said and then he turned around to leave. He stopped at the door. "I'll see you around the neighborhood, Beth Rivers."

And then he winked. I was stunned speechless as I looked at Orin and then at Donner and Randy. They didn't seem to have noticed. Orin nodded and sent me a two-fingered peace sign before he walked out the door. He could have just been being friendly, being himself, but I sensed he was telling me he knew my secret. I thought about the prickles on the back of my neck as I'd been inside the *Petition*. Had Orin been watching me? Eavesdropping? Raw fear skipped up my spine.

Hang on, I silently demanded. There was no reason to jump to conclusions.

It looked like paranoia was my new normal.

And who wanted to live that way?

"Want two pairs of those jeans?" Donner asked, bringing me out of the stupor.

"Yeah, I do," I said before I turned and went back into the dressing room. It was as good a place as any to calm down.

"That guy," I said from behind the curtain when I thought I could manage an even tone, "he looked like Willie Nelson."

"Yep, but he doesn't like that pointed out to him."

"Really? Seems like he works at it."

"Yeah, he's an odd one," Donner said. "But we all are. You'll get used to it."

He was so matter-of-fact, I wasn't sure if he was attempting to be glib or just stating the things as they were. Yes, I would get used to "it," whatever it really was. I put on my own clothes and exited the dressing room.

"I'm going to try to do things a little differently with the *Petition*. I might try to write more articles. I bet lots of people take amazing pictures around here. What if I published some of those too?" I said.

Donner's attention was inside a barrel that overflowed with fanny packs. "Okay."

"And I want to write something about Linda Rafferty. Of course, I didn't know her. Would you tell me about her?"

Donner turned his attention to me. His eyes were now their familiar perturbed, but maybe even more so. I couldn't tell if he was bothered by the question or the fact that I'd put my other clothes back on. "You need a source?"

"Yes."

Donner looked at Randy, who shrugged and said, "That's not how Bobby did it."

"I know, but it wouldn't hurt, would it? I bet people would like to know what happened to Linda," I said. "There's some question as to the manner of death. I didn't know Linda and even I wonder."

Randy harrumphed as he waved away my idea and turned his attention to the shelves behind the cash register, where jars of jerky loomed large.

"I think that's going to be an uphill battle," Donner said.

I nodded. "I get that."

Donner held his arm toward me, displaying the socks he still had over it. "You'll need at least a few pairs of these."

"Sounds good." I nodded, hearing loud and clear the words he wouldn't say. He wasn't going to talk to me about Linda. "What else?"

"I think we've done all right. Randy has some plain underwear over there, but I'll let you pick those out yourself."

"Will do."

Fortunately, the Mercantile also had a few shelves of generic gray sweats. Instead of the clothes I'd worn for three days in a row, I grabbed some sweats and ran back to the dressing room. I'd never been into fashion, but my new wardrobe would take that to a new extreme. I asked about a laundromat and learned there was a small one behind the school. I didn't wonder aloud how I would get there, but I didn't think the bike was going to be enough.

I kept the Cubs cap, but purchased one emblazoned with the silhouette of a moose. It was actually cute, tourist-like, and it would probably sell well in the lower forty-eight.

"Much better hat," Randy said as I approached the cash register. "You still look like a salmon out of water, but it's better."

My bags were packed with underwear (long and regular), jeans, T-shirts (both long- and short-sleeved), socks, boots, a parka, gloves, hats, scarves, and the orange onesie. It was almost like shopping for a new winter term school year, except for the added snowshoes.

"You never know when you'll need these," Donner said as he held them up. "Take them with you out to the *Petition*."

"All right."

Donner walked me back to the Benedict House and to my room. We made a pile of the bags and items and he turned to leave.

I realized that other than the interruption from Orin, I'd just spent the last hour in a haze of normal, mostly without fear buzzing inside me.

Stay busy. Keep busy. It wasn't a revelation, but reinforcement. Even my mom had given me the advice.

"Thank you," I said as Donner made it to the door.

"You're welcome." He stopped, turned, and studied me.

"What?"

"I'm driving out to the Rafferty place tomorrow morning, un-less . . . well, that's the plan right now. You can't go inside, and I'm not going to give you a quote for your story, but I'll show you where Linda lived. Want to go?"

"Why?" I said. "I mean, yes, thank you."

Donner didn't smile. "I don't exactly know why, except there are questions. I don't think your ideas for the *Petition* are going to work, but if you're truly curious, I'm all about getting answers."

"Great. Yes. Thank you. What time?"

"Right after breakfast."

"I'll be ready."

As he left, I wondered about what he'd said. I thought maybe he felt sorry for me; maybe some more time with him in his truck was a good chance for him to share some survival techniques with the new person, the "salmon out of water." No one else was going to show me, it seemed.

I was okay with that.

Ten

The pounding was persistent.

"Hey, Beth, wake up and get yourself out here right away. Dining room, stat."

It was Viola's voice. As I'd done the previous night, I'd fallen into a deep, carefree sleep. With the chair under the doorknob and Levi hopefully in the lower forty-eight, I'd lulled myself into thinking I could finally get some rest.

Apparently not.

The rude awakening sent my heart into overdrive and my confused senses searching for some understanding of what was going on.

Okay, it was two in the morning according to my phone. And it was really cold. Leaving the comfort of the thick blankets and the bed was not appealing, but something was going on. Something Viola demanded me to be a part of.

I'd given it some thought. If Gril hadn't expressed such confidence in Viola, I wasn't sure I would have stayed at the Benedict House. An extra room at the Harvingtons' would get me away from pickpockets and thieves. And blackmailers, from what I'd witnessed between Willa and Loretta.

But I liked Viola, and I liked that it seemed like she would protect me to the best of her ability.

I hurried into some new sweats and the moose cap, and moved the chair. I opened the door slowly and peered out into the starkly lit hallway. No one there. I closed the door behind me and double-checked that it locked before I made my way to the dining room.

I was the last one to arrive.

"I have no idea!" Trinity, the mousiest of the felons, was protesting. Even her squeaky voice seemed to fit.

Viola turned to me. "Sit down, Beth. I've already gone over this once, but I'll do it again."

I took a seat at the end of the lined-up row of three criminals. Everyone in the room but Viola looked like they'd been awakened and dragged from bed. Willa's short hair stood on end, Loretta's ponytail was messy, and she currently wore no makeup. Trinity wore flannel onesie pajamas that were decorated with dinosaurs. She was small enough that she might be able to shop in the young girls' department. Even with a quick glance, I thought I saw a twitch at the corner of her eye.

Viola frowned at the lot of us, her eyes stopping on mine. "Beth, did you purchase some snowshoes from the Mercantile today?"

"I did."

"I thought that might be the case," Viola said. She sat on the edge of a table and reached into a large bag, pulling out a snowshoe. "These them?"

I blinked. "They look like them. What's going on?"

Viola sighed. "I take it you didn't throw them out back into the dumpster."

"Of course not."

"Someone did."

"I'll go check my room." I stood. Even Viola's gun couldn't have stopped me.

I made a quick run and fumbled with my key in the lock. When I managed to get inside, I hurried to the stack of gear I'd purchased but hadn't put away yet.

Relief flooded through me when I saw that the snowshoes I'd purchased were still there, at the bottom of all the other things, well hidden by the orange Carhartt. They hadn't been taken from my room, which to me simply meant my life hadn't once again been somehow invaded.

I made sure the door locked again and went back to the dining room.

"Mine are still there," I said.

For a moment, Viola looked perplexed, but she brought back the consternation quickly as she turned to the other women.

"I heard someone out in the dumpster about an hour ago. Which one of you put these brand-new-tags-still-on snowshoes in the dumpster? Who did you steal them from? I want to know."

"Maybe it wasn't any of us," Loretta said.

"Some stranger put some new snowshoes in my dumpster? That doesn't make much sense," Viola said.

"Viola," Willa said. "Why did it take you an hour to check?"

Viola glared at her. "Good question, Willa. In fact, I should have checked earlier, but the noises took about an hour to register."

"Well, if you'd gone out when you first heard the noise, you might have seen that it wasn't one of us," Willa said.

I held my breath. I couldn't tell if the other women did the same. Maybe they didn't care how Willa spoke to Viola.

"Willa, you're skirting the edge of acceptable tones here," Viola said.

Showing a glimmer of intelligence, Willa pursed her mouth closed, crossed her arms in front of her chest, and nodded once without saying anything else.

"Viola," Trinity pleaded. "I don't think it was any of us, and her stuff is all okay." She nodded toward me. "We're not going to go into her room and take her things, no matter what you might think.

We all want good reports from you. You know that. Besides, snow-shoes? Who in the world would try to take something so big? Not how we usually work."

Loretta didn't say anything at all. She was silent, her eyes too widely innocent. She was trying too hard, but at least she didn't have an attitude.

"I will find out what happened," Viola said. "I will find out the truth, and I promise you, it would be better if whoever is behind this confesses to me first."

We could hear the motor from the refrigerator in the kitchen click on as we looked at Viola. No one confessed to anything.

"All right. Have it your way. Get to bed and get back here in time for breakfast," Viola said before she stood and marched out of the room.

The tense air left with her and the other three women relaxed. Trinity's shoulders fell, Loretta rubbed her hand over her forehead, and Willa stood.

I should have just followed Viola, but I was too curious about what would happen next. There was something else to me staying too. I wanted the three women to see that I wasn't scared of them, wasn't going to be bullied by them, if that thought had crossed their criminal minds. I *was* scared a little, but I knew enough to know you can't let bullies see that they're succeeding.

"I can't believe I'm in the middle of all this shit," Willa said as she left the room, her footfalls heavy and angry.

Loretta rolled her eyes at me. "She thinks she's something."

Trinity looked sideways at Loretta and I wondered what she was thinking.

"You!" Loretta said to Trinity. "Whatever went on to get her so mad at you, get it fixed. I don't want to do this every night."

Trinity glared at Loretta and then scooted her chair back noisily. "What makes you so sure it was me?"

"I have no doubt," Loretta said firmly.

In what I could only describe as a huff, Trinity left the room.

"What was that about?" I asked. "What do you think Trinity did?"

"Nothing. I'm going back to bed," Loretta said as she stood. She didn't look at me as she left. "See you in the morning."

For a long few moments, I sat in the dining room, making sure I wasn't dreaming. I wasn't.

Willa had a point, who would steal snowshoes? Who would throw them in the Benedict House dumpster? What did Loretta think Trinity had done to anger Viola?

I didn't know enough about anything to venture any guesses.

But I didn't trust any of my housemates, and I would make sure my door was always locked, the chair under the knob when I was inside.

I trusted Viola though. I trusted her completely.

I hoped I wasn't making a mistake, I thought, as I went back to the comfortable bed and the warm covers.

But sometimes, you just needed to trust someone.

Eleven

Breakfast was a quiet event. No one said much. The entire meal was strange and fraught with unasked questions and held breaths. I didn't really care, because Willa made biscuits and gravy and eggs, and again I ate more than everyone else. I could not seem to get filled up. No one minded my appetite.

"You've been to the Mercantile," were the only words Loretta uttered. She rolled her tired eyes at my attire and then turned her attention back to her plate. She, of all of us, seemed the most tired after our middle-of-the-night interruption.

Viola didn't stay in the dining room, but the three other women were so subdued that I didn't ask questions I wanted to ask. Something more than the late-night incident was on their minds. Or they were just all tired.

I was strangely well rested. My jeans were stiff, but the T-shirt fit well, and I liked the cap. I didn't much care what I looked like, and it was freeing not to care. I wolfed down my food amid the uncomfortable silence and then left to wait outside for Donner. I would have liked to have a private conversation with Viola, but I didn't want to miss my ride and I didn't think she'd tell me anything anyway. I was glad to leave the Benedict House, an extra sense of freedom in my bones. Not only was I away from Levi, I wasn't a parolee under whatever restrictions they were under. Was it possible I could get back to my old self simply because I recognized my own true freedom? I hoped so.

As if he knew exactly when I'd be done eating, Donner's truck came into view from down the paved road that lead to the dock just as I stepped outside. I still hadn't ventured the direction he came from and I wondered if we'd go back that way.

We didn't. We went the opposite direction instead.

"Listen," he said, very seriously, shortly after we set out, "you need to be extra careful, and I know we don't have consistent cell service out here but you do inside the *Petition* building. You need to try to call me if you get in a bind or something."

"What kind of a bind?" I asked as I looked at the business card he'd handed me.

"You need to be careful around here. No setting off on bike rides in rainstorms, no exploring without the proper guidance and gear. You came here with no real preparation. I talked to Gril and let him know I would tell you to call if you needed anything."

"Do all the new residents get such a welcome?" I asked, suspicious that Gril might have told Donner who I truly was.

"Only the ones who show up with a brain surgery scar on the side of her head, and no luggage."

I frowned. "That's fair. Thank you."

"Good, now here's a small speech about living in the wild."

Apparently, I shouldn't have left the *Petition* until the storm passed. And, in fact, I shouldn't have gone anywhere without the appropriate footwear and clothing, all of which I now owned, thanks to our shopping spree. I should not even consider exploring the woods on my own yet, but Donner would be a willing guide. So would others. I just had to ask. I was to never go anywhere without a raincoat and boots. Ever. And when winter hit, he would give me a new set of rules.

"I'll be careful," I said.

"Good. Now, did you know George Rafferty, the husband of the deceased, has gone missing?"

"No." Gril hadn't mentioned that part to me, not that I thought he should have. "What do you think happened to him?"

"We have no idea."

"Do you think he could have killed Linda and then run away or did someone take him, someone else killed Linda and came back to kill George too?" I speculated aloud.

Donner shook his head slowly. "We're just not sure. He called in when he found her body and now we can't find him."

"That's not good, no matter what it means."

"No, it's not."

"Are you a law enforcement officer?" I asked as we rode another bumpy path through the woods.

"Gril is the chief, but we help fill in when he needs us, and when I say 'we' I mean park rangers. Sometimes we have to call in Juneau police, but though things can get dicey around here, Gril and the few of us that work with him seem to be able to manage," he said. "All of us are well trained in outdoor survival, and our training is ongoing. We take it seriously."

As we fell silent and Donner steered his truck into an even more thickly treed patch, flashes of a memory came to me, but not a bad memory. Levi Brooks wasn't part of this one.

One year, one spring break, my mother had come upon some information about my dad's whereabouts during the three weeks before he'd disappeared.

"We're going to talk to a woman," Mom had said as she'd turned onto a dirt road in Missouri. "Some loser your father met at some sleazy backwoods bar."

She'd looked at me, frowned, and then tapped a Marlboro out of the pack that had been sitting on the old Buick's bench seat. Over the years, she'd managed a few round, brown burns into the blue-and-tan striped upholstery.

She stuck the cigarette between her lips and punched the lighter on the dash. "I don't know what we'll find, but just work with me."

"I always do, don't I?" I'd just turned thirteen.

She huffed a laugh. "Yeah, girl of my heart, you do."

She lit the cigarette and sucked in hard. She talked as she exhaled. "Your dad ever talk about women to you?"

My attention jerked to her. "No!"

"Hang on, don't get all sensitive on me. I'm just curious, Bethie. He's dead and gone probably and I loved him, you know that. You know he loved us. Hell, we wouldn't be out here looking for what happened to him if we didn't love him. But he was a man, and men are led by . . . well, you'll see as you get older. But I do need to know everything. Did your dad ever talk to you about another woman?"

"No, Mom, he never did."

"You sure?"

"Yes." Something bitter burned at the back of my throat. I was old enough to wonder why I was so bothered by her insinuations. She was right, he was probably dead and gone. But that was my dad she was talking about. He'd been loyal to her. To me. To us.

"Beth," Donner said.

I blinked back to the present. "Yeah, sorry."

"I was just saying that this is an area we call the Northwest quad. I don't know why or how Benedict got split up into four zones, so to speak, but it works for us. The Raffertys have a P.O. box, but if someone were to tell someone else where they lived, we'd say Northwest quad, third right road in, road 12-60."

"Not third road on the right?"

"Nope. Third right road in."

"I can handle that."

We were under such a canopy of thick branches that the sky was barely visible. Narrow slits of sunlight made it through, but only a few. It was as dark as dusk, and even though warm air moved out of the vents on Donner's truck, the window next to my arm seemed to become colder.

"The temperature really went down when we moved under the trees?" I asked.

"Yeah, probably," Donner said.

"Can it be different by a lot in the shade?"

"Yep, and it'll rain soon, which will make it colder."

"It always rains soon."

"That's right. Good job."

I nodded but my attention was pulled to the cabin we were approaching. It was a log cabin in the classic sense.

"Did they build this, log by log?"

"The Raffertys didn't, but the previous residents did."

The square-shaped house wasn't big, and with windows on each side of the door, it seemed like it could be made into a cozy place, something that might be used in a magazine ad for a vacation destination. There was no smoke coming up from the chimney, but I could easily imagine it. I squinted at the crime scene tape over the front door. It wasn't my place to offer an opinion, but it seemed like an afterthought, not really a deterrent. It *was* the middle of nowhere though.

"How many rangers work with Gril?" I asked.

"Depends on the day, I suppose. We have four who've been deputized. I mostly help with search and rescue situations. And airport runs," he added.

"Thanks for that."

He threw the truck into Park. "Stay here. I need to check something in the cabin, but it's still a crime scene and I'm here on business."

I nodded.

I watched Donner make his way to the cabin door. I also watched as he looked over the grounds. I didn't know what had been determined so far, but Donner was alert to the world around him. He looked at the path he walked. He looked around at the surrounding woods.

I wished I'd asked more about the Raffertys on the way over. I'd been surprised by the news about George, but who knew what that meant. Donner had seemed concerned but not overly so.

Some reporter I was going to make. I looked around too. If there was a boondocks, it probably didn't feel as primitive and uninviting as this. I shivered.

I could hide here, but I could also be alone in a place like this. I doubted anyone could hear a scream from inside this cabin; even nearby witnesses might only hear something that had been muffled by all the trees, or nothing at all. I wondered if anyone had heard a gunshot. I wondered how much hunting occurred in these woods. I needed to start asking the right questions.

As I settled into the lumpy seat, something moved amid the dark patch of trees on the right side of the house. I bolted upright.

A moose? A bear? I looked back and forth between the movement and the door of the cabin. Would Donner be caught unawares, or had he lived here long enough to know to look both ways before stepping outside?

Should I get out and let him know? Honk the horn? I watched the movement as I put my hand on the door handle. I didn't know how big a deal I needed to make of this.

A man finally emerged from the woods, seemingly pushed out forcefully. He wore ripped winter gear, and again the thought that a bear might be nearby came to my mind. But if a bear's claws had sliced at him, he'd be cut up too. Bloody. He'd be about dead, right?

He didn't notice the truck at first, and when he did I thought I saw panic flash in his eyes. With my elbow, I locked the door and then reached over to the driver's side and did the same. And then I laid on the horn.

The man jumped in his skin and his eyes got wider, but he didn't run away. He blinked in confusion toward the truck and then at Donner when he emerged from the cabin. A second after he saw

Donner, the man crumpled into a pile on the ground. Donner hurried to him.

I unlocked my door and ran to join them.

"I wasn't sure what to do." I crouched next to Donner. "Do we need to get him some help?"

Donner felt at the man's neck. "He's got a pulse. This is George Rafferty. We need to get him to town for medical attention. I'll call Gril on the way. Will you just go pull the door of the cabin closed while I get him in the truck?"

I hurried to the door, satisfying a small part of my curiosity by glancing inside. From what I could discern, it still looked like an active crime scene. I did what I could to memorize the view.

Blood spatter in a pattern that told me the bullet had come from the west side of the house. I could determine where Linda had been when she was shot and where her body probably fell after the shot. I didn't spot any brain matter, or other body parts. But the blood was still there. At least some of it. I tried to burn the image into my brain for later contemplation, but if I knew anything at all it was that memory wasn't always reliable, particularly with only short glances. I also knew that without precise measurements, suicide or murder could only be guessed at—where had the gun been when it fired the bullet that killed Linda? That distance, the measurements were needed to determine the answers. They had an ME who would or hopefully had done that, but I could too. I was good at that. I'd remind Gril.

We hadn't had a lot of violence in Milton, Missouri, but we'd had some. Gramps had taken me along to a few crime scenes, the ones where math would help—measurements could be important. But it had been a long time since I'd seen actual blood spatter.

I was good at remembering things, good at noticing things. At least I used to be. But there wasn't currently time to measure anything.

I closed the door tightly and ran to join Donner and George Rafferty in the truck.

Twelve

f I wanted a story for the *Petition,* all I had to do was pay attention. One was unfolding before my eyes.

Gril met us at the doctor's office, which was simply a back room in the Saloon, a room set up like a bedroom with a cot and an old television. The most sterile item was the empty vodka bottle on the edge of an old dresser, but the sheets and blankets on the bed looked clean.

"This is where the doctor meets people," Donner explained. "He does the best he can, but we always get ahold of the Harvingtons just in case we need to get a patient to Juneau. Francis works part-time here behind the bar, so that can save some time if we have a real emergency."

I nodded, wide-eyed and silent. We were crowded in the room—Donner, Gril, me, and an unconscious George Rafferty on the cot. However, he wasn't really unconscious as much as he was just deeply asleep. Donner explained that Gril had told everyone to approach George with extreme caution. He hadn't been given the armed and dangerous designation because the gun that had been used to kill Linda was with her body and no one was aware if the Raffertys owned any other weapons.

I didn't say much, hoping only to stay out of the way, help if George Rafferty needed help.

"Oh," a man said as he opened the door. "A bit crowded, I'd say."

"I can . . . ," I began.

"No, no, it's all right. Where's my patient?"

Dr. Powder was a puzzle piece of ages. His head was old, his face wrinkled, his hair gray. His chest was wide, framed by burly shoulders that couldn't belong on someone who must be at least sixty. His waist was trim, but his legs seemed too skinny underneath his old jeans. He carried a worn doctor's bag and I wondered if it had always been his or if it had been part of a Benedict doctor's possessions for a hundred years.

"And there's Mr. Rafferty." Dr. Powder cut a short path to the man on the bed.

I found some space in a corner, but Gril and Donner stood behind the doctor and watched as he examined the patient.

Dr. Powder listened to George Rafferty's heart and lungs, then put the stethoscope to the carotid artery in George's neck. He pulled a blood pressure cuff from his coat pocket, and with quick, efficient movements checked his blood pressure.

"George, buddy, can you wake up?" The doctor gently shook his patient's arm, but to no avail.

On the way to the Saloon, George had sort of been awake but incoherent and mumbling things that included Linda's name, but no other words had been clear. Once Donner had deposited him on the cot, he'd either fallen into unconsciousness, or this deep sleep, I didn't really know the difference, and had been that way ever since, snoring once or twice every few minutes.

The doctor pulled the stethoscope from his ears and looked at Gril. "Probably a little dehydrated, but not bad. I think he'll be okay."

"Why can't we wake him up?" Gril asked.

Dr. Powder shrugged. "My guess is that his body is dealing with whatever trauma he's been through. He'll wake up when he's ready, but he's in good shape, considering."

I suspected most people in such a condition would be sent to a hospital but, again, I didn't comment.

"If he doesn't wake up by tomorrow morning, we'll get him to Juneau. As it is, I think he just needs some rest, fluids, and food. I'll grab an IV and get some good stuff in him. We can get him to Juneau if you want but I don't think we need to rush him there." The doctor looked at Gril.

"Whatever he's been through, it didn't get down to freezing last night," Gril thought aloud. "We could just watch him. I need to talk to him, see if we need to look for someone else."

"I think he's okay. He could wake up at any second. I've seen this sort of thing before. He's fine. He's resting and processing."

"Is there anything you can give him to wake him up?" Gril asked.

"Yeah, but it might not be good for his heart. I don't know enough about his medical history, and I don't have equipment to help him if he goes south."

I was standing behind them, but I could see by the set of Gril's shoulders that he was considering his options.

"We need some questions answered, answers that only George can give us," Gril said.

Dr. Powder shook George's arm. "George, buddy, we need you to wake up."

Another time, the snort from George might have been funny. Today, no one laughed.

"All right. Donner, can you stay with him while the doc grabs the IV stuff? I'll go with him," Gril said.

"Yeah." Donner looked at me and then Gril did too.

"I thought you'd left," Gril said. "You should have left."

"I, uh, sorry. I'll go now." I nodded at Donner. I had an urge to tell him thank-you, but I thought better of it. Maybe later.

Donner nodded and then his attention went back to George. As I left the small room, the only eyes still on me were Dr. Powder's. Did he wonder who I was or did he know and wanted to get a look at my scar? At least I'd know what he looked like when I went to talk to him about my situation.

It was good to get out of the small, crowded room, but the Saloon wasn't spacious either.

Two customers were huddled together in a booth along the side wall. It was dark enough inside that I couldn't tell if they were men or women. The bare wood slat walls had been adorned with a few neon signs—beer brands—but the place still felt unfinished. An old jukebox sat in a corner but it wasn't illuminated. Did it not work or was it not plugged in? I was curious enough to investigate, but I didn't get far.

"Drink?" a female voice said from behind the bar.

I squinted. The female voice didn't belong to someone who looked like a female, but that seemed too rude to even think.

The barkeep laughed. "It's okay. Yeah, I'm a girl but I choose not to look like one so much. You're not the first I've fooled."

I approached the bar. "I'd love a drink, but something light. I'm sorry if I looked . . . perplexed. That was rude."

She laughed. "Name's Bonita. Call me Benny though. I'm just being the 'me' I need to be, and dressing the way I want to dress. How about a Bloody Mary, light on the bloody?"

Dr. Powder and Gril left the small room and then the bar without seeming to notice anyone else.

"Do I look like I need some vegetables?" I sat up on a stool.

"As a matter of fact, you do." She put a bowl of pretzels in front of me. "I've heard about the scar. You fell off a horse and you're from Denver. Welcome to Benedict."

I took a pretzel and realized I was hungry. I'd lost track of the time and it must be at least lunchtime. I looked at my watch; not quite eleven. Was I ever going to get full? "Me in a nutshell."

Benny looked at the huddled customers in the booth and then leaned over toward me. "Can I see the scar?"

I took off the cap.

It was dark inside the Saloon but she could still see well enough. "Holy moly, that's a scar. How are you not dead?"

"I was taken care of quickly." My words coming out around a pretzel.

My eyes got big as I watched Benny create the Bloody Mary behind the bar. It was going to be huge, but true to her word, she put in very little booze.

For whatever reason, I suddenly remembered I still wanted to call Dr. Genero.

"And speaking of blood." Benny placed the tall drink in front of me. She reached into a cooler and pulled out two stalks of celery. "Enjoy. You want a burger or something? I can call the café and they'll bring it over."

"That's convenient." I thought about it a minute. "Yeah, I'd love a burger. Cheeseburger. Fries too. You can just call? I can walk over and order it."

"Two shakes of a cow's tail and I'll have it ordered."

Benny placed the order via walkie-talkie and then turned back to me.

"How's Vi treating you?" she asked.

"Very well," I said. "She scares me, but I like her."

"She's large and in charge." Benny laughed. "She's my people."

I looked at her. "Literally?"

"Yep. We're sisters."

"Now I see the resemblance. Did you two grow up here?" I took a big pull on the drink. Best Bloody Mary ever.

"We grew up in Juneau. Our parents drowned when we were teenagers, fishing boat. We ran away to Benedict so we wouldn't be put into foster care."

"Oh. I'm sorry."

"Nah."

"Had to be rough."

"We've survived so far." Benny eyed the door to the back room.

"I think Mr. Rafferty will be okay," I said. "The doctor says . . . well, I'm not so sure I understand the diagnosis, but he thinks George will heal."

"If Donner doesn't kill him, I suppose."

She'd mumbled and muttered the words under her breath.

"Excuse me?" I took another pull of the drink.

She lifted her eyebrows at me and then shook her head. "Nothing."

"That didn't sound like a casual comment."

"It's bad form of me to share so let me emphasize that it was just a rumor, and I have no proof of it, but there was a rumor that Donner and Linda Rafferty were involved."

Questions are important. Almost as important as the answers that go with them. It doesn't take someone with my background and in my varying lines of work to know that. But sometimes asking the wrong questions will guarantee that you never get the answers you need.

I thought about what I'd witnessed so far. Donner had picked me up from the airport and had seemed bothered to have to deal with me, but not upset, not distraught about anything. He didn't mention Linda's name. He'd hurried to help George. But why had we gone out to the cabin in the first place? He'd told me he was working but didn't give me any other details. Why would he though? He had gone inside the Rafferty's cabin by himself, the cabin that was still marked as a crime scene. But he was an officer of the law. Sort of. Or, was he trying to hide something, remove proof of some affair?

"I see," I said, still not zoning in on the right words, but hoping my tone prompted her to talk more.

"Well, I don't know, but it's all pretty weird. I can't imagine that being caught in an affair would cause Linda to take her own life. I can't imagine anything that would make her take her own life. Now, at least. She made it through a tragedy some years ago. She was still sad but not suicidal."

"The loss of her son?"

"Yeah, you heard."

"Yes. It's very sad. You knew Linda well?"

"Sure, we all know each other around here. You'll see."

I nodded. "It can be hard to know if someone is hurting enough to take their own life."

"The day before she died, she came in to tell me she'd help out around here part-time. She was going to start tonight. Is that something someone who is going to kill herself does?"

I shook my head once. "I don't know."

"I don't think so," Benny said.

"Did you tell Gril?"

"I did."

"How did he respond?"

"Thanked me but didn't get too wound up about it."

I cleared my throat. "George looks significantly older than Donner."

"So was Linda."

She made no further comment about the age differences and I didn't either, but it was interesting food for thought. And Donner and George were in a room alone. If there had been an affair, did that matter?

As I took another sip, Loretta came through the bar's front door, bringing my cheeseburger and fries.

"Hello there, roomy," she said as she placed the plate in front of me.

"Oh. Hello. Thank you."

"Yeah, yeah, you're wondering if parolees are allowed to have jobs while we're getting free room and board. Well, we are, encouraged to, actually, but this is not a job. I'm volunteering, because they need some help over there, and I'm all about helping where I'm needed. I'm allowed to take tips, but no one's paying me for this."

I was so lost in smelling and inspecting the mountain of food before me that her words didn't immediately register.

Loretta cleared her throat.

"Oh. Of course." I reached into my pocket and pulled out some bills. But as I extended them to her, I had a thought and I pulled them back. "What was going on this morning? Breakfast was strained. What were you talking about last night, something between Trinity and Viola?"

Loretta looked at me with question and then admiration. She looked down at the five on the top of the stack. "Gosh, I'm not sure I can remember the 'more' you're talking about."

I displayed a ten and looked at her.

To her credit, Benny walked away. Her sister had been involved in whatever had been going on—sometimes curiosity did kill the cat, and ruin relationships.

"Right," Loretta said. "Well, I remember a little. Yesterday, during the day, Vi was upset at one of us. It wasn't me." She raised her eyebrows.

I brought out another five and added it to the stack.

"It wasn't Willa either," Loretta said. "It seems that one of us had an argument with someone here in town, and it was loud. Too many people might have heard it. That bothered Viola. She came back to the House yesterday, fit to be tied. She and the one I didn't name, in turn, argued. Loudly."

"I see. Who did Trinity have a public argument with?" I didn't wait for Loretta to prompt, I brought out another five.

"Linda Rafferty."

Oh. I thought about Viola's visit to the *Petition* and her sudden need to leave, right after I told her Gril might suspect Linda Rafferty was murdered. "Any chance you know what it was about?"

"Wish I did, but even though it was gossip, I never caught the deets, you know. Willa doesn't know either, at least that's what she says."

I nodded. "Anything else you'd like to tell me?"

"No, just that the three of us girls were scared shitless this morning, because of that argument and because of the late-night weirdness that was all about some snowshoes." Loretta looked up at

Benny, who was ignoring us, and then back at me. "We don't even think the snowshoe incident was real. We think it was just Viola's way of rattling our cages after yesterday's confrontation. Viola is in charge of our freedom, you know that, don't you? Her being angry can delay that freedom. None of us wanted to spark the fuse we'd heard explode with Trinity. Willa and I wouldn't have even gone to breakfast if we weren't required. We got through it okay, but I hope things are better for dinner."

"Me too. Thanks, Loretta." I gave her the money, plus a little more.

She smiled at me. "Thanks, doll, you're a peach."

I smiled and turned back to my food as she sauntered away. I put my wallet securely into a front pocket.

"You might want to make sure she didn't take your whole wad," Benny said as she rejoined me.

"I checked," I said around a bite of the burger. "I'm good."

"Alrighty." Benny smiled.

She watched me eat for a moment, her eyes squinting. "You know, there's a community center. It's just an outbuilding down the road a piece. We do all kinds of things there. Evening craft things. Meetings. I hear you're going to be writing the *Petition*," Benny said.

I nodded as I chewed.

"You'll hear a lot about the community center, and you might want to check it out. Everyone spends some time there. Everyone."

"I will. Thank you."

Benny looked over my shoulder as the door opened, filling the dark space with harsh light yet again.

"Hey, Doc, Gril," Benny said as they came inside with the bags of fluid that would be IV'd into George.

It was a strange set of circumstances, but if anyone other than me thought so, they didn't show it.

The door to the back room opened just as the Saloon's front door closed.

Donner leaned out. "He's awake, and he's talking."

Gril and Dr. Powder hurried to the back.

I looked at Benny.

"This could be interesting," she said before she excused herself to attend to something somewhere behind the bar.

I wondered if she was somehow eavesdropping on the men in her back room. And I really wondered how I could get in on that action too.

It wasn't meant to be though. Other customers came in and Benny reappeared and did all the bartending and table waiting. I realized I might not be made of the right reporter stuff when I didn't want to hang out in the bar to wait for the medical report. After I ate, I was full and tired. I finished the drink and wiped off the celery with a napkin.

No one was paying attention as I left, but, happily, the three horses were hanging out by Ben, the fake bear. All I had to do was hold up the celery and the three large animals approached. They were gentle as they took their quick snack and then done with me when the celery was gone.

As they walked away, I looked up at the blue sky. I was glad it wasn't raining, but at least I'd have been ready this time. I had my boots on.

Thirteen

I couldn't sleep. I'd tried. And tried again, but it was a battle I wasn't going to win easily. Too many things were running through my mind. Mostly, I wondered what George Rafferty had said when he'd awakened. I'd spent the rest of the day cleaning up the *Petition*, enough work to keep my mind occupied but not enough to tire me out. I needed to get some exercise.

Finally, at just after midnight, I moved the chair away from the door and ventured out to the hallway. The space was illuminated with night-lights intermittently plugged into the walls. I hadn't noticed them the night before. As my eyes adjusted, I wondered if I could find any food or something to do to keep my mind off my once again hungry stomach.

My first stop was the kitchen, but that and the dining room's doors were both locked tight. I really needed to get some snacks for my room, as soon as possible.

For a long moment, I just stood in the hallway and listened. Wind rattled something, but I wasn't sure if it was rafters or a loose window, or maybe a loose door somewhere. I didn't hear televisions or music coming from anywhere, but I didn't know how the parolees' rooms were furnished. Were they allowed to use laptops? I hadn't asked Viola if there was any Wi-Fi in the building, but based upon everything else I'd seen in Benedict, it wasn't likely.

I wasn't even sure which room was Viola's. I crossed through the lobby and then down the other hallway, the one I'd first seen Willa walk down. Viola had mentioned that the parolees were all upstairs and that the stairway was at the end of the hall. I moved slowly with my ears perked. I didn't get right up next to any of the doors, but I veered close to them, making a serpentine all the way to the stairway. I still didn't hear any electronics, but I was pretty sure I figured out which room was Viola's when I heard a snore coming through. If I'd had any doubt after that, I just had to read the plaque adorning the door.

THE BOSS.

And she was.

Her room was at the end, right next to the stairway. Either she snored loudly, or her room was like mine and the bed wasn't too far away from the door.

I took the stairs up to the second floor, two at a time. There was no light in the stairwell, but I could tell that dark carpeting covered each step. It muffled my footfalls. Upstairs, the hallway looked just like the one downstairs, and was similarly lit with plugged-in night-lights. I found the item that was making the noise. A window at the far end was partly open, about six inches up. Even from where I stood, I could see it moving with the breeze coming through.

It was cold outside. I crossed my arms in front of myself and hurried toward the window. Surely even parolees shouldn't have to be too cold.

But as I went to push it closed, I glanced outside. This part of the Benedict House backed up to thick woods. I couldn't tell if there was a moon or if it was covered by clouds, but I could see the darkness of the woods; it was endless.

Except, there was a small light in the distance. A white circle moved back and forth, up and down, and around the trees. Who was in the woods with a flashlight?

"Why do I care?" I said aloud.

Maybe it wasn't an unusual sight anyway. I reached again to close the window.

But then I saw something else.

"Uh-oh," I said when I noticed a rope had been tied to a hook that jutted out from the side of the building. The rope reached to the ground. I looked back out toward the moving light. I couldn't tell how quickly it was approaching, but it was still moving. Either someone from inside the Benedict House had left, using this rope, or someone had or was using it to come inside.

I looked back over my shoulder at the parolees' doors. I knew I should wake up Viola immediately and let her know what I'd found.

But I didn't want to. It wasn't that I sympathized that much with the parolees. I didn't, not really. But where could they go? They weren't violent offenders and there was no way to easily leave Benedict. However, was I seeing the person who'd stolen the snowshoes?

I hoped that whatever was going on didn't require a gun to squelch potential trouble that might be bubbling up, but I wanted to know.

I turned and made my way back to the stairway, taking a seat on the first stair down. I put my back against the wall. All I had to do was lean a little to the right to be able to see the window at the other end, and chances were good that I wouldn't be noticed by anyone coming in; the hallway was too shadowed.

It didn't take long to feel the cold air seep under my skin, but I didn't want to leave my spot to gather some of my warmer gear. I rolled my eyes at the idea that Donner would be irritated that I hadn't been more prepared to snoop.

I settled back and hoped I wouldn't have to wait long for whatever it was I was waiting for. After I rubbed my arms and then sat back again though, I hit the back of my head on the wall. It hurt, sending a different sort of blinding pain up around the sides of my head. I hadn't hit it that hard, but it must have been at just the right spot to cause the pain.

Mine. You are mine. You will never get away from me. You are mine forever.

Panic stopped my heart, or that's what it felt like. I wanted to open my eyes and prove that Levi wasn't there in front of me. But the pain kept my eyes closed; as it took an eternity to dissipate, I realized I could smell him too—the same smell I remembered when I'd seen Hank's lumberjack coat. A distant sort of fascination overtook me. That smell—so bad, and so real.

What the hell? Why couldn't I get my eyes to open? But then, somewhere in my mind, I recognized that the pain was dissipating. If I could just not panic, I would be okay in a minute. Levi is not there. He's is not *here*.

"Hey!" a voice whispered forcefully. "Wake up!"

It was a female voice. It wasn't Levi.

"Come on. Open your eyes," the voice said, gently but filled with concern.

Once the pain faded to a soft beat, I could get my eyes open.

"Loretta," I said. "Hey."

"Hey, yourself, crazy girl from Denver. What the hell happened?"

She was sitting above me on the landing. I'd never seen her in so many clothes. She wore jeans, a sweater, and boots. I could smell the cold, outside air coming off her and it wasn't unpleasant. A flashlight was propped upright on the floor next to her.

"Just a headache," I said. "I'm okay now."

"No, no you're not. I don't know what's wrong, but you're not well, girlfriend."

I managed a quick look down the hallway. The window was closed.

"Were you out for a run or something?" I asked.

Loretta sent a glance toward the window. "Something like that." She looked back at me. "It's my freedom. I like to get out and walk around without anyone in an authority position knowing about it.

Gives me some control over my life." She looked at me and half-smiled. "Weird, huh?"

"I don't know."

"I thought that's why Viola called the middle-of-the-night gathering last night, shoot me or at least yell at me. Imagine my relief when that wasn't it."

I looked at her. "Was the timing right? Could she have heard you and thought someone was rummaging around the dumpster?"

"Yes ma'am. I already thought of that."

"You should tell her."

"No ma'am." She shook her head. "I didn't steal no stupid snow-shoes and I didn't throw them in the garbage. I don't know who did, but like I already told you, I think she made it up."

"It might put you on her good side if you tell her. She might understand."

Loretta laughed once. "No. You know, Beth from Denver, life sure can suck sometimes. When I roam around at night, I feel free, like I'm not the idiot who keeps getting caught and either locked up or sent to some bumblefuck in the middle of nowhere. I don't want that taken away."

"You weren't meeting anyone? What about the wildlife out there? All of it?"

Loretta shrugged. "I'd rather get eaten by a bear than miss my midnight walks." She squinted at me. "I want to be a better person, Beth. But it's not that easy sometimes."

I nodded.

Another memory swept through my mind, one I hadn't thought about in a long time. A good one.

We're gonna try and help some of them, Beth, but some are beyond help. Breaks my old heart right into a million pieces.

Tears sprang to my eyes when I thought about my grandfather. Still, even after all these years, and after the terror I'd been through, memories of Gramps brought me to tears more than any other memories. I blinked them away quickly.

"You just walk around?" I said.

"I do. That's it. I couldn't run farther into the woods if I wanted to, but I don't really want to. If I watch my p's and q's, I should be free in a few months. And, again, I'll try to do better. We'll see."

I nodded again. Gramps wouldn't think Loretta was a hopeless case, but I wasn't sure what he would do or say to her. I wished I did. I wished I knew some magic words that would help. But I didn't.

"Hey, I heard George Rafferty was fake sleeping today," Loretta said. "You know anything about that?"

"I don't know about it being fake, but I know he woke up. I don't know what he said to the police. You think there's any chance he could be responsible for his wife's death?"

"I have no idea. I didn't know them like Trinity and Willa seemed to."

"What do you mean?"

She shrugged. "It's just that . . . I don't know, I'm not good at friendships, getting to know people."

I laughed once but then covered my mouth with my hand. For a few long beats, we listened, but it seemed no one else was awakened. "You seem like you'd make a lot of friends."

"No, Beth. I'm friendly, but I don't make friends. There's a difference."

"True." I felt sorry for her, but I didn't really know why. If Gramps were alive, he'd tell me not to.

Stay on your toes, Beth, criminals work hard at getting sympathy. Most of the time, it's undeserved, but we'll still try to help.

"Want to tell me more about the stuff I paid you for earlier?" I said.

"Why, you got more money?"

"No."

Loretta laughed this time, but it was quieter than mine, more practiced at laughing furtively probably. "Well, I don't have any more scoop. I'll let you know if I hear anything else, but none of that stuff is as interesting as me getting out of here as soon as I can. My only vice is my night walks."

"I understand." I wasn't so sure I believed her though.

"Are you going to tell on me?" Loretta asked.

"No," I said easily, but I wasn't sure what I would do.

"Thanks. Now, let's get you back to your room. You need rest. Actually, you probably need to see a doctor, but from what I've seen, there are none of those around here," Loretta said.

I stood. "I can get back on my own."

"Uh."

"If you get caught downstairs, you could be in trouble, right?" Loretta shrugged again.

"You stay up here." I paused as I looked at her. "Be careful out there."

Loretta laughed once. "I'll be fine. Until I'm not, and that's okay too."

I nodded slowly, in deference to the slight pain still in my head, and made my way downstairs. I could tell that Loretta waited at the top of the stairs, probably wondering if I'd stop by Viola's door more than if I'd make it to mine.

I walked right by the boss's room, hearing the same snore I'd heard earlier. I didn't smell Levi anymore. I didn't hear him either— for now at least. I was finally tired. I went to my room, closed the door, put the chair underneath, and wished for snacks for only a few more minutes before I finally fell fast asleep.

Fourteen

Dear Baby Girl,

Boy, oh boy, do I miss you. Call me when you can.

Quick and dirty update. Detective Majors—and isn't she something else?—too young to be doing what she's doing, that's for sure—told me about a van sighting over in Weyford. I went out to explore. Twice now, actually. The first time I met the old woman who'd seen the van outside her farmhouse. Geneva Spooner. We don't know that name, do we? I don't think so. Anyway, she's exactly what you might expect; old, all about the Bible, and living in a house full of doilies.

Anyhoo, there are tire tracks across the old highway in front of her place. I talked to her and it sure sounds like the van you were in—old, brown, Chevy or something like it. It might be a real lead. Majors thinks so too.

I talked to Geneva the first time I stopped by, but I forgot to go over and take pictures of the damn tracks. So, I went back the next day. Turns out it was a good thing I went back. That second time, Geneva came at me from across the road like a woman with a mission. She told me that she thought the van had been there again, the night before. She'd looked out her window and saw what she thought—but it was dark and all—was someone walking on top of that goddamned van. At first she didn't recognize that's what it was, but after she thought about it, that's the conclusion she came to. She was going to call Majors and tell her, but she hadn't yet. We went to look together, and I'll be horse-tied but that old woman helped us find something good. Maybe.

Up in the trees was a pink blanket, or something.

You can bet all your money and your love that I called Detective Majors and her merry band of idiots, I mean officers, right then and there. Even I know a good lead when I see one. Do you remember anything about a pink blanket?

I don't know what will come next, but I used some Bible talk on Geneva—eye-for-an-eye shit—and told her to call me first if she sees the van again. Don't know if she will, but if so, I'll hightail it back out there and take care of that mother-fucking piece of shit. We're getting closer, I can feel it.

I'm heading over to Milton to talk to Stellen the stud too. Want to make sure he's keeping the secret as to who you really are. I'll let you know.

Call me as soon as you can.

Love, Mom.

I was both pleased about a possible lead—though I didn't remember a pink blanket—and nervous that my mother was on the loose.

Damn. I was worried, but probably not as much as I should have been.

I read the email twice more, and then thought again about a pink blanket. I had nothing. Not one pink thing came to mind.

I needed to let Detective Majors know about the email ASAP. But I also wanted someone to take care of Levi Brooks, and I knew my mother didn't have to follow police procedures. Besides, she'd do whatever she wanted to do anyway. I had complete faith in Detective Majors, in all the police, in fact, but maybe I just needed to let this one play itself out. I wasn't sure.

"Stellen the Stud" was Chief Stellen Graystone, the police chief of Milton, MO. He was the man who still sat behind the desk my grandfather used to sit behind, at least that was the case about eight years ago when I last went to visit my old stomping grounds. He was a good man, a good police officer, but he couldn't possibly make sure everyone in the town of Milton, MO, kept my secret. It was an angle I hadn't considered much—I had thought about it some, but maybe not enough. Most of the residents of the small town knew *their* Beth Rivers, the beloved granddaughter of Dusty Sherwood, the best lawman in the history of lawmen, was the author Elizabeth Fairchild.

However, keeping my identity a secret had been a sort of unspoken bargain I'd made with the town. They were protective of me—because they'd loved my grandfather—but who knew what they thought of me or my secret all these years later? Mom wanted to make sure that at least the Milton police force was remaining mum. That might not be possible. In fact, I wondered, maybe they needed to become involved in the investigation. Now, there was an angle I hadn't thought about, but maybe *because* they knew me, they should be helping, or conducting their own investigation.

I didn't know. And I didn't know exactly what to do. I was far away, thankfully. Mom had dealt with so many different police over the years. For now, I'd just let her handle what she needed to handle. She was good at calling in the authorities when she thought it necessary. I hoped.

Considering the lack of sleep the previous two nights, I woke up with an even bigger sensation that I was on the road to healing, in many ways. Physically, the wounds were continuing to fade, little by little. My emotional healing would take longer, but I would work on it.

Last night's time with Loretta made something else clear too. Busy was good, very, very good. I needed to stay as busy as possible and I was intrigued enough by the local mystery to want some answers, maybe for an article, maybe not. I needed my own form of midnight walks, a good sense of my own freedom.

I *was* convinced that if Linda Rafferty had been murdered, it had nothing to do with me or Levi Brooks. Her death was no less tragic because of that realization, and I still wanted to know what happened to her—now, more than ever. It wasn't the writer in me. It wasn't the budding journalist (whatever form that would take), it was that cabin. I'd seen the inside of it. I'd seen Linda's blood. Maybe my grandfather's determination to find the truth, solve crimes, and try to reform some of the criminals, was something he'd instilled in me more deeply than I'd recognized before now, before I'd heard his voice in my head last night.

As I'd finally slept some the night before, I hadn't dreamed about Linda, Gramps, Loretta, Levi, or even that mysterious phone call Detective Majors was investigating. I'd dreamed about my father. Almost every day of my life, I had fleeting thoughts about him, but it had been a long time since he and my mother's obsession over where he'd gone had loomed so large in my thoughts that I remembered complete scenes from the days we were an intact family.

Last night, though . . . It hadn't been a misshapen dream, but a replay of something that had actually happened.

"Bethie buttons, sit right there and let me practice on you." He lifted *me up to the hood of a car, my dirty legs hanging over the side.*

I'd been playing in the mud, like any normal country girl who lived near a Missouri river.

"Practice?" I said.

"Yes. Now, what is it that I sell?"

"Cleaning supplies, Daddy!"

"No." He held up a serious finger. "I sell so much more than that. I sell extra time, I sell pride in your home, I sell luxury, baby girl. Luxury! I make women's' lives better, more beautiful."

"Cleaner!"

Dad laughed. "That's right."

But then his face fell, as if a cloud of sadness came over him suddenly.

"Daddy?"

He shook his head. "I'm sorry, sweetheart. I was just remembering a time when I didn't make a beautiful woman's life better." He forced a smile. "And that's why I need to practice, I suppose. Here we go."

I wasn't aware if I'd ever before remembered that moment in time. Was it significant in any way, to what happened to him, or what recently happened to me? Were my tragedies overlapping or elbowing each other for space? Was it all just random stuff or would it come together to mean something important?

Over the years my mother had asked continually if I remembered my father behaving strangely or differently in any way. I had called up a few moments, but never that one.

To my knowledge, my father had never before asked me to watch him rehearse, and I still didn't remember what happened next. Had he actually rehearsed? I didn't think so, but I couldn't be sure.

I shook my head and thought maybe I was getting too much Alaska fresh air. I sensed that I was spending too much time away from the current moment in time. Memories, flashbacks—they weren't overtaking all my hours, but it seemed like they were with me too much.

I double-checked the lock on my room door, grabbed a burner phone, and dialed Dr. Genero.

She answered after three rings, her voice hesitant. "This is Dr. Genero."

"Hey, it's Beth."

The doctor sighed. "I wondered. Are you okay, Beth? Hang on." I heard noises as if she was moving to another space. "Okay, I'm in my office alone now. Talk to me. Tell me everything."

I told her I had flown to someplace far away and that I was safe. I didn't tell her where I'd gone, but I tried to make my destination sound more rural than urban. She interrupted to ask if the flight, the altitude had bothered my head.

"No, and I'm feeling very well right now, but I had a couple of moments of white-hot pain. I've never had a migraine before, but I wonder if that's what they were."

"Probably. How long did they last?"

"Only a few minutes."

"Just two times?"

"So far."

Dr. Genero sighed again. "It's probably nothing to be concerned about. But, Beth, I really wish you'd come back. I'd like to be able to observe your progress for a few months at least."

"You said I was going to make a full recovery."

"And that is true, but, still, I'd like you to be close by just in case. It *was* brain surgery," she said.

"I'm not coming back, Dr. Genero, so we'll just have to make it work. There's a city close by. I'll find someone."

"A city, not a local person close by?"

"I'm not so sure about the local doctor."

"Did the headaches send you to her or him?"

"No, it's just a small town, and I ran into him already. He was busy. He didn't even ask about the scar yet."

"I'll get in touch with him if you'll let me."

"No, I'll talk to him soon."

"You'll tell him who you are?"

"No. I'm telling everyone I fell off a horse."

"I suppose that's plausible. Have you ever ridden a horse before?"

"No."

"Hopefully, you haven't escaped to a ranch somewhere."

I laughed. "I haven't."

"Good." I heard the smile in her voice. "I'm glad you're okay."

"I'm sorry I ran away, but I hope you understand how necessary it was."

"You did what you had to do. I'm glad you called."

"Dr. Genero, along with the headaches, I'm also remembering other things, in flashbacks and dreams."

"About your time with Brooks?"

"Some, but there are other things too. Childhood memories; things I hadn't remembered before."

"I see. Any disturbing images? Scary stuff?"

"Any memory I have of my time with Levi is bothersome, but not graphically exaggerated. Not yet at least. You know my father disappeared when I was young?"

"Yes, your mother told me."

"Right. I'm remembering him, and my long-dead grandfather too. Moments I don't remember thinking about before. They are surprising, though not all bad."

"I see. Well, the brain is a mysterious thing. At the risk of over-simplifying, you stirred things up in that noggin of yours. Who knows what's going to rise to the surface. Are the memories disturbing your sense of well-being, your sleep?"

"No. I wasn't tired last night until late, but when I was tired, I was able to sleep and the dream I had was good, though vivid and more a memory than anything imagined. I do feel safe here."

"Write everything down. That's for two purposes. One, it helps put memories in order, but secondly, I believe that writing these things down gives them less power over you. Give it a try at least. I do think you're still healing. I think it will get better."

"I will write things down."

"All right. How's your vision?"

"Fine."

"What? I hear something else in your tone."

I hesitated as something occurred to me. "I wonder if I'm re-membering my father, my grandfather, so my brain can avoid re-membering the man who abducted me. I'm a little afraid of what I'll remember next about him, and, yet, I want to remember something that will help the police find him. Could my brain be reaching for other things, so the horrific things don't get top billing?"

"It's possible, but anything is, at this point. I wish you were here, Beth. You need to have someone to talk to about this stuff on a con-sistent basis. Someone you can be honest with."

"I'll work on finding someone."

"Have you started writing your books yet?"

"I'm going to try again today."

"That would be good. Jump in, see what happens, and call me if you need me."

"I will. Thank you."

"I can talk more, I don't have to hang up yet."

I thought a moment. "I'm good for now, Dr. Genero, but I'll call back if I need to."

"All right. Take care, Beth."

"You too."

I disconnected the call and then immediately dialed Detective Majors.

I was disappointed when the call went to voicemail this time, and I left a message.

I put the phone into my pocket, found the moose cap, and checked the time. Breakfast should be just about ready, and I was starving.

Fifteen

Willa was still the cook, and waffles and bacon filled serving platters on the table in front of us. Viola randomly chose one of each of the foods and leveled a plate toward Willa. She survived the taste test and we all dug in. Loretta and I shared a look, but we didn't let it linger. Viola was too observant to let any look linger. Besides, my attention was almost completely on the food. I ate an inordinate amount again.

Daytime at the Benedict House, the outside light automatically made the atmosphere cheerier, the criminals less criminal-like. However, Viola was still her intimidating self. Even though there wasn't as much strain this morning as there had been yesterday, she spent much of the meal deep in thought, maybe distracted.

I enjoyed the food and finally got to a point where I didn't think I would fade away from hunger. I knew I might ruin the easygoing mood, but I was okay with that.

"Hey," I said, garnering everyone's attention, "who here was friends with Linda Rafferty?"

"That would be only me," Viola said dryly. "The three other

women in this room are only here temporarily and haven't lived here long enough to make such friendships. Why?"

"Have the police determined if it was suicide or murder?" I asked.

"Suicide," Viola said quickly.

"Really?" I hadn't expected that answer. "For sure?"

"For sure. I talked to Gril late last night. He got some information back from the medical examiner from Juneau. Something about blood spatter measurements. But it's confirmed." Viola sent Trinity a glare that made me think that the determination of the cause of death was the only reason Viola hadn't shot the swift-fingered Trinity.

Or that Gril hadn't arrested her.

I was still curious though. "Trinity, what was the argument you and Linda had? What was it, a day or two before she died?" No need to beat around the bush if all gossip spread around Benedict with the same speed as the gossip about me had.

Viola sent me a long, dark look. Willa put her fork down and seemed genuinely curious. And, Loretta and I avoided looking at each other, which probably only made it more obvious as to how I'd learned about said argument.

"Oh," Trinity said meekly. She sent a flittering glance at Viola before she looked at me. "It was absolutely nothing. She thought I'd taken her wallet." Trinity laughed. "Blame it on one of the criminals, you know."

"Why were you the one she blamed? Why not the other two?" I asked.

"Because I was the one sitting behind her at the Saloon. You know those booths over there?"

"I was in there yesterday."

"Right, well, we were back-to-back." Trinity looked at Viola. "And I was only having a soda because I'm not allowed to drink alcohol but there aren't many choices where to go in this town if you want a soda." She turned back to me. "Anyway, we were sitting back-to-back and at some point, her purse fell to the floor. I reached down and helped her pick things up." Trinity shrugged. "When she went to pay, her wallet was missing. Thought I took it. I can see why she might have thought so, but I didn't take it. She chased me out and yelled at me out in the middle of the street. It was embarrassing."

"I see," I said, watching her body language. It didn't tell me anything. She seemed calm and not defensive, if still mousey, trying to fold in on herself, make herself smaller than she really was. I looked at Viola, who was still watching Trinity too. I'd talk to her later. Is this why she'd hurried out of the *Petition*, to talk to Trinity about this argument, yell at her? Did they yell at each other?

"But," Trinity said, "it sounds like everyone was worried about the argument for no reason. Linda Rafferty killed herself. Unless it was because she thought I was lying about her wallet, then I had nothing to do with her death—if that's what everybody was thinking, and it sure seems like maybe it was."

Viola shook her head.

"That sounded . . . wrong. Sorry," Trinity said.

"Did she ever find her wallet?" Willa asked, but I noticed she kept her head down, didn't look at anyone.

"I have no idea," Trinity said.

I looked at Viola, but she might not know either. She didn't look at me. If Linda had killed herself, the case, as it was, was now closed.

Everyone went their own direction after breakfast. My bike had been stored next to the front desk in the lobby. I'd walked by it the night before but hadn't noticed that someone had wiped it clean. I looked around a moment but there was no one to thank.

I grabbed my backpack filled with my laptop, scanner, and two more burner phones. I slung the heavy pack over my back and carried the Olympia under my arm as I climbed aboard the bike, balancing the typewriter on the bar in front of me. I'd need a basket, at least. I'd pocketed some apple slices from breakfast, but the horses weren't around when I left downtown.

I quickly decided it'd be a miracle if I made it to the *Petition* in one piece.

It was cool and cloudy, but thankfully not raining. I recognized two trucks I'd seen parked on the street the day before, but I didn't know who they belonged to. I didn't see Donner's truck. I peered toward the Saloon, where the neon OPEN light was illuminated. I might check in on Benny later.

As I pedaled down the road toward the woods, I caught a glimpse of Willa walking around the corner of the Mercantile. Her arms were crossed in front of her and a look of irritation downturned her face. She'd been fine at breakfast. I stopped the bike but was far enough away that she'd have to look up to notice me. I didn't call out but watched as she yanked open Benedict House's door and disappeared inside.

I had no idea why she seemed upset. I decided I didn't need to know.

It was an anxiety-riddled ride to the *Petition*. I felt exposed. I felt stupidly out of shape, ridiculous as I maneuvered around the dirt road's divots and fallen foliage. No one was watching me, but it felt like the world was. I didn't know what parts of "all the wildlife" lurked behind branches, but no animals showed themselves. If they were watching, they were probably too amused to attack.

By the time I was inside the leaning walls, I was relieved to be there, happy to be behind a locked door, and grateful to get to work, occupy my mind.

With an energy that had eluded me for weeks, I cleaned, organized, and filed. I found an old boom box and a drawer full of seventies CDs, and played a soundtrack I hadn't heard in years. As 38 Special and the Doobie Brothers serenaded me, I put the office all the way together, setting up my typewriter and laptop on the desk that faced the door. No one could come in without me seeing them. The one window would be to my side, no longer to my back.

It's not that I expected Levi Brooks to break down the door or peek through the window, but if he did, I'd hopefully see him in time to fight back.

Remnants of Donner's lecture rang in my mind, preparedness for the wilderness. He hadn't mentioned self-defense. I'd thought about my lack of defensive skills since waking up in the hospital. Could Donner help me with those? What about shooting a gun? As I prepared to get to work, a new resolve built in my gut. I had much I wanted to do, to learn, to keep myself safe, not just run away to Alaska.

Just as I fired up my laptop, someone rattled the locked doorknob and then knocked.

"Hey! I have an announcement! Open up."

As I went to answer the door, I wondered about adding a peephole.

I unlocked and opened it. A middle-aged woman held a piece of paper in the air. "What the hell? Why is the door locked? I have a knitting class."

"Come on in," I said.

She introduced herself. Serena Hollister had lived in Benedict for twelve years, having come from Seattle. Her husband had beaten her one too many times and she'd needed a place to hide. She told me the story so matter-of-factly that I almost spilled my secrets to her. For an instant it seemed like the right thing to do. Instead, I just told her I was sorry for what she'd been through.

She shrugged and said it had turned out okay and that he was dead now.

I envied the outcome.

"I've been knitting since I moved here. I was told it would help me get through some of the lonelier hours. I've never been lonely, but I'm not sure if that's because of the knitting or something else." She pushed up some heavy glasses. "I never married again. Went on a date with Benny but realized I'm not a lesbian no matter how much I like her, so we just stayed friends. I'm happy. Happier than I ever thought I could be, was happy here even before my husband died. There's just something about this place. It works for me."

"That's great. I'm jealous. I hope I find that kind of peace someday."

"What are you running from?"

"Nothing. I just wanted to see this part of Alaska."

Serena smiled. "Sure. Whatever you say. And the door was locked . . . why?"

"I just forgot." I shrugged.

"Uh-huh. Anyway, can you put this in your next edition, about my knitting classes? It's different nights every week and I'm tired of trying to get ahold of everyone to tell them when it is. Here's the next six weeks' schedule. I'll be glad the *Petition* is back."

"Sure." I looked down at the torn piece of paper and decided I could interpret the scribbles. "How many people come to the class?"

"Up to ten or so."

"How do I sign up if I'm interested?"

"Just come." Serena shrugged. "We're not too formal."

"How much do you charge?"

"Just for the yarn. And the ferry trip to Juneau to pick it up. Turns out to be about ten dollars a class, but that's different every time. You don't have to pay right away. I can bill you."

I wanted to know how she paid her own bills but I didn't ask.

She answered anyway. "I work at the visitors' center in the summer. I make enough. My cabin is long paid for. Turns out my ex had some money. We weren't divorced so I got it when he kicked the bucket. Win-win, I say."

"I agree."

"Oh!" She rubbed her finger under her nose. "We're down one. Lost a member. Tragically. A few days ago. We still don't have all the details."

"Linda Rafferty?"

"Yeah." One of her eyebrows rose.

"I heard. Did you know her well?"

"We all know each other, some."

"I heard that Gril determined it was suicide."

Serena's suspicious eyes gave me a long once-over. Whether she'd put together she was talking to "the press," I couldn't tell.

But she didn't know me. I was the outsider, the new girl. I waited and was surprised when she continued.

"No. Linda Rafferty didn't kill herself. Gril will figure it out."

"I think that *is* what he figured out."

"No. I don't care what you've heard, she didn't kill herself."

"What makes you so sure?"

Serena laughed once. "You writing an article or something?"

"Maybe."

We looked at each other another long moment.

"Last week, she came over to my house. She was excited about a baby blanket pattern she found. She was hoping to get the yarn for it. Wondered if I'd pick it up on my next run into Juneau."

"She had plans."

Serena shook her head. "It was more than that. She had a baby . . . I mean, there was an important baby in her life. One that was going to be born in six months. She was excited."

"Grandchild?"

"That's what I asked. But she didn't answer. Who would hide a grandchild though? Most people can't stop talking about something like that."

I thought about my mom. She'd be happy for me, but maternal instinct didn't run deep in her bones. She wouldn't make much of a babysitter. But maybe I was underestimating her. And, Serena was correct, most women would be thrilled about a new baby in their life, particularly a grandchild.

"Any chance she was the pregnant one?" I asked.

"She was in her early sixties."

That was about where I'd put George. I wondered again about Linda and Donner's relationship. "Did you know anything else about her family?"

Serena shook her head and then looked off toward the door briefly. "Nothing."

"Did she have any close friends here in Benedict, closer than others?"

"No one more than anyone else, but lately it seemed like she'd been spending time with one of Viola's girls."

"Which one?"

"Mean-looking one. Short hair, always a sour expression on her face. I've invited the Benedict House women to knitting but they rarely come. I'm okay with this one not coming."

I nodded. "Willa?"

"I think that's her name. Anyway, I don't have anything to tell you for any article or anything, but, no, for whatever it's worth, I don't think Linda Rafferty killed herself."

"Thanks for being so honest."

"I'm all about honest. Have to be." She stood. "You really shouldn't lock the door. If you feel the need though, get a gun. We all have guns."

"Um, okay," I said. I didn't mention that I'd just been thinking about weaponry and my lack of skills with any form.

"Someone can teach you to shoot," she said, sensing my concern.

"I'll keep that in mind."

Serena bid me good-bye and I watched her as she walked away from the building.

"You walked here?" I yelled.

"Yeah. It's a short walk."

It was a short walk when you took into account how big Alaska geography was, I guess. I felt like a wimp. I felt like an even bigger wimp when I decided I really wanted a truck. If I stayed, I'd have to figure out a way to get one. Preferably an old one.

I closed and locked the door before I moved back to my laptop and opened my new email account. I was thrilled to see that Detective Majors had written.

Call me, I have news.

I grabbed a phone and hoped she'd answer this time.

Sixteen

"Hey, Beth, sorry I missed you earlier. We traced the call that went to your burner," Detective Majors said.

My hands iced, and I sucked in and held my breath as she paused.

"It was an accident. Some guy thought he'd left the message for his friend," she continued.

"Are you . . . sure?"

"Yes. The guy's in Philadelphia. We sent some uniforms out to talk to him. The police came close to breaking down the door. The guy, about twenty-five, was trying to hide some weed in his night-stand when they barreled in. Scared him to death. Almost. He survived, and when it was all said and done, he was relieved not to be arrested for either the weed or the misdialed call."

Disappointment plummeted my stomach. "Damn. I hoped it was a lead."

"Me too." Another pause. "I'm sorry, Beth."

"It's all right. Anything else?"

"I have more to tell you, but before I go into detail, just know that we still don't have him. We have a few more things to explore, but we don't have *him*. Okay?"

"Got it."

"Okay. Remember the tire tracks?"

"Yes."

"The tracks at the place where the old brown van was reportedly seen matched the tracks by where we found you. They were a match, Beth. We can be sure of a couple of things now: one, the van must have skidded either as you were jumping out of it or afterwards, but more importantly, we are now sure that that was the same van that was spotted in Weyford. We have that eyewitness, an older woman, nosey, always looking out her window."

"Thank God for nosey old women."

"Right, but there's a little more." Detective Majors cleared her throat. "I told you that I told your mother about the sightings. She went out to talk to the witness, a woman named Geneva."

"She emailed me. I know she talked to her."

Detective Majors hesitated. "Okay. Well, your mom went out two days. Geneva didn't get a good look at the man who was driving the van, she didn't let us know that she'd seen the van again the night in between your mom's visits, but she had. And she did see something else."

"Mom wrote something about seeing someone walking on the van."

"Right. That's what Geneva, the woman, thought she saw. It also appears that when he visited this time, he left something behind."

"The pink blanket?"

"Yes. She told you."

"She did. However, is everyone sure it wasn't there already?"

"Yes, we know we didn't see it the first time we were out there. We looked all around, including up. Do you remember it or something like it?"

I sighed. "I wish I did."

"Well, even if you don't, it's covered in possible evidence. It's in the lab right now, a priority."

"DNA stuff maybe?"

"It's a good possibility. Bodily fluids, blood . . ."

My stomach turned, but I ignored it. "Why would it be *there* though?"

"I have no idea, except that Levi is a sociopath. Maybe leaving it there instead of destroying it was just part of his messed-up head. If . . . if it has some of you on it, maybe he wanted to save it for later but he knew that having it with him was asking for trouble. He scoped out the location one day, left it there the next. Maybe he didn't know about the nosey woman across the street. We're lucky Geneva was paying attention."

"Jesus."

"I know. Levi is arrogant."

I'd been listening, conversing easily with the detective. My head was clear, no pain. But as she said the word "arrogant," something else filled my mind.

I was suddenly in the passenger seat of the van, tied to it, a rope wrapped around me and the seat three times. I could *see* the three lines of rope, feel the roughness under my filthy shirt. I looked out the passenger side window and saw a mailbox—a single box nailed to a leaning piece of wood. I heard his voice.

"Ignorant country folks don't check their mail on time," Levi said. *He opened the box door, reached in, and pulled out a stack of mail. "Lookee here. Let's see what we've got."*

One by one I could see the envelopes flutter to the ground as he complained about the contents. But then he whooped with joy. "Found something good, Ms. Fairchild."

The sound of an envelope ripping open led to another cheer. "A fucking credit card. We are so set. I'll have this activated and ready to use by dinnertime. My dinnertime. You get crackers again. You were a bad, bad girl."

I couldn't see him. I could only hear him and see the box and the fallen envelopes. Why couldn't I see him?

The memory was a part of the past, I knew that, but the sensations I'd felt—the fear and disgust—were with me now, fully formed. And, there was something else. I remembered thinking, on top of all his evil, he was arrogant too. Yes, he was most definitely so, so arrogant.

"Beth!" Detective Majors said.

I snapped back to the present. "Yes," I said weakly, but I sat up and found my voice. "Yes, Detective, he is arrogant."

"What just happened?"

I told her what I'd "seen."

She listened closely and then asked evenly. "Can you remember a name on an envelope, an address on the mailbox?"

I thought so hard, but it didn't help. "No."

"What about what happened right before? What did you do to be so 'bad'?"

I closed my eyes. I'd started the day on such a positive note, but now I felt depleted and defeated. "No."

"Okay, that's okay. Are *you* okay?"

I opened my eyes, relieved there was no pain behind them. "I'm fine. It's . . . good to remember."

"It's also tough, going to be tough. That's to be expected."

She said the words carefully. I wasn't delicate. I'd been through a lot, and I wasn't in the best physical shape, but I'd never been delicate.

"I know," I said. "I'm good. Really."

"Look, we now have an idea where Levi Brooks and his van were two days in a row. Maybe he was seen too. We will bleed that area dry for information. We aren't done out there."

"Good. Yes."

"I'm hesitant to go on, but there's a little more. Do you need a break?"

"Not at all."

"I was contacted by a man in California. He used to be a writer. About ten years ago he was stalked for a couple of years and then someone tried to abduct him from outside his house. He got away, but he wondered if maybe the guy who took you is the same one that tried to get him."

"That's interesting."

"I know, and apparently there's a sketch of his alleged attempted kidnapper."

"I don't know if it will spark any recognition, but can I see it?"

"The second I get it, you'll get it. It's currently being searched for." Detective Majors seemed to cover the phone to clear her throat.

"Files, bureaucracy, red tape," I said. My mother's mantra, usually uttered with disgust, and the reason she didn't like, trust, nor believe the police.

"Yeah, something like that. The file was closed and sent to some box in some building somewhere. It wasn't downloaded to any computer. It's my experience though, that even that might not have helped."

"I suppose it's a possibility. He wasn't young," I said. I'd already told the police that I was pretty sure the man who'd taken me, the one I thought was named Levi Brooks, the one whose face I still couldn't picture, was at least fifty years old. I was even more sure of that now, but I didn't know how I could be so sure.

What I'd told the police was that I was unsure about almost all of my three days in that van, but the things I was sure of, I was one hundred percent certain they were true. Later, after I'd made that proclamation, even I'd wondered how I was so sure about anything. I never voiced my later doubt, but I felt it again now. I still wouldn't voice it though. There comes a point when you have to stick by some story. That was my story, and I was sticking to it.

Detective Majors continued. "I know. I'm not discounting it, but I have a hard time believing Levi was in California ten years ago.

I've got it in my mind that he's a Missouri boy, has been forever, but I don't want to have my instincts make that call. I'll look into it closely."

"Good. Thanks."

She gave us both a beat but finally said, "So, how's it going?"

"Fine. This is an interesting place."

"I hear it's beautiful."

"It is. It's also big and . . . remote."

"Gril, the police chief. He a good guy?"

"I think so."

"You hesitated."

"No, he seems like a good guy, but I'm not sure he's smart."

"Oh, he's smart," she answered quickly.

"How do you know?"

"I know. Trust me, and you can trust him. Like I told you, I researched him. Came from Chicago. Put some really bad folks behind bars. He's a good one."

"Good to know. Did you find out if he was running away from something? Apparently, lots of people think this is a good place to hide."

Detective Majors laughed once. "No, I didn't find out anything specific, but if I were to guess, I'd say that fighting crime in Chicago got old and tiresome, and frightening."

"Probably."

"Oh, hey, I gotta go. Call coming in from California."

"I'll call—"

But Detective Majors clicked off before I could finish telling her I'd call her back soon. I didn't tell her about my mom visiting Stellen Graystone or my thoughts about him becoming involved in the investigation. I still might, but I definitely leaned toward just letting that play itself out.

I sat back in the chair. The police had a line on Levi Brooks, or where he'd been, within the last week. I was relieved and excited, scared and cautiously optimistic.

But he still hadn't been caught.

Keep busy, Beth, keep busy.

I looked at my Olympia, my laptop, the scanner, and out the window.

And then I screamed.

Seventeen

What the complete fuck?" I said to Orin Capshaw.

"I am so, so sorry," he said, his face pale with genuine regret. "I was just looking in to see if you were here. I came over from the library and the window is on this side of the building."

"You were just looking in the window? Is that something that's acceptable here?"

Orin looked confused and then shrugged. "Well, yeah, it is, actually."

I took some deep breaths, trying to key in on the clean outdoor smells and make myself calm down. I'd seen a face peering in the window. When I recognized the braids, I'd leapt out of the building and almost ran him down. We stood out in the woods as I yelled at him.

"Hey, I'm so sorry," Orin said. "I'll come directly to the door next time."

"Do you need something?" I snapped.

"I was just coming over to say howdy. It's my lunchtime. I've eaten. I close the place for an hour."

I looked over at the library. There were no vehicles parked out-side. "Everyone goes to the airport for Internet during lunchtime?"

"Yeah, unless I can get someone to work for an hour. That hap-pens sometimes."

"You can't just hire the help?"

"Not really. We all help out when we can, but it depends on what else is going on."

"Huh." I still felt my heart beating in my chest, but it was slow-ing to normal. I looked at Orin, who seemed to still be waiting for an invitation. It was all I could do to keep irritation from my tone. "Want to come in?"

"Yeah, I haven't seen the place since Bobby died." Orin smiled and led the way. I blinked at his back and followed.

If contact high was a real thing, I was pretty sure I was getting one of those. Orin lived in a cloud of weed. Was that sort of lifestyle required if you looked like Willie Nelson or did the lifestyle lead to the look? I knew medical marijuana was legal in Alaska, but I didn't know Orin well enough to ask about the affliction that managed the prescription. If there was one.

"I love this place," he said as he sat on a chair, his feet propped up on the other desk. I'd poured him a drink and he was sipping slowly.

"You used to hang out here?"

"I did. Bobby and I would share stories. He was a Vietnam vet, you know. He had some stories."

"You too, I imagine."

"Oh yes, I have worked for the government, still do sometimes. I can't tell everything I've done and seen but I can tell some of it. Bobby and I would talk about every manner of thing." He took a sip as his eyes saddened. "I miss him."

"I'm sorry."

"S'okay. That's what friendship and love are all about, right?

Being grateful for it while you have it because it can disappear one heartbeat later."

"That is true," I said. I sat back in my own chair. "Care to share an adventure with me? Doesn't have to be juicy, but I'd love to hear a small one."

Orin studied me and then said, "There was a time, I was part of the Sky Mission."

I nodded.

"When UFOs are reported, the sightings are investigated. I was once one of those investigators."

"The X-Files?"

Orin laughed. "No, not really. That would have been fun though."

"So, what did you find?"

"Not one damn alien, I'm sorry to say. I had two cases that were never conclusively determined, but all the others were easily explained."

"So, the two might have been aliens."

"Or, they might have just been people making things up."

I looked at him a long moment. There was a squint to his eyes. He was a good liar, but not as good as he thought. Although, I wondered how hard he was really trying. Maybe he was telling me there really *were* aliens. I didn't push it.

"Orin, were you looking in the window day before yesterday?" I asked.

"No ma'am. Why?"

"I felt prickles on my neck."

"I see." He sent me a serious look. "Always pay attention to those."

"I do."

He hadn't said that he knew who I was. I couldn't tell if he was behaving coyly or not. But I had something I wanted to do.

"Hey," I said. "Have you done any extra research on Linda and George Rafferty?"

"May she rest in peace. No, why?"

"I believe her official cause of death is suicide, but I've heard that many might not believe that's possible, including maybe the police chief."

"You want to know what's in her past." It wasn't a question.

"I do."

"For an article?"

"Maybe."

"You like to be busy, keep your mind on . . . something else?" Orin sent me focused and even more squinted eyes. He was holding back, but I wasn't going to give him any easy answers.

"Yes." I fired up my laptop and saw the icon for the library's Wi-Fi in the bottom corner. "Do I need a password?"

"Bears eat people. One word."

"Okay. That keeps the tourists on their toes."

"That's the point."

"All right. I'm on. I'll do what I would do and then you can work some of that government-secret magic."

"Deal. I'll just sit here with my drink until you run into the dead ends, dead ends that I, by the way, will be able to break right through."

"How much more time do you have?"

"Half an hour."

"I can work with that."

Orin seemed comfortable as I got to work. I'd done plenty of re-search over the years, but inside the *Petition,* I was working with the slowest Internet connection since I'd had dial-up. However, I started at the end, with their names along with "Benedict, Alaska." I found an announcement about George, accompanied by a smiling black-and-white photo, and his employment with the Glacier Bay National Park Visitors' Center from three years earlier. It was short and sweet.

"George Rafferty joins us from Charleston, South Carolina, where he and his wife ran a watch repair shop. Though they hadn't spent

much time watching time tick away, they were pleased to join us in the wide-open air and outstretched ocean in the shadows of our glaciers. Come say hello to George and don't forget to ask him about his lifelong passion for woodworking."

I didn't know if the snippet meant to imply that the Raffertys had moved to Charleston before their move to Alaska, or simply hadn't had the watch repair shop for long before moving to Alaska. But another step deeper into the search, I found the tragedy I'd heard about.

Dated three months earlier than the note about the visitors' center, and part of a Charleston news site, was an article about a young man named Dylan Rafferty, a seventeen-year-old high school junior who had been killed in a car accident by a distracted driver. Though George and Linda weren't mentioned, considering what I already knew, it seemed feasible that they were somehow all related. I needed more pieces of that puzzle just to make sure though, so I searched for Dylan's obituary. It was easy to find, and I zoned in on the parents' names—George and Linda Rafferty.

"Reading about this is tough and reason enough to run away from the real world," I said.

"Mmm-hmm."

"You sound doubtful," I said as I turned to Orin.

"No. Well, yes, it does seem reason enough, but was it?"

"What do you mean?"

"I just think a deeper look is always called for. I can do that." Orin stood. "But I'll have to do it on my own. If I don't open the library on time, I have a bunch of unhappy people."

"Will you let me know if you find anything?"

"Sure, what's your number?"

"I don't have one. I'll just be here."

"Alrighty. We don't have the best cell phone service here anyway, so I get it, but let me give you the library's phone number. It's a landline."

Orin wrote the number on a piece of scratch paper and then made his way to the door. He stopped there and turned.

"Do you care if I stop by every now and then? If you're busy, just send me away."

"Stop by anytime." I smiled. "But, don't look in the window. Come to the door and knock."

"Door's going to be locked?" he asked.

"For now."

He looked at me a long moment, as if he was debating with himself whether or not to protest. "Got it."

I felt such a sense of comfort with Orin Capshaw that the possibility of a friendship was intriguing. Or maybe it was the contact high. Either way, I liked the guy—and it seemed he liked me. Unquestionably, he loved the old tin hunting shed that now housed the town's unusual newspaper office.

"Later," Orin said with what had quickly become his signature peace sign before he pushed through the door and out into some falling rain.

"Later."

I needed to figure out where to buy more whiskey.

Turning back to my laptop, I tried to find more about Linda, maybe a picture with a welcome article for her, but I found nothing else.

I wished for an image in my mind, a face, a crooked smile. Maybe Orin would find one.

I stood up to relock the door, but I opened it first. Rain was starting to fall. Thunder rumbled but I couldn't pinpoint where the lightning was coming from; blinding flashes of light filled the whole woods directly on the tail of each rumble.

I thought back to the fear I'd felt as I'd tried to bike through the rain. It didn't seem unreasonable yet, but it was clear that everything was simply something to get used to. I knew this—I'd known it before. But sometimes there was just so much to get used to that it was easy to forget how adaptable one could be.

A different sort of light pulled my eyes down the dirt road, now becoming increasingly muddy. A truck was coming this way. I stiffened and squinted, but it only took me a moment to realize it was Gril's truck.

I hoped he was bringing good news.

Eighteen

"Got any coffee?" Gril said as he came inside from the rain. He had a file tucked under his arm. He set it on the desk, but didn't say anything about it.

"I think I still have some whiskey."

"No, coffee would be better."

"I don't . . ."

It wasn't a roomy space, but somehow I'd missed the coffeepot sitting on a stand behind one of the file cabinets. I watched Gril walk over, plug it in, grab some water from the watercooler he had indeed refilled, open a can of coffee, sniff it satisfactorily, and put the ingredients in their appropriate spots before pushing the button.

"It'll be a minute," he said as he turned and rolled the chair around where he could sit and face me.

"I'm glad to know about it. I was afraid I was going to have to work on my drinking skills. My visitors have preferred whiskey," I said.

"Orin?"

"And Viola."

"Viola visited?"

"She did, the first day, actually. She recognizes me, but she can't place from where."

"She might figure it out."

"She made me promise to tell her if she gets it right."

"Be prepared."

"I'll do my best."

When he seemed to fall into thought I asked, "Have you heard anything new on my case?"

His attention popped back up to me. "No, nothing. I saw a television news clip of Detective Majors being interviewed by reporters as she was walking back into her precinct. But she didn't offer up anything new, other than a possible van sighting. I haven't tried to call her today and I haven't heard from her."

"I talked to her earlier and I'm hopeful the van sighting will lead to something. I didn't know the press was still interested; that's probably a good thing. They haven't forgotten about it yet. Detective Majors found a blanket out by where the van was sighted."

"Okay? Tell me more."

I brought him up to speed. He listened unemotionally, even when I mentioned my mother, the civilian and her curious nature, and with such a locked-in focus that I wondered if he was able to remember conversations word for word.

"You doing okay?" he asked when I'd finished and he'd poured us both Styrofoam cups of coffee.

"I think so. I don't know. Probably not, but I can tell I will be okay someday."

"You're alive. You're safe. I'm watching manifests, et cetera. I've got this too, Beth. I'm watching."

I nodded and put my hands around the warm cup. "I know. I mean, I really do know that, but I can't seem to control . . . me."

"That's how it works. Don't deny your body the right to get through its stuff either. I'm not saying you shouldn't seek help, ask questions, I'm just saying that it's all a process. And it will get better."

I looked at Gril. He needed a haircut and a shave. His glasses were probably beyond help. They would never be clean. He needed a new pair, one that wasn't so bent and had some new lenses. His clothes were rumpled. He smelled like laundry detergent tinged with cigar smoke. I wondered where and when he smoked, and I wondered if Orin's weed smell still lingered. Even though Gril's glasses were grimy, the eyes behind them were not only intelligent, but kind. How did that work for him?

"Detective Majors told me you came here from Chicago," I said.

"Yes ma'am."

"You were a police officer there?"

"I was a police chief."

"It was a tough job?"

"Yes ma'am."

"Why'd you leave?"

"I saw too many kids get killed. Couldn't take it anymore."

"Seems like a good reason to head for Alaska."

He smiled. "No, I did that because my wife wanted to come here. She loved fishing."

"Loved?" I asked, but sadness pinched the corners of his kind eyes.

"She passed a couple years ago. This is home." He looked out the window. "You might not believe it right this minute, but this place grows on you. If you stick around awhile, you'll see."

"Yes, we'll see." I took a sip.

"I wondered . . . ," he said. "I need something, and you mentioned . . ."

"I'm listening."

"It's about Linda Rafferty."

"I heard COD is suicide."

"Yes, that's what the ME determined."

"But you still don't think that's correct?"

Gril rubbed his stubbled chin and shook his head slowly. "I just can't buy it, Beth."

"It's hard to know what goes on in people's lives. I read more about her son's death in South Carolina."

"Right."

"What?"

"Linda Rafferty wasn't sad."

I blinked.

Gril continued. "She wasn't sad. She was . . . angry and wary sometimes, but never sad."

"Everyone handles grief differently." I sat forward. "And anger can be part of grief. We can't always see suicide coming; that's the biggest tragedy, the awful hindsight we have to carry with us and second-guess."

"Yes, you're right. And I know what you're saying, but . . ." He paused, seemed to be silently building a case. "But that aside, you said you're good with numbers, measurements?"

"Yes."

"All right. Well, the ME is basing the COD on the numbers involved with the blood spatter measurements. She said that it's completely reasonable to assume that Linda held the weapon that killed her. In fact, she concludes that it was most definitely suicide."

"I'm following, and I *am* good with measurements."

"Okay." Gril reached for the folder. "I brought them and wondered if you could take a look."

"Just the measurements? Not the whole report?"

"That's correct."

I reached out.

"This won't be upsetting?" he said.

"Numbers on paper? No. In fact, the whole report wouldn't be upsetting and might be better for me to look at. But I'd be happy to take a gander at the numbers."

He handed me the file.

Along with the numbers, there were a couple of quickly sketched diagrams. I studied the few pages for a few minutes before, and like riding a bike, formulas made it to the front of my mind.

"This number right here tells me about the blood spatter." I pointed with my finger. "This number is associated with the spatter on the other side of the wall from where the gun was located. Right?" I felt like I was speaking too simply, but I was doing that for myself more than him. The formulas might have come back, but the wheels in my mind that cranked them were definitely rusty and moving slowly.

"Got it," Gril said.

"Okay, these numbers, the measurements of the spatter on the opposite wall, tell me that the gun, along with the distance of thirty-two centimeters," I pointed the pencil, "that this spread could only have occurred this way if the gun was right next to her temple. I don't see anything here about bullet angles, but the ME must have done some other measurements to be certain it was suicide."

"She said she did."

I looked at the numbers again and then back up at Gril. "I wish I had something else to offer, but if the ME did what she said she did and these numbers are correct, it does seem that suicide is a possibility."

"Possibility?"

"Well, someone could have been forcing Linda to hold the gun there, or if someone else was holding it, they might have done so without contributing fingerprints and holding it at the right angle. Did she leave a letter?"

Gril frowned and fell into thought. "No."

"That always leaves questions . . ."

"Again, though, only a possibility?"

"Yes. It's probably too late for me to investigate the scene?"

"It is. It has been cleaned."

"Well, without that and without an investigation of Linda's life, talking to the people she knew, I can only say it was a possibility. There must be a reason that the ME is sure."

Gril frowned at me, but it took a minute for me to read his thoughts.

"You think maybe she was being lazy?" I said.

"Not lazy so much as in a hurry."

I nodded. "I know the type. I'm good with this stuff, but you knew Linda. What has George said?"

"That he walked in on his wife's body, lost his mind, and left. He can't remember his time in the woods. The next thing he remembers is someone honking a horn. Donner said that was you."

"It was. That was all he said?"

"Yes."

"He can't remember any of his time in the woods?"

"Correct, except that he's certain he was on his own. He's sure no one abducted him."

"Well, if anyone can understand trauma-induced amnesia, it's me, I suppose."

Gril squinted and looked at me a long moment. "Do you want to remember?"

"Yes and no." I wasn't going to continue, but then I did. "He kept me tied up a lot, even in the van, tied to the seat, I just remembered that part recently." I swallowed hard and then my throat tightened. "He wanted to own me, I think, but I can't quite understand how I know that or what it means. Maybe I will someday. There's no evidence that he . . . raped me, but . . ."

Gril leaned toward me, resting his elbows on his knees. "That's good, but he was still an evil son of a bitch."

"Yes."

"He will be found and taken care of."

Neither of us needed further clarification.

"I hope so."

"I'm sorry, Beth. I'm so sorry," Gril said.

"I appreciate that. Anyway," I waved away the conversation, "what about gunshot residue on Linda's hand?"

Gril sat back in the chair. "Yes, there was some, but she was a hunter, and she'd been out hunting that morning. Doves."

"Right." I thought about my quick visual of the inside of the

Rafferty cabin. I remembered the colors, the dingy wood walls, the wood floors.

"A barrel burn on her head?"

"She had a hat on."

"I see."

"George and Linda were solid from what I could see," Gril said. "A good couple. Not over the top lovey-dovey or anything, but if you've been around long enough, you pick up tells. There's a choreography that goes along with people who genuinely care about each other. It's the space between them, you know. You can read the space—it seems comfortable or not—and you can figure out the couple from there."

"You're intuitive?"

Gril smiled. "I'm old."

"What about their background? Their son? That had to be a terrible time."

"They came from South Carolina, used to own a watch shop." Gril continued the story I'd read with Orin just a short time ago. "Until Linda's death, I'd never had a conversation with either of them about their son. I'd heard about the tragedy, but I respected their privacy. I asked George if he thought that's why Linda killed herself. When I asked the question, it seemed like he had to remember it happened. It was three years ago, but you never forget something like that. He said it *might* have contributed to her wanting to end her life, but he didn't say much more than that."

"What about the baby? Serena stopped by to place an ad about her knitting class and she told me about the baby pattern Linda was interested in knitting. She said she told you."

"She did. I asked George and he said he didn't know anything about any baby."

"That's strange," I said.

"You think so? Maybe they didn't listen to everything they said to each other. I asked for Linda's email, but he said she didn't have one."

"That's strange too."

Gril laughed once. "Not really. Internet access isn't easy up here."

"Maybe a paper letter somewhere?"

"Maybe, but we jumped in quickly and searched the house for evidence. We didn't find anything to help us, including a letter about a baby. In fact, we didn't find anything written anywhere. No clues on her cell phone either."

"What about Linda and Donner?"

"What?"

I opened my mouth to tell him what Benny had told me, but he stopped me with a hand up in halt. "You talked to Benny?"

"Yes."

"Benny says that stuff just to stir things up. She's not a trouble-maker really, she just likes to keep things interesting."

"I'll get used to her?"

"Yes."

"Hmm. Okay, well, I think I'll try knitting."

"We all have. Wasn't my cup of manly, hot, strong coffee, you know?" Gril puffed his chest and smiled.

"Yeah, I get it."

I liked this man, this officer of the law who was smarter than he looked. He was kind and cared about the people in his community. I hoped I never had to test his skills, his real strength. He wasn't a young man, but some good things came with getting older. Orin seemed so different from him, but I noted to myself how I'd quickly grown somewhat fond of these two men who had visited me today.

Friendships and trust are formed fast in Alaska, Francis had said.

"Thanks for your help, Beth." Gril stood and gathered the papers and the folder, and I walked him to the door.

"Thanks for . . . ," I said.

"Don't worry about it. Call me if you need me," he said.

I cleared my throat. "You still don't believe she killed herself, do you?"

"No. I'm stubborn though. Maybe I just need to give in to the so-called experts."

I shrugged. "Maybe not. My grandfather never did, from what I remember."

"See you later, Beth."

"Later." I watched him walk to his truck and then left the door unlocked as I went back to my desk. A few moments later, I got up and locked the door. I'd keep working on me, but I wasn't ready for an unlocked door. Maybe tomorrow.

Nineteen

decided to skip breakfast the next morning, but not because I finally wasn't hungry. I was just as famished as I'd been for days, but I wanted to get something done early. I pulled out a burner phone and called Donner, who answered with, "Who's this? How can I help you?"

"Beth Rivers. I really need a truck."

We were both silent a long moment, but he came back with, "Give me fifteen minutes. I have an idea. It's not the best, but it might serve the purpose. You'll need cash. About a grand."

"I can do that. I'm at the Benedict."

"No, we call it the House, not the Benedict. I'll come pick you up."

"Oh. Okay. Thanks."

True to his word, Donner was there when he said he would be.

"Bringing one over on the ferry from Juneau is usually the way to go, but I did think of one idea that might be quicker. You sound like you wanted it today," he said after I hopped into the passenger side.

"Today is good."

"All right."

"Ruke is a Tlingit," Donner said as he steered his truck toward the ocean. He pronounced it Klink-it. The ocean grew bigger, wider as we approached. Under a temporarily sunny sky, the horizon seemed a universe away. "His father was good with herbs and medicine, and recently passed, but Ruke carries on."

"A medicine man or a shaman?"

"I don't think those are titles that are still used, though I think they used to be. I just call him Ruke. His father, Tenet, was a good man. Ruke is too, but he's young. It will take some time for him to be as talented as his father was."

"How young is he?"

"Thirty-five."

"I thought you were going to say teens or twenties."

"No. You'll see. Ruke's sister drove the truck I want to show you, but she recently married and moved, didn't want to take it with her." He sent me a quick look and then continued, "The Tlingits have tribes. Marriages must bring together two tribes. You're not allowed to marry within your tribe."

"Ever?"

"That's the tradition. Anyway, it's a bad-looking truck but it's reliable. For another couple years, I think."

"Interesting. Okay, I'll take the truck."

"Well, you should look at it first."

"Right." I looked at Donner's profile. He wasn't the same irritated man who'd picked up a potential felon from the small airport. I was going to buy the truck even if it was loud and barely moved. Barely was still better than the bicycle. "Can I ask you some questions about Linda Rafferty?"

"Only if you're okay if I choose not to answer."

"Were you good friends with Linda Rafferty?"

Donner sent me a quick look. "What do you mean?"

"Were you two friends?"

"Yes, we were friends. Why do I think you're asking something else?"

"Benny said it was rumored that you and Linda had an affair."

"What?" Donner laughed. "No. I'm not going to dignify this with any further comment."

"Got it. Thanks for answering."

Donner shook his head. "Damn Benny."

I thought I'd heard the same sort of thing said about Benny's sister. Maybe the two of them did just like to keep things lively, but I sensed there was something more substantive there.

"Gril still doesn't believe she killed herself," I said.

"No. Me either. There was nothing that I knew about Linda that made me think she could kill herself but I know she and George saw tragedy back in South Carolina."

"Their son."

"Yeah. I know it was horrible and painful, but I still don't know much. They never talked about it. Even when Gril asked George about it—you know, when he woke up from that weird sleep—George didn't say much. It was different—they were upset, but . . . well, it was like they'd worked to forget about it and didn't like being reminded."

"Something might have reminded Linda, and the pain was too much."

"That's possible, but I still don't think so."

"Do you think Linda was scared of anything, anyone?"

"Interesting question." Donner thought a moment. "She did act jumpy sometimes, like she was looking over her shoulder. Not always, but I did notice it sometimes. In fact, I noticed it recently."

"What were the circumstances?"

"Yeah." Donner fell into thought. "I don't know off the top of my head. I can't quite remember the moment. It'll come to me. I'll probably tell Gril before I tell you."

"That works for me."

Donner laughed. "Not going to be the type of reporter who goes for the jugular?"

"I'd prefer just to help illuminate the truth."

Donner laughed again. I smiled.

"Sounds over the top when I say it that way, but I do mean it," I said.

"Alrighty then. Illuminating truth is good."

We'd moved even closer to the ocean. A muddy beach led the way out to dark water. My stomach fell with what seemed like a never-ending depth. I smelled something briny, but I didn't know if it was a real scent or my imagination.

Something occurred to me at that moment—not a memory so much as a realization. My imagination. It had been wild, out of control all my life. I hadn't noticed it was any different than anyone else's until a friend had mentioned it right after my first book hit big.

I could never write a book. I have no imagination, he'd said.

Sometimes it feels like all I have is imagination, I'd responded.

Maybe that was part of my current problem. If my imagination wasn't so busy all the time, maybe the flashbacks and memories would slow down. Also, maybe I wouldn't be able to write any longer either. Everything's a trade-off.

"Beautiful," I breathed as I looked at the far horizon. "Terrifying too."

"Yes, it is."

A rise of land made a hill up from the beach. Half a dozen or so small houses appeared that couldn't be seen until we came around a curve.

"Huh. I would never have guessed," I said.

The houses were all bright colors—red, yellow, green, and blue. A number of cars and trucks were parked willy-nilly around the houses. There were no concrete driveways or sidewalks, but gravel and dirt walkways and parking spaces seemed purposefully placed.

My eyes went to the oldest truck. Parked in front of a yellow house, the truck had probably been red at one time. Now, it was faded, rusted, and spotty with paint. My heart swooned and I hoped that was the truck we were coming to talk about.

"That's it." Donner nodded to the truck.

"If it gets me around, it will be perfect."

"I agree. Come on."

As we stepped out of Donner's truck, I noticed movement in the window of a blue house.

"I think we're being watched," I said.

"Of course. And discussed, and then later gossiped about. You and I might be an item by the end of the day. Particularly if Benny hears we were together." He rolled his eyes.

The gravel crunched underneath our feet, but the noise was muffled by ocean sounds. The waves coming ashore weren't big, but they hit hard, bringing windy roars and foamy splashes.

"You okay?" Donner said.

I blinked and looked at him. "Sorry, just taking in the sights."

I'd seen the ocean before, but that one was on the east coast of the lower forty-eight and populated with umbrellas and sunscreen. This one was so abandoned, seemingly untouched, I wondered if prehistoric fossils stuck up from the sand.

"It's something," Donner said. He turned and continued toward the house. I followed.

Donner knocked on the door. "Ruke. Hey, buddy, we're here about the truck."

The door opened a moment later, slowly and without a person on the other side.

Donner looked at me. "Come on in. You might see something weird in here, but you'll get used to these things." He turned and I followed him in.

I was more curious than concerned, and then I tried not to gag.

"Ruke, man, what is that smell?" Donner's arm came up to cover his nose.

I plugged mine with my fingers.

"Oh, sorry. It's . . . well, it's a dead loon," Ruke said.

The house was dark, the smell making the space feel even smaller than it probably was. Ruke's features were difficult to distinguish, but I could tell he was tall with wide shoulders. I wished I could see his face better but it was hidden in shadows.

"How do you stand it?" Donner asked.

Ruke's wide shoulders shrugged. "It was worse with the beavers, I suppose."

"We're going to have to go talk outside." Donner turned and directed me to lead the way.

I didn't need to be told twice. Once out, I gulped in some of the cool ocean air, but I tried not to overreact. I didn't want to offend anyone, but particularly someone who knew herbs. I might need this guy. Hopefully not for something dead loons or beavers would cure, but he still might be better than Dr. Powder.

After a couple of deep breaths, I turned around again to face the men.

"I'm sorry about that," Ruke said. "So you know, I don't kill them. I found them dead."

He looked younger than his thirties. His wide-set eyes glimmered with intelligence, or maybe that was wisdom. His dark skin was smooth and his dark ponytail fell past his shoulders.

"It's fine, Ruke. I understand. This is Beth Rivers," Donner said. "She'd like to buy your sister's truck. Beth, this is Amaruq, Ruke."

The introductions were oddly out of place, even in this only place where they could happen. A surprising wave of peace filled my chest as I looked into Ruke's kind eyes.

"Beth Rivers. Where are you from?" Ruke asked.

"Denver. I'm in Alaska for a while and I need transportation."

Ruke looked over his shoulder at the truck and then back at me. "You could do better in Juneau."

"Does it run?"

"Yes, it runs well." He studied me again, but the peace I felt was beginning to transform into uneasiness. What was he seeing?

"I'll take it."

"You haven't driven it. You haven't even asked how much," Ruke said.

"Donner said about a thousand. That work?"

"Half that."

I smiled. "You drive a hard bargain. If it doesn't start, deal off, okay?"

He didn't smile back. "What happened to you?"

"Oh." I put my hand on my cheek, the side with the scar. It was an oddly feminine gesture but only because I consciously stopped my hand from making it up to the scar. I curled my fingers into a fist and lowered it to my side. I'd forgotten the hat and I kept forgetting what I looked like. In the midst of the moment, a ripple of humor made a smile pull at my mouth again. "I fell off a horse."

Ruke nodded but I sensed he didn't believe me.

"Let's take a look at the truck," Donner said as he turned and walked toward the vehicle.

"Sure," Ruke said as his eyes squinted at my scar.

I sent him a quick smile and then followed Donner.

The truck was far worse inside than anything my grandfather had ever driven. The upholstery was worn thin, except for the spots where it was worn all the way through, white fuzzy stuffing and a wire or two sprung up from the bench seat in the middle. Two people could sit on the bench; if they each stayed well on their sides, they wouldn't be impaled.

"I don't think the odometer works," Ruke said.

"Is that legal?" I asked.

Ruke and Donner looked at each other and shrugged.

I peered at the odometer. 298695. "Does it really run?"

"It did last time I tried it. Jump on in and start 'er up."

I held out my hand for the keys.

"They're in there," Ruke said. "Didn't want to risk losing them in the house."

I hopped in and turned the key. It purred to life quickly and easily and sounded great.

"New tires," Ruke added.

The tires were worth the price of the truck.

"Want to drive it a little?" Donner asked.

"Nope. It'll do."

The transaction was quick and painless. Ruke transferred the title to my name. I thought Donner seemed extra curious to see what I wrote on the buyer's line. As I printed Beth Rivers, I was once again glad for my mother's advice about the pen name. And then I had a stab of guilt that I hadn't called her yet.

I gave him the money, and he gave me back a hundred, bringing the total down to four hundred dollars.

"It wouldn't be right to take more," he said.

"Like I said, you drive a hard bargain. Thank you."

"Thank you."

"You know how to get back to town?" Donner asked.

There was only one choice, I thought. Well, that or into the ocean. "I think so."

"Good. You have my number. I need to get back to it."

"Thanks, Donner," I said to him as he took quick steps to his truck.

Once again, I'd interrupted his day, but I was thrilled to have wheels. I turned to get into my own vehicle, but Ruke took hold of my arm.

My initial reaction was to yank it away, but the old, polite me surfaced and I just looked up at him.

He pulled his hand away.

"I'm sorry," he said. "I have something to tell you."

"Okay."

"I don't expect you to understand this completely, but I'm an intuitive."

"I know what that is. It's kind of a psychic."

"Kind of, but not really." He took a step back away from me and placed his hand on his chest. "I was taught by my grandfather, but part of his lessons was about learning to listen to and understand our intuition. I sense things."

"And what do you sense about me? What do you need to tell me?"

"I sense a lot about you, and I'm sorry for what you've been through. It's not as if I can see anything specific, but I know you are hurting. You were hurt."

I nodded slowly, but I wasn't going to tell him what happened. I didn't think he really expected me to.

Ruke sighed. "I have a strong sense that you should stay away from the bay."

"The Glacier Bay park?"

"The bay itself. Many people kayak over the water. You should not."

"Oh. That's not even a possibility. I've never done anything like that. I never would. I have a healthy fear of the water."

Ruke nodded. "That is good, but if you are here for very long, you might be tempted. Do not ride the water in the bay. In fact, stay out of it completely."

I crossed my heart. "I promise."

We locked eyes and I worked to read my own intuition. Was this guy blowing smoke? Was he taking advantage of the new girl in town, using some Tlingit tricks on me?

"I'll be careful," I said.

I moved farther back from him. He wasn't in my space too much, but it felt invaded, nevertheless.

"Good." He took a step backward. "Thank you for buying the truck. I think my sister will be happy you are the one who will be driving it. She loved this truck." He smiled playfully. "She almost didn't marry her husband because he didn't want her to take the truck to their marriage."

I smiled back. "Hopefully, she made the right choice."

"So far. But time will tell."

"I'm not giving the truck back if she gives the husband back."

"Then, she'd be even happier you got it. You are committed."

I smiled. "Nice to meet you, Ruke. Thank you." I got into the truck and pulled the door shut. The window crank fell off and onto the floor. I didn't want to make a big deal about it in front of Ruke, so I just slipped it out of the way with my toe.

"Be safe," Ruke said.

I turned the key and backed out of the gravel driveway. As I put it into Drive and took off toward the road Donner had brought me down, I felt another layer of freedom. Any freedom was sweeter after it had been taken away.

As I turned out onto the main road, I realized there were no other vehicles in sight. There were no dwellings, no people. I veered the truck around and faced the ocean. I wasn't sure how I'd get the window back up with the crank sitting under the seat, but I'd worry about that later. I was glad it was currently down as I turned the engine off.

I was alone. I could see no one and nothing other than the waves in front of me, the ball of the sun as it was rising. Trees amid foliage that mingled with the sandy, rocky beach. It was an unwelcoming beach, but that was okay. I was alone. At that moment, the entire human population could disappear and I wouldn't be witness to its demise. Like an explorer on a different planet, I could be by myself. Without anyone else. Without Levi Brooks.

"He's not here. He's not going to find me here," I said to myself. Just when I thought I'd moved forward, something rose inside me, reminding me of evil and horror and making me so very scared. Could I ever face what had happened head-on? Would that help? The world was still turning and I was still on it. Far away from Levi Brooks.

I took a deep breath and closed my eyes. Could I remember if I really tried? Relaxed in a place where I was alone?

I took my mind back to the moment Levi had knocked on the door. I answered it and then things happened so quickly.

I'd looked out at the van. In fact I'd seen the license plate but none of the letters or numbers had stuck with me. It was still a blur.

The trip to the van, me screaming and yelling and kicking and . . . biting. My eyes flew open. "I bit his hand."

I could taste it now. I could taste his skin, his blood, the grime of him.

I bit hard. I drew blood. I rubbed my tongue on the roof of my mouth as if trying to taste him again, as if that would help in any way. It wouldn't.

But maybe he had an injury? I closed my eyes. Yes, he'd had to bandage his hand later. I could remember his hand over my mouth at some point later, stopping my screams.

Don't you even think about biting me again. I can make this worse, you know.

His hot breath in my ear. His Southern, alcohol-infused drawl.

My stomach roiled, but I knew I was just remembering. It wasn't happening now. And, I bit him! I had hurt him. A small ripple of satisfaction ran through me.

I didn't know if this new information would mean anything at all to the investigation, but I would let Detective Majors know. It might not be an important piece of the puzzle, but it was a piece nonetheless.

"Okay, what happened after him getting me into the van, after biting him?" My eyes were still closed.

He threw me in the back. I could hear the clink of the back door locks. I think I tried to scramble up to the front, but he made it around to the driver's side door before I could get much of any-where. Once he was inside the van, he pushed me, forcing me to fall back hard. I hit my head and saw stars. I remembered the pain.

You are mine, might as well not fight it.

He pulled out a syringe. In my mind's eye, the needle was huge, oversized, but I *knew* it had just been a regular-sized syringe. Had I really seen it or had my head been hurting too much to open my eyes and I was now just guessing?

And then my memory began to sputter. With my eyes closed, I gripped the steering wheel and gritted my teeth.

"Face it. Look at it."

As he held the syringe with one hand, he flipped me over onto my stomach with his other one and sat on my back. Still, I squirmed and kicked and yelled.

"No," I muttered, but now I couldn't let myself stop remembering.

Another part of me was working to remind myself that memories couldn't hurt me. I was free. I was free.

And then I felt the sting of a needle in my neck. My world went black.

In my new truck, in the now, the place where I was an explorer on a different planet, I opened my eyes and tried to slow both my breathing and my heart rate. I pounded on the steering wheel. I yelled, I screamed. I cried. How had I not fought him off?

I propelled myself out of the truck and threw up on the side of the road. It was all so fresh still. *It was the freshest of hells*. I hiccupped as the phrase ran through my mind.

I looked out at the endless ocean and wiped my mouth with the back of my hand. Goddammit, I wasn't in that van anymore! I wasn't with that monster.

But for now, I decided to be done remembering.

Twenty

Though the ME had concluded that Linda Rafferty killed herself, and though I leaned toward believing her conclusion, Gril still didn't. I didn't think it was because he didn't want to, because he was fond of Linda. Something else was keeping him doubtful, and that felt like something I could put my energy and expertise toward looking into. Well, my police secretarial expertise was certainly outdated, but I knew how to research. I was also the voice of the *Benedict Petition,* as it was. I had a duty to investigate and report.

And now I had a truck.

If I boiled it down to the brass tacks of the whole thing, I wanted to think about something other than myself, and my curious nature decided what I should do.

I steered the truck to a parking spot outside the Glacier Bay National Park lodge, where the visitors' center was on the top floor, and the restaurant on the bottom floor. There were no glaciers in sight, but through the woodsy surroundings as I walked along a deck, I could spy a ship out in a bay, docked and welcoming a line of tourists. I guessed the ship would take its passengers to the glaciers.

I didn't see any kayakers, but the ship might have been blocking them. I wouldn't be interested in kayaking anywhere, no matter what Ruke had said, but I wouldn't mind a trip on that ship to see the glaciers. Next time I saw him, I'd ask Ruke if he thought that would be safe. The only ice I'd experienced so far in Alaska were my icy palms whenever the fear pumped up my adrenaline. I would see glaciers soon, I promised myself.

A chill raised goose bumps along my arms. Though the setting for the lodge was woodsy, in between it and the beach, there was a walking path. It stretched both directions as far as I could see. To my left was another small building, but I couldn't tell what it housed. To my right, I spotted two totem poles and buildings that reminded me of modern versions of Native American longhouses. Along with the glaciers, I hoped to explore the walking path too. But I had other things to do today. I turned away from the view and made my way inside, dodging more tourists.

I climbed the stairs. The visitors' center was crowded with people asking questions and looking through brochures. Time-line pictures lined a wall, racks held souvenirs and books. As curious as I was about the history of my new home, I only scanned the pictures along the wall.

I spied one woman behind a counter who wasn't currently helping anyone. She was reading a copy of the Juneau newspaper, the *Juneau Empire,* and I realized it might have been wise to have already taken a closer look at the *Empire,* as the voice of the *Petition* and all. If nothing else, I had a way to begin a conversation.

"Hi," I said as I approached her. "I'm Beth Rivers. I'm new in town and it looks like I'm taking Bobby Reardon's job at the *Petition.*"

"Okay," she said when I didn't continue.

Her smooth, dark skin reminded me of Ruke's, and her brown eyes were surrounded by lashes so thick, I was momentarily jealous.

"Do you mind if I ask what you're reading?" I said, forcing a weird smile to hide my lack of finesse.

"Juneau paper."

"Is there a place to get those locally?"

"My brother brought this one over yesterday."

"The ferry?"

"No, he's a pilot." She put the paper down. "Can I help you with something?"

"Yes, actually. Do you mind if I ask you some questions?"

"Of course." She nodded toward the pictures. "If you need information on the glaciers, we have a full historical display. You might want to look over it first, but I can answer whatever you'd like to know."

"Right. But actually, my questions are about Linda Rafferty."

"Oh. Okay. Did you know her?"

"I didn't. But I thought I'd write something about her."

"For the *Petition*?"

"Yes."

"Bobby didn't do it that way."

"I've heard. But I thought I'd give it an extra zip of local flavor, you know."

The woman looked at me. Her mouth remained in a straight, serious line.

"I don't think so," she said a long beat later.

I nodded, but determination built inside me. "I heard Linda killed herself."

She didn't want to respond, but she finally *pffted* away the idea. "Don't think so."

It occurred to me that this was bigger than Gril's instincts then, more than Donner, Serena, Viola even. If I hadn't thought it before, I now wondered if murder was a widely held opinion. Universal even, except for that Juneau ME.

"Does anyone think Linda killed herself?"

"Of course not."

"What does everyone think happened?"

"That someone else killed her."

"Who? Why?"

"Last I heard it was the police's job to figure out that sort of thing. Or for all I know, maybe now it's the new journalist in town who'll do the job."

I wasn't making a friend, and I knew I should be bonding with my new neighbors. But now I smelled something even more than a story. I smelled a real mystery. Were the people of Benedict, Alaska, just stubborn, or were they right and the ME so wrong that even the numbers lied?

"Linda worked here, right? So did, does, George?"

She shrugged.

"I'm on your side," I said. "Even if I don't get a story, I'm all about the truth."

It didn't sound quite as ridiculous as when I'd been talking to Donner, but it still didn't ring as genuine as I would like either. I was sincere though; I just needed to stop trying so hard to prove it.

She stopped short of rolling her eyes at me before she leaned over the counter and gazed hard into my eyes. "You are a stranger in town. How do I know you didn't kill her? How do any of us know you didn't kill her?"

"I wasn't in town yet when the murder occurred. I was on my way here. You can ask Gril or the brothers who run the airport."

She stood straight but continued to remain wary. "Can I get you any brochures on the park? I can sell you a boat ticket if you'd like."

"I'd really like to do that someday, but not today. Thanks though." I didn't have a card and I wasn't going to give out a burner phone number, but I was pretty sure everyone knew where I worked. "Look, if you think of anything I need to know, you can find me at the *Petition* most of the time."

"And when you're not there, you're staying with Viola and her felons."

"Yep. I have a truck now too. It's a sight for sore eyes. If I'm not at the places you already know about, I'll be in it."

"Good to know." She turned and moved her attention to something along a back shelf.

I looked around. I would go downstairs and try the café next but as I turned to leave, the unfriendly woman behind the counter said something.

"There was an argument."

I turned back around quickly. She'd just wanted me to work for it. I was willing to oblige. "Linda was in an argument?"

"Yes."

"Do you mean the one downtown, out in the middle of the street?"

"No."

"Okay, who was Linda arguing with?"

"Well, Lois Lane, that's what I've been trying to figure out too."

I nodded and followed her lead by lowering my voice. "Okay, what else do you know?"

"A small guy is the best I've got. She was arguing with a small guy." She shrugged.

"Clothes, skin color?"

"Dark clothes, probably white skin, jacket, knit cap."

"You saw it?"

"No, one of the girls at the café *heard* it, saw some of it. She was coming to work when she heard something by the side of the building. By the time she came around to where all the yelling was coming from, the guy was hurrying away. Linda was trying to hide being upset, so the girl just decided it must have been a customer."

"Who was the girl?"

"Teresa. She's my niece, that's how I heard. I've already asked around if anyone else saw anything. I think Teresa is the only one though."

"Did you tell Gril?"

"Of course."

"Did Gril talk to Teresa?"

"Yes, but she didn't tell him any more than she told me."

"Thanks . . ."

"Maper."

"Maper. Is that a native Tlingit name?"

"It's short for Maureen."

"Makes sense." I smiled, not too weird this time.

"You need to work on your style," she said. "You're new in town and you're nice enough. But you can't just go around asking the 'tough' questions. At least not without buying drinks first. You haven't built up any trust. Basic new girl 101. You got me though when you didn't back away after I said you could be a killer. Good job on that, but you still need to work on easing into things better."

"I know. But I've got to start somewhere. I appreciate you telling me about the argument."

"You going to write about it in the *Petition*?"

"I don't know."

"It's okay if you do."

"Thanks."

Again, Maper turned to focus on something on a back shelf.

The café's front podium was hidden by customers waiting to be seated. If Teresa was working this morning, she would be busy for at least a little while. Maybe the rush would subside in a few minutes.

I moved out the back door of the lodge, where the deck I'd been on continued around. I came to a plank board stairway that led down toward the ocean. I couldn't resist exploring—but I wouldn't go too close to the water.

"Wow," I whispered as I emerged from the trees onto the wide beach.

I'd never seen anything like it, even with all I'd already seen in Alaska. The bay stretched out toward another part of the infinite ocean. The cloudy sky both darkened everything to a deeper hue and brightened the edges, giving everything more definition. Wooded coastline, as well as islands in the distance, popped with green against the monochrome.

More spots of color showed with some kayakers I now saw. Even if Ruke hadn't told me not to go on the water, the picture of adventure before me wasn't appealing in the least.

Besides, I couldn't even handle an Alaskan rainstorm yet.

I tried hard to breathe in some calm, breathe out whatever wasn't. It wasn't a winnable battle yet. My gaze landed on the sightseeing boat. It was moving toward the mouth of the bay. I could almost make out the name of the ship. Did it begin with a W?

I took a step forward; my foot slipped out from under me but I caught myself before I went down. I wasn't close enough to the water for there to be any concern, but Ruke's warnings echoed in my head. I stepped back before I looked out at the ship again, and then I went inside. Maybe Ruke meant I should also stay away from the beach. It wasn't worth risking. For now.

Twenty-One

Teresa wasn't working today. At least she wasn't working at the restaurant in the visitors' center. A woman at the front desk told me she was at the airport, helping them out for an hour or so.

I knew exactly how to get there. As I steered my new-to-me truck down the road Donner and I had first taken, I looked over to where I thought I'd spotted the daisy. There were no daisies there. There were no flowers.

At the airport, there were no airplanes, and since it wasn't lunchtime, there were no customers in the café.

In fact, there was only one person in the place. A young woman was in the luggage room next to Frank's office, lifting boxes from one older freezer and putting them into another, newer one.

"Teresa?" I said as I approached.

"Yeah?" She turned and faced me. "Can I help you?"

"I'm . . ." I wasn't sure how to introduce myself.

"You're that gal from Denver, the one with the cut-up head?" Teresa wiped her hands on her jeans and approached. She didn't extend her hand but crossed her arms in front of herself and looked at me. "What's up?"

She was young, probably not even twenty. Tall and thin but with wide shoulders, she looked like she should be a swimmer. Her dark eyes and hair didn't match her aunt's exactly, but her long eyelashes did. She'd been working hard, and a thin layer of perspiration covered her forehead. She blew up on her bangs.

"That's me," I said. "I was just over talking to your aunt, Maper."

"Yeah?"

"You heard the argument between Linda Rafferty and a man the other day?"

She blinked at me. "Well, yeah, but I'm not sure why I'd talk to you about that." She turned and moved back to the freezers.

I hurried to her side. "Can I help?"

"Sure. I've just got to get these moved or they'll thaw. The old freezer broke. This one just came over on the ferry today."

We got to work moving the heavy boxes.

"I'm going to be working at the *Petition*," I said. "I thought I might write an article about Linda. I don't know, but I hear no one thinks it was suicide."

"Can't imagine why you'd write an article. But, no, I don't think she killed herself, but maybe we're all just in denial. Maybe we all wish we could have helped her," Teresa said.

"How old are you?"

Teresa sent me a small smile. "I'm twenty-one, studying psychology at U of A in Anchorage."

"Very impressive. Nonetheless, you heard the argument?"

"I did. Gril knows all about it."

"Small guy in a knit cap?" I said.

"Yep. Orange knit cap. It was so bright; that's probably why I even noticed it. Gril knows that too."

"Right. How close were you with Linda?"

"Friendly, not friends." She heaved the largest box from the freezer. I took one end to help maneuver it.

"Good grief, are all of these boxes full of fish?" I said.

"Yes. Tourists come up here, fish for salmon, halibut, even crab and other stuff. Pip cuts them all up and we store them here in the freezer until folks leave. They don't even need to be flying. We'll store for the ferry too. If Pip runs out of space, this is second choice."

"That's a good service."

"Well, none of us want stinky fish, and we like the tourists visiting. It's good for everyone."

I felt the perspiration begin to bead on my forehead and it felt good. I really needed to get more physical activity back in my life. "If you don't think Linda killed herself, who do you think killed her?"

"Gosh, I don't know." Teresa stopped working and put her hands on her hips. "Gril didn't ask me that one."

"She and her husband get along?" I asked.

"Far as I could tell, but there was someone . . ." She paused a good long moment, long enough to wipe the back of her hand over her forehead. "No, those gals aren't violent."

"The parolees at Benedict House?"

"Yeah, there's always an interesting group there, but it's rare we get a 'violent' offender, at least that's what Vi tells us." Teresa reached for a box.

"But you think maybe one of them there now could have had difficulties with Linda Rafferty?"

"I don't know. That one, the one with the short hair, the one who always looks so darn mean, had been hanging out with Linda more than I would expect."

"What's more than you'd expect?"

"Well, I guess any. Unless we're working together, which happens— we all help out everywhere—I can't think of any reason they should have been hanging out together at all. None of us are scared of Viola's girls, but we all cut a pretty wide path around them, you know."

"I do. So, Willa, that the one?"

"I think so."

"You saw her with Linda?"

"Yeah, quite a bit actually. In fact . . ."

"What?"

"It just occurred to me that that could have been the one Linda was arguing with. I saw the back of the person, the cap and the jacket. I thought I was seeing a guy, but maybe not. Shoot, I'm not sure."

"You should tell Gril," I said.

"I will, just as soon as Francis gets back, I'll head down to Gril's office."

I thought about telling her I would cover for her, but other than moving boxes of fish, I didn't know what her job entailed. If airplanes were involved, I didn't want to cause any problems.

"Good idea," I said. "If I run into Gril, mind if I tell him too?"

"Not a bit. Here, help me with this one." She'd pried the corner of another big box up from the bottom of the freezer.

I reached in and grabbed the other end.

I could see the wheels turning behind Gril's eyes. Regret? Did he wish he hadn't involved me in his investigation into Linda Rafferty's death? But he surprised me.

"Really?" he finally said. "That's interesting. Maybe Willa?"

Gril's office was located in a log cabin not far from downtown, but hidden well amid some thick trees. Five worn and sagging steps led up to a wraparound porch and the door to the old, small building. Inside were four unoccupied desks pushed together to make a square and a glass-walled back office where Gril had been working. He'd seem surprised to see me but then relieved when I told him I was fine. He said he hadn't yet heard from Teresa, but I wasn't surprised. I'd left her alone as a small plane had landed; she was going to have to help deplane and get everyone and their luggage to all the right spots. I'd offered to continue to help but she'd sent me on my way.

I nodded at Gril. "And the argument with Trinity? I can't jump to the conclusion that either of those women killed Linda, but isn't it strange that they were involved in any way with her, other than in passing? Teresa said that most people just keep clear of Viola's parolees."

"That's true. They're usually not here long."

"Was the wallet ever found?" I asked.

"Not to my knowledge."

The phone on Gril's desk jingled. I was glad landlines were still a thing in some places.

"This is Gril," Gril said as he answered. "Hey, Teresa. Yeah, Ms. Rivers is here now. Uh-huh. That's interesting." He grabbed a pen and scribbled a note on the corner of a notebook on his desk. "I'll ask Vi. Thanks for calling. All right. I'll be in touch."

Gril hung up the phone. The only ways I would know what he scribbled were if he told me or if I stood and looked.

"Teresa said your conversation with her jogged another memory. She said that talking about the orange hat again made her mind stir things around. Not only was the hat orange, there was a word emblazoned on the back of the jacket. 'Tigers.'"

"Gril, the day after I arrived, I accidentally kicked a small plastic tiger in the lobby of the Benedict House. I thought it was some sort of toy, you know, a novelty thing. I didn't say anything to anyone, but just placed it on the counter. I mentioned it to Viola and she said she didn't see it. We didn't discuss it much. It didn't seem to be worth anything, but now . . ."

"Tigers everywhere," Gril said thoughtfully.

I wondered why he wasn't dialing Viola, asking her if she knew if one of the parolees had any sort of connection to a tiger mascot. Detroit Tigers? But I knew all the parolees were from Anchorage. Still, whoever now had the toy might also have the jacket and the orange cap.

"Gril, the Raffertys were from South Carolina? Any tiger teams there you can think of?"

"I'm not sure," Gril said.

"Me either."

"No, I'm not sure that they really are from South Carolina."

"What? I found information about them on the Internet."

Gril sat back again. "I found the same information, I bet. After you and I talked yesterday though, I wondered about something else. Did you find a picture, other than the one with the article welcoming George to town? Can you be certain that the Raffertys on the Internet are the same ones here in Alaska?"

"You're doubtful because of missing pictures?"

"No, I'm doubtful because this is Benedict, Alaska, where people run to hide sometimes. Have you tried to find Beth Rivers on the Internet?"

My mouth opened as I blinked at him. "You think they changed their names?"

"I think it's a distinct possibility."

"Holy—"

"Exactly."

"There has to be a way to figure this out."

"They might have covered their tracks well. You would know something about that too."

"It didn't even occur to me, that they might not be who they said they were."

"Well, maybe. I still don't know for sure."

The possibility of them lying about themselves was right there in front of me the whole time. I was living that life and I didn't give even a second's thought to someone else doing the same.

"Do you know something more?" I asked. "You suspected this yesterday?"

"I made some calls to South Carolina yesterday. I've got people there working on things. They'll get back to me."

"Maybe Viola has seen the cap or the jacket."

"Maybe. I will ask her, but I'd like to hear back from the South Carolina folks first."

I wanted to ask why, but then my intuition told me what he was doing—not stirring up possible problems for Viola or the parolees. If Gril was anything like my grandfather, and I thought he was, he needed a little more information before he started asking questions that might cause more trouble than help figure out a mystery.

Another long beat later I said, "I'm going to the knitting class tonight."

"To learn to knit or to research your article?"

"Neither. I'm just going to see if I can learn anything that might help. Is that okay?"

"Probably not, but if you're careful and don't do anything stupid, let me know if you find out anything."

"I will."

Gril continued. "Please don't write an article about this. Not yet. Let's see if we can find a killer first, but the *Petition* can survive a little longer without adding some investigative journalism. Hang on and maybe write something later. But not yet."

"Okay," I said without even a tiny urge to fight.

"All right. Beth, go to work or go back to the House and get some rest. Maybe you could work on a book."

"A good idea." I stood to leave, but as I reached the door, he stopped me.

"Beth, you okay?" he asked.

"I feel better than I have in weeks." I smiled ruefully.

"More like yourself?"

My smile faded but not because I was sad. I didn't even think about lying though. "No, Gril, she's gone forever, I'm afraid. I'm going to work on making a somehow better version of her though."

Gril nodded.

As I got into my truck, I decided that it was time to talk to my mom.

Twenty-Two

"You're where?" Mill Rivers said.

"Far away."

"For fuck's sake, Beth, tell me where. You're on a burner phone and I'm on a safe enough line. Tell me where you are."

She was on one of the last pay phones left in the United States. I'd sent her a text code indicating that she head out to the Hillside Diner on I-44. On the edge of the parking lot and in between the diner building and the road that used to be Route 66, one lone phone booth still stood. Mired in weeds and insects, there was probably some sort of infection risk in just entering it, but Mom was glad it was still there, probably forgotten by the people who had been tasked to get rid of them. There was a time when she sometimes couldn't pay her phone bill and she had calls to make. If she took me with her, we used to grab some fries or some ice cream just to make the trek more enjoyable.

I'd started paying her bills a long time ago. I didn't even tell her. I just started paying them. We'd never discussed the transition, but that was okay. I knew she was grateful. She had her own phone now, but this was the one I'd wanted to talk to her on.

"I'm in Alaska, Mom."

She whistled. "I'll be! That sounds like an adventure. Or maybe a crazy plan for someone not quite in their right mind yet. I'm not being critical, dolly, but you were terrorized. Scared is normal, but they were doing an okay job for you and you didn't heal all the way."

"Not good enough. I needed to be in some sort of control. Maybe I'll come back soon." I thought about Loretta's midnight walks. Control over anything was better than no control at all.

"But maybe not." I heard her suck on a cigarette, heard the sizzle of the tip. Or maybe that was just the old telephone line.

"Maybe not right away." I paused. "Hey, Mom, I talked to Detective Majors. She told me about your blanket find. Good work."

"Credit goes to an old woman I usually wouldn't have the time for. Geneva put two and two together and we both looked up. Weird one though. I'm guessing Brooks put it there to save it for later. Majors thinks the same, probably."

"I think that's a good guess."

"Anything else coming back to you?"

"Not really."

"Might be a blessing."

"Yeah, I thought about that. Hey, how are you?"

Mill laughed. "Gosh, I'm fine, honey. Worried a little sick about you, but I'll be all right. I'd like to find the son of a biscuit eater who had you. I'm not giving up. In fact . . ."

"Yeah?" I said, trying not to smile at one of the phrases she'd starting using it when I was a kid and my grandfather had told her she cursed too much in front of me. She'd slanged son of a bitch, but could never quite get comfortable with "flip" or "fudge."

"I talked to Stellen."

"How'd it go?"

"Originally, I went to talk to him about keeping the secret of who you are. You know, him and his band of merry gun-toters."

"That was a good idea. What'd he say?"

"That your secret was safe with them."

"Good. You said 'originally' though. What else did you talk about?"

"He recognizes chicken balls' name."

"Chicken balls" was one of her less offensive nicknames for men she didn't like. She might have used it on a few women too if I thought about it.

"Levi? He knows Levi? Has his name been released?" Panic zipped through me again. Apparently, panic was just like any learned skill—it got easier every time.

"No, see, that's the thing. Detective Majors-Minor didn't go talk to him. It seemed like the right thing to do to share it with him so I went and did the deed."

"I agree that it was the right thing to do. What did Detective Majors say when you told her that Stellen recognized the name?"

"Well, that's the other thing. I didn't tell her."

"Why not?"

"Two reasons: One, Stellen couldn't place how he knows the name. He's researching and will get back to me. And, I want a shot at him first, Beth. You do what you need to do with Majors. If you feel the need to tell her what I just told you, do it. But I'd really like a shot at Brooks first. I've got that woman Geneva on my side, I think. She'll call me if she sees him. I think I convinced Stellen not to jump to call Majors, but I could be wrong. But, really, Beth, I want my shot. I can taste it. He's close, I can feel it. Could you grant me that first shot?"

I'd heard her words, but was caught back on the fact that the Milton police chief thought my abductor's name was familiar. "Do you think I knew Levi way back in Milton? Maybe we knew him? Is he someone from a long time ago?" Scenarios ran through my mind. Did he hold a grudge against my grandfather, my loud, opinionated mother, or me? Did I know him before I became Elizabeth Fairchild? Did he know Beth Rivers?

"I don't know, Beth, I just don't know. But I'm going to find out, even if . . ." She might have said *if it was the last thing she ever did*. I was glad she didn't finish the cliché. "Will you give me that shot?"

"I don't know, Mom. He's evil. He's dangerous, even to you. I can't promise I won't tell Detective Majors about Stellen knowing the name. I'd be surprised if Stellen doesn't tell her himself. He's loyal to you, but he's an officer of the law. He has a responsibility."

Because of his respect for my grandfather's legacy, I tended to think that Stellen would grant my mother any favor she asked, but this was a doozy.

"All right. Fair enough for now." She fell into a coughing fit. It didn't sound good, but I'd heard her cough that way for years. After she cleared her throat, she said, "I want to come see you, but I'm not leaving while I've got Brooks's sour smell in my nose. If I don't find him soon, I'll visit."

I didn't want to worry about her, but there was nothing I could say that would deter her from doing anything. I'd played this game all my life—I couldn't allow myself to dwell on the situations she put herself into. It was probably because of my imagination again, but she was way too easy to worry about.

I also didn't really want her to come see me. She'd be too big for this part of the world, too big even for Alaska. I loved her and would take care of her forever, but she and I didn't need to spend a lot of time together in the same one hundred square miles. I couldn't say that aloud.

"Okay," I said. "We'll talk about that when the time's right. Hopefully, I won't have to stay too long."

"Right."

We were silent a moment, neither of us wanting to hang up. We were dysfunctional in the sweetest way. Sometimes we didn't want to talk to each other, but we didn't want to end the call either. Gramps would roll his eyes if he could see us now.

I said, "Hey, I'd like to talk to you about something else."

"I'm listening."

"There was a death here, and the local lawman doesn't think it was a suicide. Could I tell you the details?"

"Hell yes. I'm definitely listening." I heard a match flare and her lips pop around a new smoke as I told her all about Linda Rafferty.

"Blood spatter measurements might only tell part of the story," she said when I finished. "Sounds like an ME who just wanted to be done. Sounds too fast."

Mill didn't have any formal forensic training, but between her father's position as police chief and her obsession with finding my father, she'd taught herself quite a bit.

"That's what the local police think."

"If there was no note from the victim, it's important to make sure. I understand why he can't just be done with it."

"Yeah. The police chief knows these people, even if the victim wasn't all that forthcoming with her past."

"That's where the answer is, somewhere in her past, but you gotta know who she is to find her past. I'm sure the police are trying to figure that out."

"Any ideas to help with that?"

"Well, good old-fashioned snooping, of course. If possible, you need to search the cabin yourself. I'm sure the chief is good at his job, but you could look at it with different eyes. Because of all your research, you might see something the chief doesn't even realize is relevant."

"I think the chief respects my opinion but I doubt he'll let me search the cabin."

"Well, be careful, of course, but if you feel that strongly about it, I bet you can find a way."

I didn't know how many places my mother had "searched" on her own, but I knew she'd been caught a couple of times, inside houses belonging to people who purchased cleaning supplies from my father. She'd always been able to talk her way out. I didn't have quite the same skill set.

"I'll think about it," I said. I paused again but not for long. "Anything new on Dad?"

"No, ma'am, that old man is on my back burner, for a while anyway."

Was there a chance that Levi Brooks would be such a distraction that she might finally give up searching for my father? If so, that was the silver lining of this very dark and cloudy mess we were in. However, I didn't think anything would deter her—forever.

It was time to let her go, for now.

"Hey, Mom, send me emails, okay? Phone stuff is spotty up here and you don't need to keep going into that booth. Send me email updates. I'll do the same."

"Dealaroo, Baby Girl. I'm working 28-8. You know that, don't you?"

I sighed. "Be careful, Mom. Please."

"Always."

Our call ended as they frequently did, with the sizzle of a cigarette tip.

Twenty-Three

As I looked around the room, I realized that my mother had never purchased even one skein of yarn. I'd heard of crafters, seen plenty in my small Missouri town, but Mill had been more about smoking cigarettes and listening to country music from a car radio while driving down long, dark roads at night. I'd never even thought about any sort of crafting.

Considering my own background and preconceived notions, I was surprised by the different personalities who enjoyed or wanted to learn how to knit.

The community center was the place to be. Another building hidden in a pocket of woods, I'd struggled to find the place with "community" in its title. It hadn't been down the left dirt road, but one farther to the right. I'd cursed Viola's directions but then remembered she'd warned me from taking the left path, not told me that it was the way to go. The truck and its new tires took the roads well and I'd been right on time. I only had to put the radio button back into place twice, but I didn't mind. I already loved my old truck.

The community center was another industrial building located on a cleared patch of ground. When I finally found it, I wished for an aerial view of town. If there was some sort of grand plan as to where things were located, I couldn't pinpoint it.

The inside was sparse with a few tables and lots of chairs, but at least the chairs were comfortable. One of the bulletin boards was pasted with old copies of the *Petition* and I studied it for a while.

Ten eager students, Serena and me included, were there that evening. The eight others included two guys who worked on an oil rig but were home for a break. They looked exactly like I would guess guys who worked on oil rigs would look. Burly and hairy. They were both making sweaters. Honestly, Lyman and Randall initially struck me as so out of place that I probably stared at them too long. They didn't seem to care.

I can't get my sleeves to be the same length. I'm about to go with it and just roll the long one up.

Na, you can do it. Pay better attention to your stitch markers.

They both wore sweatshirts with the sleeves cut off, exposing their big arms and muscles that contracted as they deftly moved their yarn over and around their needles. Lyman wore a pair of reading glasses on the end of his nose; the plastic frames and the glass were smudged and crooked.

Benny was there too. So was Loretta, who seemed to be trying to get either Lyman's or Randall's attention. Neither of the guys seemed to notice her obvious flirtations. They only had eyes for their sweaters. When Loretta had delivered my lunch to Benny's bar, I'd noticed that they seemed to be friendly toward each other, but not quite friends. Tonight, they spent a long few minutes discussing Viola's dinner rules.

"She's in charge, Loretta. And it's her job to make sure you all don't screw things up. You have to listen to her," Benny said.

"We are adults who have, for all intents and purposes, been put on a stranded island surrounded by shark-infested waters. Or at least whale-infested. No matter, they are unfriendly waters. We can't get *a flight out of here and the guy at the ferry watches for us like it's his mission in life,"* Loretta replied.

"Viola said she'd shoot him if he let any of you get over to Juneau."

"She would too, I bet."

"Of course, she would."

I still wanted to know if Viola had shot anyone, but I still didn't ask. I'd ask her myself if the timing ever felt right.

The last two members of the group were a mother and daughter. I guessed they were Tlingits, but I didn't know yet if it was okay to inquire. They and Serena seemed to be friends, and once the class got under way, the three of them sat in a corner and chatted quietly as they worked on their projects.

Larrie, the mother, pronounced like Larry, and Janell, her daughter. Janell was blind but seemed to out-knit everyone. Her needles clicked and flew, quickly creating perfect rows of stitches.

I was only learning to cast on tonight, and I played the roaming student, the one curious about everyone else's projects and if I was finally getting my own simple—but only after I did it a few times— task down correctly. As I turned the yarn and made the knots, I wondered why anyone enjoyed such silliness when there was a perfectly good mercantile in the area selling lots of different kinds of winter gear, but I didn't voice my thoughts.

I wasn't really there to learn to knit anyway, but a voice in the back of my mind suggested that it might be something I'd enjoy, particularly if I could move my needles like Janell.

"Hey." I held up my yarn-looped needle as I again roamed toward Serena, Larrie, and Janell. "I think I'm getting it."

"You are doing great. Here, sit here." Serena patted an empty chair on her other side.

Larrie sent me a considerable frown.

"I don't want to interrupt," I said.

"Not at all," Serena said.

I sat and looked over the other projects. Larrie moved her focus back to her scarf.

"You are new in town," Janell said to me. "I heard you have a scar on your head from a horse kicking you."

"No, I fell off a horse," I said, but immediately liked the exaggeration it had become. Much more exciting to be kicked in the head and recover.

"Oh," Janell said. "I'm sorry you were hurt." She put down her knitting and held her hands toward me. "Let me see your needle."

I handed her the one I'd been working on, and she ran her fingers over the loops of yarn.

She smiled. "You just need to slow down, be more patient. These will be more even in no time at all." She extended the needle back to me.

"Thanks."

"Sure. I love to knit."

"I can tell. You're very good. You can't even be sixteen."

"I'm fourteen." She smiled. "And I'm the best in town. Better than Serena even."

"True story," Serena confirmed.

"I love it. It gives me pictures in my head, patterns, lines, and rows that make other pictures. Something organized."

"That's interesting."

Janell laughed. "You don't need to be extra polite to the blind girl. You can ask for clarification. What I mean is that when I knit, I see scenes in my head. I haven't always been blind. I remember people and places and colors. They are locked in time in my head, and I can see the old scenes when I'm knitting, make new scenes up. Dr. Powder says it's a gift, not something normal, just a gift."

"I agree. Pictures in the mind are wonderful things. How did you become blind?" Since we weren't being polite or anything.

"Detached retinas. It happened during the winter and we were in the outback at the time. We couldn't get to a doctor."

I swallowed hard the pity that found its way into my chest. She spoke of the tragedy with such an accepting tone. She didn't want pity.

"It looks like you've made the best of it," I said.

Janell shrugged. "Nothing else to do."

"True."

"Are you ready to learn to knit?" Serena said.

"Yes." I wasn't, didn't really want to, but I needed to ask everyone more questions, and I couldn't just walk around casting on all night.

After I endured—and then a few rows into it, surprisingly enjoyed—learning the knit and purl stitches, I thought it would be less jarring to jump into the real questions. There had been no class end time mentioned, and I thought that it just went on until everyone was done or wanted to go home. I figured I might have about an hour left when I got to the real questions.

"What do you all think about Linda Rafferty?" I asked as casually as possible.

"Well, I already told you, she didn't kill herself. Couldn't have," Serena said. "She had plans."

"Right. The baby blanket. Does anyone know who the baby belonged to?" I asked.

Serena and Larrie shook their heads.

"I don't know exactly," Janell said, "but it was for someone in Detroit, Michigan."

Serena, Larrie, and I turned our attention to the girl, and those alarm bells rang noisily in my head. Hadn't the Detroit Tigers recently come to my mind?

"How do you know that?" Serena said.

Janell smiled. "I listen."

Larrie finally spoke to me. "As you might imagine, she listens to everything. She credits her blindness for giving her the gift of hearing things the rest of us miss."

"That makes sense," I said.

Larrie sent me a raised eyebrow. "Yes, but Janell is particularly afflicted with it."

Janell laughed. "What my mom is saying is that I am too nosey for my own good."

"You never know when your nosey might help someone," I said.

"Or get you hurt," Larrie added.

"Oh, Mom, I'm careful, you know that," Janell said.

She was a kid. Kids were never as careful as they should be, even if they were considered careful people. That probably still applied to a kid who couldn't see.

"What did you hear?" I asked.

"Oh," Janell said. "Everyone heard it, well, could have heard it, everyone except Serena. She wasn't feeling well so she didn't show up that night. We didn't get any calls to cancel so the rest of us showed up."

"That's right," Serena said. "That's why she came to my house. I missed class and she wanted me to see the pattern and get the yarn. That actually makes sense. I should have remembered to tell Gril that part."

Janell continued. "We were sitting around in a group together. All of us." She nodded toward where the men were sitting. "Lyman and Randall were sitting with us too, but we were just sharing patterns; we do that sometimes. We sit in a circle and talk about what we want to make, we show each other. Linda pulled out the baby blanket pattern. I was sitting right next to her. Since I couldn't see the picture, after she showed it around, she leaned toward me and tried to describe it. Everyone else kind of ignored us, had moved on to someone else's pattern, but she was talking to me specifically. After she told me about the stitches and the pattern, I asked what baby it was for. She said that her niece was having the baby so it would be a blanket for her grandniece—back in Detroit."

"Detroit?" I said. "Michigan?"

"I don't know of any others. It wasn't even something I thought much about, and I didn't ask for the state. I just told her it sounded beautiful."

I looked at Larrie.

"I didn't hear anything," Larrie said.

"She didn't tell me and I'm pretty sure I asked what baby she was talking about when she came over," Serena said with a shrug before her attention went back to her project.

"Hey, roomie," Loretta said as she pulled a chair next to me. "Are you guys talking about Linda Rafferty?"

"We are," I said. "Why?"

"It's so darn sad."

"She sounds like she was a nice person," I said, though I was wary. My lack of trust for the parolees had only grown.

"It's extra sad when someone kills themselves," Loretta said.

I caught Serena's side-eye toward Loretta, but she didn't say anything. She'd mentioned that she didn't go out of her way to invite the parolees to the knitting classes, but Loretta seemed pretty comfortable. I wondered how many classes she'd attended.

"She didn't kill herself, Loretta," Benny said, still sitting in her chair. She stood and stuck her bag of yarn under her arm and walked over to join us.

I noticed the guys were curious enough about the gathering to look over, but they remained where they were.

"Linda Rafferty didn't kill herself," Benny said again as she nudged a chair with her foot to join us.

"Who killed her, then?" Loretta asked.

Benny shrugged. "Who knows. None of us knows everything about everyone around here. We all know that many of us have secrets. We always have to be alert and careful, no matter what."

Larrie, now fully engaged, leaned over to talk to me specifically. "We find the people we trust, and we trust them fast. Have to. This place can be brutal."

This was becoming a common refrain. I nodded.

"But some people plain don't want to trust or be trusted. They hide away, live on their own, don't want help from anyone. That doesn't make them automatically bad or killers or anything, but you just never know," Larrie said.

"Hell, you never know even if you know someone. Everybody hides things," Benny said.

"Speaking of," Serena said to Loretta. "I just remembered this. I thought I saw your friend in a little tiff with Linda outside the Mercantile the other day."

"Who's my friend?"

"That other criminal. The scrawny one with the short hair."

"Willa?"

"Yeah, that's the one," Serena said. "I don't know about her."

"Oh, she's all right," Loretta said unconvincingly. "You know, I noticed that Willa and Linda Rafferty seemed to hang out a little, like they knew each other or something. I didn't think about it much, because mind your own business and everything but, yeah, it was kind of weird. What were they arguing about?"

"I don't know. They were quiet, but you know how you can tell when even whispers are mad whispers? You know what I mean?" Serena said. "I can't believe I didn't remember it until right now."

Loretta nodded.

"Hang on. I thought the argument was between Trinity and Linda—about Linda's wallet," I interjected.

"No, for sure I saw Linda and Willa—the one with short hair—arguing," Serena said. "I didn't think much about it, but I didn't hear any words about a wallet. I know Gril said it was suicide, but I'd better tell him."

Every pair of eyes looked at Serena. It felt like the story wasn't over, but she didn't continue.

The two men finally stood and came over to join the rest of us. They moved like big, burly men, even with their needles and yarn in tow.

Lyman, the bigger of the two, spoke up. "Hey, we've been listening and we both saw something. We didn't think anything of it, but now we wonder."

"What did you see?" Benny asked.

"We saw Willa"—he looked at Randall, who nodded—"come out of the Benedict House. She hurried over to that big garbage can in front of the Mercantile. She threw something away. Don't think she even saw us see her and she didn't act suspicious or anything. We just thought she was throwing away some trash. Probably was," he laughed once, "but Randall and I actually joked about it being a gun or something. It might not be important, but maybe we should have told Gril, just in case."

"Did it look like a gun?" I asked.

What would it mean if it were a gun anyway? The weapon that had killed Linda had been with her. However, a parolee having a gun in itself was not a good thing, no matter what.

"No, it didn't look like anything," Randall said. "But it was about that size, it was in a black bag or something. She pulled it out of the bag she had over her shoulder and put it into the garbage can."

Lyman shouldn't have said the word "gun," but he had. Our collective curiosity was set in motion, and there was no stopping it.

"Let's go look," Loretta said.

That wasn't the right thing to do, I wanted to say. I wanted someone to say it.

"No!" Benny interjected a beat later. "You know what, everybody, sit tight. I'm going to run into town and call Gril."

I relaxed in relief.

Twenty-Four

The evening was illuminated by three trucks and Gril's flashlight, though it wasn't as dark as the middle of the night.

"For Pete's sake, everybody from the knitting group, go home," Gril said as he stood next to Donner and faced us.

We were lined up along the rough concrete walkway. As he faced us, his figure became lost in the flashlight's white glow.

None of us moved.

The members of the knitting class had all come downtown, and we'd been joined by Viola, Trinity, and Willa, though Willa had been the only one given a chair, and an admonition from Gril to "sit there."

My truck's lights were part of the illumination. It was barely after 9:30 P.M. and had only just gotten dark. In fact, a thin layer of light still glowed up from the western horizon. If it weren't for the nature of the gathering, it might have been a beautiful sight to behold.

"All right," Gril grumbled when none of us moved. "Stay out of my way, then."

It was cold, almost freezing, I thought, but I didn't take the time to check the temperature. I was glad for my gear as the cold bit at my nose.

"What the hell," Viola said quietly as she sidled up next to me. "Someone saw Willa throw something away and now she's been sat down in the corner, like a bad girl?"

This was the first time I witnessed that compassionate side of her, and she reminded me of Gramps. She might be in charge of the parolees, but she was on their side too, when necessary. I wouldn't have guessed she had it in her.

"I don't think Gril's ready to find her guilty of anything. He has to check things out," I said just as quietly.

"She said she didn't remember throwing anything away," Viola said.

"Do you believe her?"

Viola hesitated. "No, but I still don't want her getting in trouble for something she didn't do. What's the deal with throwing around the idea it was a gun?"

"From what Lyman and Randall said, she purposefully walked out of the Benedict House and threw something away, that it only might have looked like something the size of a gun. I agree, though, jumping to conclusions is bad. We'll see."

"Hmm. Good guys, but I'm not sure. Lots of people automatically don't like my girls."

"Do *you* like her? I mean, I know it's your job to . . . well, do you like some of the women?"

"Rarely. And, I don't know if I like Willa or not. She's a tough one to get to know. Some of these girls talk to me. Not Willa. In fact . . ."

"What?"

"Nothing," Viola said.

I remained silent, hoping she'd want to get whatever was bothering her off her chest. I gave her a good long minute, but she didn't continue.

"You don't think that garbage can has been emptied, do you?" I said.

"I know it hasn't. It's only picked up once a week. Pickup is later tomorrow. The timing is good."

My eyes angled toward Lyman, who stood at the end of the group. I wondered if one of the big guys who liked to knit set something up to make Willa look guilty of something. Gril was smart enough to wonder that too. As I looked at Lyman though, he didn't seem anything but wide-eyed curious, like the rest of us.

I'd wished for a chance to tell Gril that the baby Linda was knitting for was in Detroit, but a good moment didn't present itself.

Since the light was no longer in our eyes, we could better see what Gril was doing. It had been quite a production to find some gloves. Ultimately, pairs from the Mercantile were procured. With gloved hands, Gril and Donner sifted through the garbage can contents, taking things out and placing them on the ground. Beer cans, food wrappers, typical stuff.

My eyes moved to Willa. She sat quietly with her head down.

I returned my attention to Gril and Donner. Gril pulled out a small black bag. A collective gasp moved over the gathering, but Viola remained silent and still next to me. She watched, but might not have been breathing for her focused concentration. Gril and Donner looked at each other and then carefully opened the bag.

It was too shadowed to clearly see the looks on their faces, but their body language screamed surprise mixed with disappointment.

"What is it?" Viola said, firmly and loudly.

Gril and Donner looked at each other but didn't respond. Viola pushed her way around Benny and walked toward the officers. Her hand rested on the gun in the holster on her hip.

Gril reached inside the bag and then pulled something out. I couldn't quite tell what it was, but I didn't think it was a gun, or any sort of weapon. It seemed pliable.

Because Viola had a big voice, we could all hear her say, "Whose is it?"

Gril unfolded what I could now see was a wallet. I took a step toward them, but then remembered his command and stepped back.

It had to be Linda Rafferty's. Who else's could it be? But hadn't I just been thinking that no one should jump to conclusions?

Gril talked to Viola and Donner and then re-deposited the wallet back into the black bag. Donner made a beeline for Willa.

"You need to come with me," Donner said to her as he lifted her up by her arm. She didn't struggle. She nodded but didn't look at him.

Someone made a noise beside me, a squeak. I turned to see Trinity, her thin fingers worrying together up around her mouth.

"What?" I said. "Do you know what's going on?"

"No!"

"If you know anything, now would be the time to tell the police," I said.

She sent me a withering look and then walked away. It was in that small moment that I suspected she was faking the diminutive act. Of course, she was, I thought to myself. She *is* a criminal. She wouldn't be here if she wasn't good at faking some things, and then failing at it. I watched her walk into the Benedict House. She didn't look back once.

I shook my head. I was trying too hard, looking too suspiciously at everything.

As Donner put Willa into his truck, Gril pulled out his cell phone, and Viola started walking toward me.

"I want you to meet me in my office in five minutes," Viola said to me.

"Yes ma'am," I said as I watched her walk inside the Benedict House.

"I don't know what's going on here, but you might want to find another place to stay. I can help." Viola had taken off the holster and placed it on her desk. The mess I'd seen a few days ago was now cleared away and there was only her phone and an old lamp on the desk with the gun. The lamp's base was a cracked globe, and its small shade leaned to the left. I hadn't noticed it before.

"Are you kicking me out?"

Her mouth pinched as she thought a moment. "No, I don't think so, not yet, but I might have to."

I nodded. "Whose wallet was it?" But I knew the answer.

"Linda Rafferty's."

"And Willa threw it away there?"

Viola shrugged and sat in her chair. Defeat flitted over her face, but only momentarily. "I think that's what Gril will try to determine. Again, Beth, I don't know what's going on, but it could be something worse than bad pickpocket behavior."

"Or that's all it was. Someone stole Linda's wallet and then tried to get rid of their crime so they wouldn't get caught when Linda died."

Viola squinted and ran her tongue under her cheek. "Who are you?"

"At one time, I was a secretary in a police department," I admitted and shrugged. "I guess I've seen a few things."

"Okay." As suspicion left her face, I decided I'd done the right thing by offering her that small truth. "Well, you might be correct, but things are uncertain at best, and you can probably understand my concerns."

"I do, but I think I'm okay. I like it here. That bed is comfortable." Also, I didn't want to move in with the Harvingtons, though they were nice men. I didn't want to move in with anybody. I'd discovered some joy in having a small space to myself, a door with a lock and a chair to put under the knob. I didn't have to take care of a yard, and I didn't have any spaces that would serve as hiding places. I felt safe and secure at the Benedict House.

"Right," Viola said distractedly.

"Trinity was acting weird out there."

"How so?"

I told her about the brief exchange out front.

"I'll look into it."

I sat still. She clearly had more on her mind. If I played my cards right, she'd keep talking. I didn't really know which cards to play, but silence sometimes prompted the right deal. I clamped my teeth tight.

"I think Willa and Linda Rafferty knew each other, before Benedict, I mean," she finally said.

"How? What makes you think so?"

"I've been wondering about an exchange I saw between them two days before Linda died. They were walking toward the Mercantile, shoulder to shoulder. Their heads were down and they looked to be talking. I thought there might be tears, on Linda's part. They stopped outside of the Mercantile and hugged."

"Why couldn't that have been a relationship that was developed here? I mean, they could have met here."

Viola shook her head twice. "Willa's only been here two weeks. There was something so . . . I don't know, intimate, about the way they walked together."

"Did you tell Gril?"

I hadn't asked anyone how long Willa had been in town. I should have. It had already been noted that they'd been "hanging out" together. Two weeks definitely was quick to form that sort of relationship, in my opinion.

"No, but I suppose I need to. It was just a hunch, and I thought I'd do some research first. I need to talk to an officer of the court in Anchorage, Leslie, the woman who chooses which girls to send here. She and I usually talk before any new girl is sent. She was on vacation when Willa was sent. I got some emailed paperwork one day, and the next day Willa was here. I didn't get the extra scoop on her that I normally get. I just left Leslie a message tonight. Hopefully, she'll call first thing in the morning. I don't have her home number or I'd call it tonight."

"That's what's been bothering you? You don't have the information on Willa that you usually have?"

"Yes."

"What about Trinity? What did your contact say about her?"

Viola huffed one laugh. "That she was the best pickpocket she'd ever seen."

"Manipulative?"

Viola laughed again. "They're all manipulative, Beth, but, yes, that word did come up with Trinity."

"Huh."

"What are you thinking? That Trinity and Willa are in cahoots?" Viola asked.

It wasn't the exact thought I was having, but I shrugged. "Do they get along?"

"They don't *not* get along, I guess."

"They're all from Anchorage?"

"Yeah . . . but . . ."

"What?"

"I don't know." Viola shook her head. "On Willa's paperwork, 'Anchorage' was handwritten in, not filled by the computer like it usually is. I'll have to ask Leslie, but it's rare she handwrites anything."

"She might have been in a hurry, her computer was down or something."

"I'll ask her when she calls."

I couldn't think of any way to help. "Well, I'm staying here for now if you're not kicking me out."

"I'm not subtle. If I was kicking you out it wouldn't have been a suggestion."

"I'll be careful."

Viola fell into thought and looked at her phone on the desk. It always made for a long night when you were waiting for a phone call.

"Maybe Leslie checks her messages at night," I said.

"Never has before."

"Maybe Gril could get her number, police business or something."

"I thought of that. If he doesn't get what he needs from Willa, I'll let him know. My intuition could be all off anyway, and who's to say that the found wallet has anything to do with Linda's death?"

"True."

"All right, if you're staying, lock your door. Put that chair under the knob too. If there's a fire, I'll break it down."

I believed she would, and I did what she said.

Twenty-Five

The next morning, I woke up with an idea. I got ready quickly and set out to find Orin.

At only seven-thirty, the Benedict Library already showed signs of life. Three vehicles—two trucks and an old Honda Civic—were parked along the undefined parking strip, but the front door was still locked. Posted hours said the library would open in thirty minutes.

I stood on the stoop and peered in through the window on the top part of the door. At first I didn't see anyone, but just as I was about to turn away, Hank Harvington walked out from behind a half wall.

He pushed through the front door, not noticing me until he was outside.

"Well, hello there, how goes it?" he asked.

"Well. Thanks."

"Good. Excuse me."

"Do you work here too?" I asked as he walked around me.

"Volunteer. We only have one librarian, but the place couldn't stay open if we all didn't help."

"Is Orin inside?"

"Sure is. Here, I'll let you in." He walked back to the door and unlocked it, using a key from a jam-packed ring.

"You flying anywhere today?" I said.

"Not today." He smiled. "I'm glad you turned out not to be a criminal. That room my brother told you about is still available, but he told me not to bring it up again, because it might make us look creepy. We aren't creepy. But, here I am, bringing it up again. Sorry about that."

"You're not creepy at all. Thanks for the offer. I'll keep it in mind."

He pushed open the door and I walked through. "Thanks."

"You're welcome." He turned and hurried to the Civic. I never would have guessed that would be his car, but as I watched him get into it, I realized how well it suited him.

I snaked around a few shelves full of books and long tables with chairs neatly tucked in. The linoleum floor looked freshly mopped and I smelled Pine-Sol. Had Hank been cleaning?

As I approached a closed door, the bass beat of "We're Not Gonna Take It" grew louder and deeper. I knocked forcefully, bringing the music to a quick halt.

"Come in."

I opened the door slowly, a little worried I'd find him smoking, thankful he wasn't. The room smelled of weed and patchouli, but Orin was at his desk, reading glasses perched on the end of his nose, as he looked at his computer screen.

He took off the glasses and smiled. "Well, hello, neighbor. Hank let you in?"

"He did. Is that okay?"

"Of course. Have a seat. I was going to come see you today."

The office was small, but comfortable, decorated with shelves full of books and a large variety of peace signs—paintings, carvings, macramé. His desk wasn't really messy, but not cleaned off either. Just right, with books and a few folders.

Whenever I visited a library, I couldn't help but indulge myself by searching for my own books. I wouldn't do that at this one, not obviously, at least. As my eyes moved quickly over the books on the desk though, I didn't see any of mine. A good sign, I thought. If he knew who I was, he might have gathered my books to take a closer look. Or maybe not. Orin was pretty sharp; maybe he wouldn't be so obvious in researching me.

I sat in the only other chair in the room. "Why were you going to come see me?"

Orin sighed. "Something's up."

"What do you mean?"

"I can't find anything else on George and Linda, nothing that matches them, I mean. No pictures, nothing anywhere, even in the secret places."

"That's kind of why I'm here. I have news, and I need more research, deep research probably."

Orin smiled, put his glasses back on, and cracked his knuckles. "I love going deep. Where do you want to begin?"

I told him about Gril's suspicions—that George and Linda might not be who they said they were. I told him that I had a hunch that Detroit was a good place to search for their real identities.

"Can you search for George and Linda Rafferty in Detroit, Michigan?" I asked.

"Sure. How far back . . . never mind, I can do a pretty broad search. One second." He continued to type. "I've found some George Raffertys and one Linda Rafferty, but it looks like none of them are connected."

"Pictures?"

"Only of two Georges, and neither of them is ours."

"Okay, let's go at a different angle. How about you search for car accidents that resulted in death," I said. "Go back from five years ago to three years ago."

Orin typed away. "Too many to even begin detailing. At least two pages."

"Can you narrow your search to anyone killed in the crashes being under twenty years old?"

Orin looked at me around his screen. "I can do anything." He typed some more. "So you think George and Linda came from Detroit, not South Carolina? And that they're not George and Linda?" He peered around the screen again. "Imagine that, someone coming here, changing their name, and hiding."

"I think it's a possibility."

He moved his attention back to the screen. I tried not to roll my eyes at myself.

"Wow," he said a moment later. "Thirty-five under-twenty deaths."

"Okay, this is probably the hard part, but how can we figure out if any of them are linked to our George and Linda? One at a time, find pictures?"

"Well, I can do some merging with a handy program that I have that those of you mere mortals aren't allowed to have."

"Will you get in trouble?"

Orin *tsked*. "I *am* the trouble, Beth. You'll see."

I was suddenly even more curious about Orin. What had he done for the government? Did he still do top secret stuff? If I stuck around awhile, maybe I'd try to get more out of him. I did, in fact, have a bargaining chip. Well, sort of. I could confirm that I was who he probably thought I was in exchange for him sharing some secret stuff with me.

I suddenly froze in the chair. Hang on, maybe he could find Levi Brooks. If I was here much longer and if I decided I could trust him as much as it seemed I could, I would ask for his help.

Not today, though. Besides, I wasn't sure I could trust him.

"What's your program do?" I asked.

"I can link directly to obituaries, and then it gives me other links too, to places with pictures of those named in the obits."

"Handy. Let me know if you see—"

"Got 'em! Lookee 'ere."

I stood and moved around to his side of the desk.

Our George and Linda Rafferty were actually Greg and Sharon Larson, onetime residents of Detroit, Michigan. There was no doubt in either of our minds.

The gist of their actual tragedy was that Linda/Sharon had been driving their car, George/Greg in the passenger seat, when it T-boned a teenager's car, killing the driver, Travis Butterfield, instantly. They weren't related to the teenager and it seemed that they weren't parents to anyone. Linda had tested negative for alcohol and drugs, but evidence showed that she'd been on her phone at the time. She'd been charged with involuntary manslaughter and found guilty. She hadn't been sentenced to serve any prison time, but she'd been put on probation and was required to give her time to public service. If my calculations were correct, Greg and Sharon left Detroit before any community service was done, but it wasn't clear why they'd taken the Raffertys' names. Orin and I decided to keep calling them George and Linda, since that's how we knew them.

They hadn't lost a son, but someone else had. There was no way to weigh the tragedies. Nothing worse than losing a child. Nothing worse than killing one. In the category of worst tragedies, these probably topped the list.

"Why did they run away? So Linda wouldn't have to do community service?" I wondered aloud.

"Na," Orin said. "My bet is that she was embarrassed, maybe being harassed, just couldn't live there anymore, they didn't want to be them anymore."

"I can see them running away, but without changing their identity. It takes a lot to make those big changes. And just leaving the place where people knew who they were would have probably solved their problem. Something else was going on, I bet."

Orin sent me one lifted eyebrow, but he didn't comment.

I kept my eyes level. "So, here's some news you might not have. Have you heard about the wallet from last night?"

"No."

I told him, and then I told him about the tiger toy, the orange cap, the Tigers-emblazoned jacket, and the baby blanket.

"They've seemed to be acquainted with each other, according to some," I said.

"What's Willa's last name?" Orin put his fingers on his keyboard again.

"Fitzgerald," I said. "But I doubt it's her real name."

Orin looked at me again. "If that's not her real name, how did she get here? She's a felon, right?"

I shrugged, liking that I still knew more than him. "There are some paperwork questions. I couldn't find Viola this morning, so I don't know if she's figured that out yet or not."

Orin whistled. "Really? Well, that could end up being a very big deal indeed."

Orin worked to find a Willa Fitzgerald in Detroit. There wasn't even one.

"Oh what a tangled web we weave." Orin pushed back from his desk. "You think Willa killed Linda?"

"I don't know anything," I said. "But there are some connections that seem suspicious. I think I'll track down Gril and talk to him. Want to come?"

"No, go talk to him. Have him call me if he needs anything else, landline to landline. I've got a library to run."

"Thanks, Orin."

"You're welcome, neighbor." He winked as he sent me his now familiar salute. I would have been disappointed if he'd forgotten.

I was pretty sure he knew who I was. I had no idea if that was something to be afraid of, but now I just wanted to talk to Gril.

Twenty-Six

Gril's eyes were ablaze, lit with a combination of things—anger, panic, concern. He hid the panic from his behavior, but I could see it in his eyes.

Willa Fitzgerald had escaped police custody. In a series of events I still didn't quite understand, the front door had been left unlocked. Willa had just walked out, and couldn't be found anywhere. I didn't understand who'd left the door unlocked or who was supposed to have been watching her, but Gril wasn't in a good mood. My news didn't help much, even if it was helpful information.

"Linda and George were from Detroit, not South Carolina?" He said after I finished telling him what Orin and I had found.

"No, a Linda and George Rafferty lived in South Carolina and did run a watch repair shop, but I don't know where they are now. Our Linda and George are, were, actually Greg and Sharon Larson. They took George and Linda's names at least, maybe identities I guess, before moving here. You were right about them not being who they said they were." I cleared my throat. I hadn't meant the flattery to ease his irritation, but that's what it sounded like I was trying to do.

"And Linda, as Sharon, killed a kid?" he said.

"Involuntary manslaughter."

"Goddammit," he said with a sigh as he ran his hand over the top of his head. "I can't find George. We've lost Willa and I can't find George. What is going on?"

"You can't find George?"

Gril shook his head. "I don't know if he's missing, but I've been trying to check on him. I haven't been able to track him down. He hasn't been seen in a couple days."

"I . . . have a theory," I said.

His panicked eyes zipped back to me. "What?"

"I think Willa might have been related to the kid Linda killed."

"You think Willa killed Linda?"

I thought about the hug they shared that I'd heard about, the close conversation. "I just don't know, Gril. Linda might have killed herself because Willa brought back bad memories. I . . . I'm just about ninety percent sure, though, they all knew each other. Finding what's behind their relationship will probably answer all your questions, including whether Linda was murdered or not."

"Except where the fuck Willa is." He blanched and then lifted his hand. "Sorry. Do you think George, or what's his name, Greg. Shit, I'm sticking with George and Linda. Do you think George has Willa or Willa has him? Is one of them, or both of them in danger?" He was thinking out loud more than asking the questions.

I shrugged, but only a little. "Dunno. I suppose anything is possible."

"Goddammit!" He said again with a fist pound on his desk.

Viola pushed through Gril's office door. "You're not going to believe this one."

Gril and I looked at her. If Gril was on the same page I was, anything was becoming believable.

"Close the door," Gril said.

Donner was in the outer office, sitting at a desk, seeming to wait for orders.

"What?" Gril asked Viola.

"Willa's not even supposed to be here. My Anchorage court officer, Leslie, remembers her, but she wasn't sent here, Gril. She came here on her own."

"How could that even happen, Vi? Start at the beginning—just a minute." Gril raised his voice. "Donner, get in here."

I wasn't asked to leave, so I didn't. We all crowded into Gril's small office instead of using the collective space out front. Gril and I were the only ones who sat. Viola told us what she'd learned about Willa Fitzgerald.

About three months earlier, Willa had approached Leslie in Anchorage, asking her questions about Benedict House in Benedict, Alaska. Willa had claimed to be searching for a place her sister could go. Leslie informed her that it wasn't really a choice, but they would note the request in the file for when her sister came to court. But when the officer asked for her sister's name, Willa never gave it. There was no sister.

Leslie suspected that when she left her office briefly to gather something, Willa swiped some paperwork to get her here. Something seemed off to Leslie, but she didn't even consider that paperwork would have been taken. *Who wants to put themselves in a halfway house?*

"But, Vi, you catch everything," Gril said. "What happened?"

"A confluence of weird shit," Viola said. "Leslie was out of town when Willa got here. I didn't even leave her a message back then, thinking I would talk to her eventually about something. Willa was right there in front of me with her paperwork. I needed to get her taken care of, situated. Dammit, Gril, just like with Leslie, it would never, ever have crossed my mind that someone would come here trying to present themselves as a criminal, but it should have, I know that."

"I dropped the ball too, Vi. I hadn't been keeping track of those coming and going very well." He looked at me. "I'm doing better at that now." He looked back at Viola. "I'm sorry."

I felt an ironic laugh bubble in my throat, but I swallowed it away. I'd actually thought Willa's plan would have made a good cover. When everyone was assuming I was a parolee because I was staying at the Benedict House, briefly I'd thought I should have used that story. Willa had done it successfully, at least for a while.

"Hang on," I said. "Why didn't she just come for a visit? Why the whole parolee thing?"

"Diversion, I suppose. None of us saw her as a visitor, but my girls get a certain wide berth, a certain attitude that they're left alone for the most part. Also, a free roof over her head and three squares," Viola said with a sarcastic laugh. "It's kind of genius if you don't get caught. The jig would be up at some point, but she's been here almost two weeks. Unbelievable."

"No good escape plan though," Gril said. "When I'm paying attention, no one comes in or gets out of here without me knowing."

"She either does have a plan we don't know about, or she didn't care," I said. "She got here, probably thought she'd figure out how to get out of here too."

"You think they're all from Detroit?" Gril said to me.

"I do. That blanket Linda was knitting, it was for a baby in Detroit. Linda told Janell but no one else. Janell told us."

Gril stood. "I need to find them." He looked at Donner. "We need to find them. Viola and Beth, back to the Benedict House."

"I'd like to go to work at the *Petition*," I said.

"Lock the door," Gril said. "You too, Vi. Make sure the other women are with you."

Viola and I nodded and I listened to her mumbled expletives as we made our way out of the cabin.

As I stood on the stairs to the porch and watched Viola drive away in her truck, I took in some big pulls of cool fresh air. I didn't feel unsafe, but I did feel vulnerable. I wondered if the sense of being watched that tickled at the back of my neck was left over from Levi Brooks, or all of these new revelations.

I looked around once more before I hurried into my truck. I picked up the radio knob that fell onto the floorboard and put it back into place before I headed to the *Petition*.

Twenty-Seven

didn't have plans. I just didn't want to be stuck in the Benedict House. If I had to be stuck anywhere, I preferred the *Petition*. Gril knew what he was doing when he offered me the job, the old hunting shed as a place all my own. Any project I might have started though was quickly forgotten when I opened my email and found a note from Mill.

Got some news, Baby Girl.

Stellen found a Levi Brooks, figured out why his name was familiar. Long story, short—he was the guy who burned down the Blankenships' barn about ten years ago. Remember that?

Here's the longer version: Blankenship used to let folks down on their luck crash in his barn for free until they could get something else figured out. One night, Brooks knocked on the front door, waking up Blankenship, and wanting a ride into town. He was already three sheets to the wind by that time and when Blankenship told him to go away, Brooks burned down the barn, killed the livestock inside too, the piece of shit.

We don't know if it's your Brooks or there's more than one bad Levi Brooks, but they're looking.

Of course, they can't find the booking photo. Remember, there was a trial but Brooks' attorney managed enough reasonable doubt, so he was let go to roam the world and maybe terrorize my baby girl. Stellen and his cleavage riddled but smart secretary Melanie are looking for the file.

Still bothers me to see someone behind Gramps' desk, but Stellen is an okay guy. Melanie can't hold a candle to you, but she's sharp, even if she buys shirts two sizes too small. You know what I mean?

Updates soon I hope.

"I do know what you mean," I said after I read the email from my mom.

Oh, God, were we that much closer to finding him? Not *we*, but my mom? Had her efforts gotten us to this point? Was Levi just around some Missouri corner that my mom was about to turn onto? I was afraid to hope too much. I was also afraid for her, but I reminded myself: there was no stopping her.

And then, there was something about the new information that sat funny with me. It wasn't the obvious—that the guy's name was Levi Brooks—that bothered me. There was something else. I couldn't pinpoint it.

I read the email again, hoping to figure out what was causing my subconscious to scream to pay attention.

What was it?

Another new email popped up before I could think too long. It was from Detective Majors.

Beth–

Here's the picture of the man from California. Just got it logged. Give it a look. Let me know.

I held the cursor over the PDF. My heart rate sped up. I would have never guessed that this would be difficult, that I wouldn't rush to open the picture and see if I would recognize the man as Levi Brooks.

But there I was.

Finally, I clicked. And it opened, ever so slowly. Almost line by line, the picture of a man who'd stalked and tried to kidnap another author came to life.

I looked hard. I studied. I blinked and squinted. I looked away and then back again. I tried as hard as I could possibly try before I hit Reply.

I'm afraid I have no idea at all. I'm sorry.

I had become so distracted by everything that I'd forgotten to tell her my recent memory when we'd spoken but I remembered it now, so I added: *He might have a bite injury on his right hand. I remember biting him.*

I still couldn't *see* what he looked like. At first I thought maybe he'd had dark hair, but now I wasn't so sure. I wasn't sure if the sketch was or wasn't him. I simply had no idea. At all. The name, that was it, that was all I'd been certain of. There was no doubt in my mind, but I couldn't remember why I was so sure about that one and only thing.

I took a deep breath and let it out through puffed cheeks.

You are mine. You are all mine.

Suddenly, pain pierced behind my eyes as Levi's voice and blurred images filled my head. Levi over me, on top of me. A bristle of beard over his face—was it dark or blond? I couldn't quite tell. His eyes, bright, as if he was fevered. His eyes were blue! His eyes were blue! I could see his eyes.

I should have seen it earlier—the evil in those eyes. At the grocery store.

I found a bug in the last head of lettuce I bought.

He'd been trying to be charming, friendly. Faceless, but for those eyes, still in the memory, but a wary sensation had run through me back then—I remembered it. A stranger. He'd been a stranger, just talking to me about lettuce. It shouldn't have been strange. It was a grocery store, after all. But it *had* seemed odd—then, not just in hindsight. When I'd left the grocery store though, I'd forgotten all about the uncomfortable moment.

Come on, come on, I need his face. Come on.

Oh my God. Once, when I was out for a walk, there he was running by. He'd waved and said hello. I'd smiled, but I hadn't pegged him as the same man at the grocery store.

Why can't I see his face? How am I making these connections?

And then at a book signing—he'd been at more than one. He'd laughed too loudly as he stood in line, laughed so I'd hear him, look at him. I'd done my best to ignore that loud voice, that laugh, but I hadn't put together all those coincidences, everywhere he'd been. Why hadn't I paid attention? Why had I ignored all those times he'd been there?

But I hadn't ignored them so much as just pushed them to the side. It had never occurred to me that I would be kidnapped—kidnapped! And, evil was even the sort of thing I wrote about, the places my always churning imagination went. I should have been paying better attention.

The pain became even sharper and I thought I might pass out at my desk. I rolled into myself as my hands bookended my temples.

It hurt so, so much.

You're okay, you're going to be okay, baby girl. Shh, rest now. You're okay.

My mother's voice forced its way past Levi's. She'd been at the hospital, she'd been motherly even, more so than she'd ever been. She'd held my hand and stroked my arm when I'd come out of the brain surgery. She hadn't wavered. There had been nothing in her voice that sounded like a lie. She'd been sure I was going to be okay. She was the one finding the leads, tracking the evil. She was on my side. Always.

And I was okay. Dammit. I was okay.

Deep breaths. Relax. I'm okay. I'm O. K.

It didn't happen instantly, but I made it through the episode. The pain subsided to a dull heaviness and I could finally open my eyes.

But then I wanted to close them again. The pain had lessened, but I was tired, bone-deep tired. I stumbled to the door, made sure it was locked, shoved a stool—the closest item I could reach—in front of it, and stumbled back to the desk.

I was suddenly so, so tired. I crawled under and pulled my chair where it would hide me, and I curled up and fell asleep.

Twenty-Eight

I woke up with something resembling a hangover. My mouth tasted horrible, my eyelids were stuck shut, and I was desert-dry thirsty. The headache, even the dull ache, was gone though.

I pushed on the chair with my toes and freed myself from under the desk. I managed my way up and into the chair and tried to figure out what time it was.

It was five, according to the old clock on the wall, but I didn't know which part of the day. A glance toward the blind-covered window didn't help. Either A.M. or P.M. would have some light. I should look at the sun, see if it's in the east or west. I wasn't sure I could figure out which way was which yet though. Donner would be disappointed.

Once I managed to get the computer up and going, I discovered it was evening. I'd slept away almost a whole day. Had George and Willa been found? I was so thirsty. I made my way to the watercooler and downed water too quickly.

I coughed, but then refilled the cup and took it with me to the door, opening it wide.

A slap of fresh air worked some magic and I stepped outside. It wasn't cold. In fact, it wasn't cool, even in the shade. It wasn't too warm either, just comfortable. Was I acclimating or was Alaska just working harder to make me like it? I sniffed in earthy scents and wondered at the continuing episodes. They had passed; hopefully, there weren't others on the way. I suspected there were, but it wouldn't do any good to worry about them. However, I felt strongly that they had to stop. I didn't want to get to that point where I lived more in my memories, the episodes, than in my real life, and I was on the verge of such an existence. That wouldn't do. I would work to get better—get rid of whatever was continuing to happen.

At least, I was now one hundred percent sure that Levi Brooks's eyes were blue. It was a good piece of information to have. Detective Majors would appreciate it. I could visualize my mother grabbing every man she came upon by their shirt collar and looking to see what color their eyes were. With the information, she might frighten the entire male population. I felt the tug of a small smile at the mere thought of it. Besides, maybe that was going to be the only way to find him.

Another scent made its way to my nose. It wasn't pleasant, and I guessed it might belong to an animal.

I stood still and sniffed some more. Oh, yes, there was something pungent in the vicinity.

I turned around slowly and inspected the trees. I wasn't far from the *Petition*'s door. I could run inside if need be.

In the middle distance between me and where I thought the river ran, I spotted something dark moving—waddling—in the other direction. I squinted and looked hard. It was the backside of a bear—not too big with deep black fur.

I was standing in the woods watching a bear walk away from me.

Missouri had bears, but I'd never seen one live and in person. I thought back to what Donner had told me. I was pretty sure the coat wasn't brown and that there wasn't a hump on the back of its neck. So, not a grizzly, which meant . . . Run or play dead? I couldn't remember.

However, it wasn't a big bear, maybe about the height of a big German shepherd, and it was moving away from me.

Then it stopped. It turned and awkwardly sat sideways, so I had a view of its profile. And then it started whining, a woeful, rattling, high-pitched moan. I couldn't tell for sure, but I thought I saw blood on the side of its head, near its ear.

"Dammit." I looked around. I didn't see anyone. I also didn't see any vehicles at the library. I thought about running inside to grab a phone, but when I was last conscious, the local law enforcement officers had their hands full with two missing persons.

It was a young bear, but it was still a bear. What was I supposed to do? Call wildlife control? Was there a way to assess if it needed—God forbid—to be put down or something? I had no idea what I was supposed to do.

I was still far away from the animal, but the step I took toward it was still hesitant. When it didn't seem to hear the crack of the foliage at my feet, I stepped again. How much did teenager-ish bears weigh?

I stepped again. The bear bleated. I was still closer to the *Petition* than the bear. I could still run back.

But then a voice inside my head said, *Don't forget about mama bears. And since you don't seem to know anything at all about this place, remember that you have absolutely no idea how fast mama bears can run. You should probably bet faster than you.*

I stopped in my tracks. "Yes, don't be a complete idiot."

I would just call someone. I would call Viola and ask what to do. I turned back toward the *Petition.*

And then the rain came down. It was as if someone dumped a giant bucket full of cold water on top of my head. In fact, it came with such a sudden and heavy force that I tried to look up and see if a bucket was there, but I couldn't look up without being blinded. I couldn't understand how this had happened again. How had I not seen the clouds coming this way?

I stepped toward the *Petition.* Wait, was this the right direction?

I looked into the wall of falling water, but I couldn't see the building. I looked around but didn't see it anywhere. I'd only been about twenty feet away from it, but the rain was so blinding that I couldn't even make out the trees that had been surrounding me. I couldn't see my truck either. It would pass. If I didn't freeze to death first and a bear didn't eat me, the rain would move on or lighten up and I would be fine.

I wrapped my arms around myself and shivered as the water sluiced down my body. I made a pathetic sight, even to myself.

Something rumbled at my feet. Confused, I spread my arms to balance and wondered if my inner equilibrium had been thrown off-kilter. I couldn't see.

Had I just felt an earthquake?

Wouldn't that just be perfect?

But it wasn't an earthquake. Another moment later, I saw what had made the ground move. Not a bear, it was a moose.

All the wildlife. All of it.

The moose's gigantic head came into view, so close to my own. I could make out the animal's big brown eyes, curiously scrutinizing me, its mouth in an odd, displeased frown. I took a muddy step backwards. My foot sunk into gooey ground; I wasn't going to be able to run. It stunk, something fierce. The pungent odor I'd smelled from the far-off bear had nothing on this creature. How did the entire woods not stink of the wildlife?

The moose took a casual step toward me, air coming hard out of its nose, making a snorting, wet noise.

We looked at each other in the rain. I had to keep wiping and spitting. It wasn't the same moose I'd seen at the airport, though I wasn't exactly sure how I knew that. This one was bigger, browner maybe. Older. Yes, this one was older than that one.

Finally, the head swung back and then forward. And then it did it again.

"You want me to follow you?" I said, ridiculously.

It swung its head again.

I pulled my sunken foot from the mud and took a step in the direction I thought I was being instructed to go. The animal started walking. It was so big, easy to see.

Only seconds later we were at the *Petition* building. I hurried inside and then stood in the open doorway. By the time I turned around, the creature was gone. I couldn't make out its shape anywhere.

Had that really happened? Had a moose just made sure I'd get safely back to shelter?

It had seemed so real, but unreal too.

I closed the door and dried off. Once the rain passed, I would go back to town, tell someone about the bear, and see what I'd missed.

Twenty-Nine

irst of all, you don't go chasing after hurt wildlife. Any wildlife. But when they're hurt, they are at their most dangerous," Viola said.

"Yes, that makes sense. I should have known that, but I wasn't sure. I . . . I know. Sorry."

"I can check on them, but you never should, not until you get better at"—she waved her hand around and even though we were in her office, I knew she meant *Alaska*—"all of this. Or until you get good with a gun."

"All right. Should I call Gril?"

"I would probably call Donner on that one. Which direction from the *Petition*'s office did you see it go?" She lifted a pencil.

"It was headed toward the river, so that would be west, right?"

"Yes. Good. I will let Donner know this time. He will look into it."

"Okay." I didn't mention the moose. "Have George and Willa been found?"

She'd avoided the question the first time I'd asked, when I'd walked into her office. She'd diverted my question with questions about why I looked like I'd gotten caught in the rain, was I hurt. When I'd seen her the word "simmering" had come to mind. She was unhappy, anger mixed with frustration and simmering just under a boiling point. I didn't want to be the one to turn up the heat. I'd tried to make myself sound less stupid than I'd been, but I probably wasn't successful. I didn't know her well enough to know if I should tread lightly or cheer her on. For now, I would just take it easy, run away if she got too upset.

But then Viola surprised me and sighed in resignation before she sat back hard in her chair. "As of a few minutes ago, they have not been found."

"Did the police find anything from Detroit?"

"I know nothing new. Gril might, but he's not in a sharing kind of mood."

"Right. Have you asked Trinity and Loretta about Willa?"

"Yes, in fact I have. They had nothing new to tell me, though I think Trinity was lying."

"Why?"

"Because I get lied to all the time, Beth Rivers."

I nodded. "Right."

"Yes."

I thought some more. I *could* just leave or sit in silent support, but something had been simmering under my skin too; something based on my gut sensing something was off with Trinity. I cleared my throat but didn't expect her to agree. "Can you call Loretta in, and then Trinity, one at a time? Can I ask them some questions? Is that against the rules?"

"Yes, yes, and yes, but I'll let you break the rules if it helps us find George and Willa."

"I'll try."

I thought maybe she'd just yell or pick up a phone to summon Loretta, but she stood and made her way out of the office, returning less than a minute later with Loretta in tow. She closed her office door, found a stool against the wall, unfolded it, and pointed. "Sit."

"Hey," Loretta said. "What's up?"

She didn't look good. With a messy ponytail and no makeup, I saw her age more. It didn't matter, but I also knew that Loretta didn't get as much sleep as she should.

"Viola, will you do something for me?" I said.

"Depends on what it is."

"I need you to promise not to hold anything that Loretta says in this meeting against her."

Viola frowned and shook her head slowly. "You all are up to something."

"Not really. It's not bad, but I want Loretta to be honest. You have to promise," I said. "It might help."

Viola shook her head again. "All right. Go."

I nodded. "Loretta, the first morning I was here, I was walking into the dining room and I overhead you and Willa talking. You accused her of blackmailing you."

Loretta laughed. "I don't remember that exact conversation, but I'm not surprised. Willa is always trying to work a deal, always trying to get money for something. If Trinity or I sneeze wrong, Willa is there, asking for money not to tell Viola."

"Why didn't you tell me?" Viola asked.

It was Loretta's turn to frown. "Because we aren't tattlers. Besides, we would have had to tell you what we were doing wrong. Trinity and I can handle Willa. She's . . . I don't know, somehow small-time. She acts tough, but she's not. If she really is a thief, she's probably been caught more than Trinity and me combined. There's not one slick thing about her."

It felt like it was too soon to get to the question I really wanted to ask so I said, "Any chance you can remember something she wanted to blackmail you about? Remember, Viola is forgiving everything in this meeting."

I looked at Loretta. She knew what I was getting at and, at first, she was angry, but it passed.

"You mean my middle-of-the-night walks?" Loretta said.

"What?" Viola said.

"I think you might have heard Loretta the night you heard someone in the dumpster," I said to Viola. "She doesn't do anything out there. It's her freedom and you said you wouldn't hold that against her."

Viola nodded once, but didn't smile.

I turned to Loretta. "Was that you the night Viola heard someone?"

Loretta rolled her eyes. "Why you need to know this, I don't know, but, yes, it was me. I was throwing away a candy bar wrapper. From a candy bar I purchased, let me add. I didn't steal it. I don't know a thing about snowshoes. Nothing."

"Okay," I said. What I also didn't say was that one reason for asking the question was to ease my mind. I didn't *truly* think Levi Brooks had been rummaging through the dumpster, but it was good to confirm it. "I think it's important that Viola knows it wasn't Willa."

"Okay. Sure." Loretta nodded and pulled her sweater tighter.

"Loretta, why do you think Willa threw away the wallet?" I put up my hand to stop her from shrugging her shoulders. "Think about it a minute. If Trinity stole it, like seems possible, why did Willa throw it away?"

"Ah. I see. You think there was some blackmail or some bargain there?" Loretta said.

"I do," I said. "Do you know what it was?"

"No," she said. "I really don't. What I do know"—she paused and looked back and forth between Viola and me—"is that Willa is always trying to work a deal, and . . . Trinity isn't mousey at all. I don't know what went on between them, but neither of them are what they seem. I'm pretty sure."

"Do you know if Willa knew Linda Rafferty before she got here?" I asked.

"No idea. Truly."

I looked at Viola. "Any more questions for Loretta?"

"Not at the moment," Viola said. "Head on back to your room and send Trinity in."

Loretta nodded and hurried out of the room.

Viola looked at me. "You know, I knew what Loretta was up to. I just let it slide. No harm, no foul."

I was genuinely surprised. "That's nice of you."

"I'm not nice, Beth. I'm fair. I didn't find any snowshoes either. I'd just bought that pair, but I knew you had too. I thought I could shake out . . . something, maybe scare Loretta into stopping her excursions."

"Why didn't you just tell her?"

"Because I would have had to fill out paperwork, harm her chances at freedom. Don't think I'm being nice though. I believe Loretta deserves a fair chance, that's all."

I nodded.

Trinity came through the door and seemed small, rat-like, nervous and suspicious. Back in my days of police secretary-ing, I hadn't been the one to ask questions of suspects, but I'd been around a few interrogations.

As a writer of thrillers though, I'd asked lots of questions. I'd even been given the opportunity to interview a serial killer. It had been a mistake, and something that I hadn't been able to shake for a long time. But now I had my time with Levi, and a serial killer had nothing on those nightmares.

As Viola leaned back in her chair, I knew I would have to exude some confidence even if I didn't feel any. I looked at the cowering girl as she sat on the stool.

"Trinity, when we were standing outside, watching Gril search through the garbage can, you behaved differently."

It was only the smallest of twitches, but I saw it in her cheekbone.

"I don't remember," she said.

"Sure, you do. It was just last night. Let me refresh your memory. You didn't seem like shy, quiet Trinity. Well, you did at first but then you changed." My words were full of a confidence I didn't feel, but I knew if I shied away from her, she'd think she'd won and would continue to lie.

"I don't know what you mean."

Viola laughed. "Good God, girly, your acting is getting worse and worse. Cut the crap."

"You know who Willa really is, don't you?" I asked.

Her eyebrows lifted high. "What? Willa is Willa."

"And you told her you would share her secret if she didn't get rid of the wallet for you, didn't you?" I persisted. "I mean, it was only fair, considering all the things she wanted to blackmail you about."

I was swinging for the fences as well and swinging in the wind. I hoped I was close to something, but I wasn't sure at all.

"What? I have no idea what you're talking about."

"Trinity," I said sternly.

"Trinity!" Viola said with doubled-up stern.

Trinity startled and looked at Viola. The jig was up. The second she looked at the woman in charge of her freedom, she let down her guard, let down that mousy, rat-like quiver. For an instant, she tried to put the disguise back into place, but she was smart enough to understand not to try too hard. Viola was the smartest person Trinity or I had ever met. Or so she said.

"Yeah, yeah, I figured it out pretty quickly," Trinity said.

I wondered if Viola would say something that would stroke Trinity's ego and the fact that she'd figured out what Viola should have immediately. She didn't. I didn't either. We both just waited and looked at her.

"She wasn't right, you know. She wasn't acting angry enough and every time Loretta and I talked to her about what she did, the story was never straight. I know an act when I see one." Trinity looked at Viola. "Her first name *is* Willa though. That part's correct."

"All right, what else?" Viola said. She didn't reach for the gun, but I could imagine her doing so.

"Yeah, she's from Detroit, Michigan, and her name is Willa Clanston, not Fitzgerald. She came here on purpose, but she never told me why. I guessed it was for Linda, 'cause I saw them chatting a lot. She's always playing the tattletale, or at least threatening to tell on me or 'Retta. She's a pain. When I saw her and Linda together, I saw an opportunity to maybe use something against her, get her to shut the hell up about things. I kyped Linda's wallet just to see if I could figure out if there was a connection." Trinity shrugged and smiled crookedly at us. "Plus those sorts of things keep my skills sharp." Neither Viola nor I smiled back. "I couldn't find any connection, but I got her to tell me her name. I told her I was going to tell you," she looked at Viola, "that she took the wallet. I wasn't ready for what she did. She took it out of my hands and marched it outside to the garbage. She came in, not afraid at all, and told me to go to hell. First time I respected her."

"Why not just return it or turn it in, no questions asked?" I said.

"Nope. Too much of a chance to be blamed for something, anything. Things get piled on, you know," Trinity said.

Viola said, "Do you know if she has a record?"

"No idea," Trinity said.

"Why did you care so much?" Viola asked. "Why in the world didn't you just mind your own business?"

Trinity sent Viola a sour look. "I have never been so bored in my life. This place has absolutely nothing going on. I just wanted something to keep my mind occupied. Teachers used to tell my mother— God rest her evil soul—that I was too smart for my own good, that I got bored easily, and that when I got bored, I got in trouble. I was trying to not be bored."

Viola and I shared a glance that verged on tandem eye-rolls.

"Let's call Gril," Viola said as she reached for her phone.

"Hang on," I said. "I saw Willa reading something at the front desk, some sort of tri-folded letter. She seemed upset. Can we go into her room and search?"

Viola's mouth pinched. "As much as I'd like to, let's let Gril do it.

If Willa isn't technically a parolee, I don't know what rights I have over her room."

I nodded.

But before Viola could dial, her phone rang. She looked at the screen and answered, "Yo, we need to talk. Hang on." She pulled the phone away from her face and looked at us. "It's Gril. Wait out in the lobby for me." She looked pointedly at Trinity. "If you run, I will make sure you are never a free woman again. Would be a shame, Trinity. You're just a petty thief; I can make the rest of your days worse than you would deserve. Stay in the lobby and wait for me."

Trinity swallowed hard and blinked slowly. "Yes, ma'am."

Where could she run anyway?

Thirty

The lobby hadn't been made for easy conversation. There was no cozy corner, no chairs even. Trinity and I stood. I leaned on the front counter and Trinity leaned against the opposite wall.

"Why are you staying here? I mean, Viola said there were no other places available when you called, but why are you here, in this godforsaken part of the world?" Trinity asked.

"Bucket list, remember?"

"Whatever. Why are you really here?"

All mousey was now gone. It had been a pretty convincing act, but this one suited her better, was authentic. I hadn't backed down but she hadn't either. She'd only become a tougher version of herself, but it didn't take a secretary or an author to know that only the biggest bullies act the toughest.

"I needed to get away. Life sometimes gets dicey, you know," I said.

"I got that part, but why, Beth, why did you have to get away?" She pointed at her head. "Was it because you got so hurt? Did some guy do that to your head?"

"No, believe it or not, this came from falling off a horse. My story is long and, like everyone else's, complicated. I wanted and needed to get away."

She nodded but her eyes still squinted suspiciously.

"Why are you a thief?" I asked. "You're not stupid. You could make a living doing something."

She huffed a laugh. "Define 'living.' I'm smart, yeah, but I'm also a high school dropout. There aren't many people opening their doors for me. The jobs I can get are stupid. I'd rather steal. I'd rather go to jail."

"You're young. You could advance your education."

"Aren't you the hoity-toity one? Advance my education. Whatever."

I looked at her a long beat. She had a point. "Sorry."

Her eyes jetted to me. She was ready to be angry, but her hackles relaxed when she saw I was sincere.

"There are two kinds of people, Beth. Those who can and those who can't, and I can't *even*," she said. A smile pulled at the corner of her mouth, but she meant what she said.

I nodded. "You're from Anchorage?"

"Well, not originally. I was born in a small town in Missouri. Washington. It's outside St. Louis a ways."

A gasp made its way up my throat, but I stopped it before it reached the top. I'd been in Washington, Missouri, more times than I could count. It had been another town in my father's sales territory, and the one he visited on the day before he died. In fact, I'd spent part of first grade there when my mother thought she found a trail of clues. Like all the other trails, this one had led nowhere important.

Did Trinity mean anything to my past, or was this a strange coincidence? I couldn't believe she and I were connected, but I didn't have time to ponder it and she didn't behave in any way that made me think she knew me.

I said, "No, I haven't heard of it. Did you like growing up in Missouri?"

"I didn't like growing up because of the people I was forced to grow up with, but the place was just a place. I like Alaska though because the people here are better; in other words, they aren't the loser family I grew up with. I also like the cold and the darkness. Don't know why but I do. Anchorage is a city. This place, I don't like as much."

I saw a tiny spark in her eyes.

"Why did you need to know what Linda and Willa were up to so badly?" I asked.

"Like I said, something to do."

I mostly believed her. But I would never trust her.

Viola opened her office door and marched out toward the lobby. The loaded holster was back around her hips. "Let's go, ladies. We're off to talk to Gril."

Trinity and I did as we were told.

Trinity had re-adopted her meeker personality when she first talked to Gril, and neither Viola nor I had patience for it.

"Stop it," Viola said to her. "Sit up and tell Gril the details you told us."

Trinity blinked as if she'd forgotten which person she was supposed to be and was surprised by which one she'd chosen. She sat up straighter, nodded, and told the story again.

Gril took notes and grumbled along the way. "The last sighting we have of Willa and George is both of them getting into his truck and driving off toward his cabin, but that doesn't mean much. Toward his cabin is toward a lot of things, and a lot of nothing. And it doesn't appear they went to the cabin."

"Did whoever saw them say they were friendly to each other?" Viola asked.

"He said they weren't unfriendly, but they didn't notice much. Randy's the one who saw them, just down the road from downtown."

"You know Donner and I were at the cabin when George appeared from the woods?" I said.

"Yeah," Gril said.

"Maybe there's a place somewhere out there that George goes. Maybe there's a shelter. George didn't seem too worse for the wear, I mean, considering everything. He was dirty and needed a shave, but I remember thinking he didn't look like he'd been out in the elements."

"He didn't say there was a place, but we wondered about that too," Gril said. "Maybe Donner knows more. I'll see if I can reach him." Gril picked up his phone and hit call. Before he spoke, the door to the small office swung open.

"What's up?" Donner said as he walked through. "I just got back from the lodge."

"What do you have?" Gril put the phone down.

"Nothing new, I'm afraid. No one there had anything else to tell me about George or Willa. Nothing."

Gril told Trinity's story yet again and we all looked at Donner hopefully.

"Don't know of any shelter. I'll check it out though," he said.

"Can I go with you?" I stood.

"No," Donner said instantly.

I wasn't going to ask again, but Gril jumped in. "Take her along, Donner. She'll stay out of the way." He looked at me. "Just take a quick look inside maybe."

"I'll stay out of the way," I said to Donner. I knew Gril was telling me to look at the reality of what he'd shown me, the space where the measurements I'd studied had been taken. But he hadn't told Donner about my input. Of course not. He hadn't told anyone who I was. I was grateful for that, even if his wanting me to go along did seem weird.

"Why?" Donner asked.

To save Gril from having to lie or come up with a good reason, I jumped in. "A long time ago, I worked in a police department."

"I knew something was up with you." Trinity smirked.

"So?" Donner said.

"Her instincts are good, Donner, and she was with you the day you found George. She'll stay out of the way," Gril said.

It was probably a rare moment when a police department was in such dire need of assistance that they'd ask the visibly injured new person in town to help with an investigation. But Gril needed help. He hid it well, but he was scared for someone—either George or Willa or both—and he was just as willing as Viola had been to break the rules to get to some answers. I was at least potential help.

Donner didn't want me to go along, but he worked to hide his irritation. Again.

"What did you do? At the police department."

"Honestly, it was a long time ago, but I'm good with numbers. Measurements. It helped sometimes. I liked the tedium and could get lost in it." I cleared my throat.

"You weren't a police officer?"

"No, I just helped." I might tell him I was a secretary someday but not today.

"Let's go," Donner said.

I followed him out to his truck.

When we were both belted in, he rubbed his hand over his beard-covered chin and sighed. He forced some words. "I appreciate your experience, but you need to stay out of my way."

"I know that, and I will."

"Good. All right, we're going to drive up to the Rafferty cabin and search behind it. You're wearing your new boots?"

"I am." I looked down at them. "They saw some mud today, but they're good to go."

"Do you have a jacket?"

He knew the answer, but I said, "No."

"Reach behind the seat and grab one of mine. In fact, here's another lesson, always make sure you keep extra jackets and bottles of water in your truck. Just in case."

Sounded like winter travel preparations in St. Louis, but I said, "Okay," as I reached and grabbed.

We were silent the rest of the way until we reached the cabin. It had a distinct look of sad abandonment. I sensed no one was inside.

"Give me a second to see if anyone is there, but then come in when I signal," Donner said as he hopped out of the truck.

He didn't lock his door and I resisted an urge to lock mine and his. I wasn't scared, but it seemed like the safe thing to do. I still didn't though.

I watched Donner open the cabin's front door and disappear inside. The loudest thing in the truck was my breathing; it was airy and accelerated. I took a deep pull of old-truck-scented oxygen and tried to slow everything down.

I looked at the trees. There was nothing out of place; no people in sight. No animals either. Just trees, dark and deep. The sky was cloudy, but it wasn't raining. It would soon; it always did. I gripped Donner's jacket tighter.

A few seconds after worry began to creep in, Donner appeared at the door and signaled me to join him. I hurried to the cabin.

"This place has been gone through, fingerprints taken. Look around and tell me if you see anything that would help us know where George and Willa might have gone," he said.

I nodded and began. "Okay."

I stood in the entryway, the spot where Linda had shot herself. Most of the blood had been cleaned away but there were still visible stains on the floor and the walls. At first it seemed like there was nothing else to see. Other than the blood, it was just the small, comfortable home of a couple of people who wanted to get away from the rest of the world.

I didn't have a tape measure. Neither did Donner, but I guessed it matched up with what I'd read.

I stepped into the living room.

One couch and one chair. A side table and a coffee table. Books stacked on a lower shelf of the side table. I startled when I noticed one of mine there. *37 Flights,* the one I'd stolen my "filing consultant" career from. It was on the top of the stack, with the back cover swung open. There, on the back flap, was my picture. The old me, the one who wasn't ever really me anyway, the person Levi had become obsessed with. Not only did I recognize her less and less as time ticked by, oddly, I was beginning to resent her more and more. I swallowed fear and bitterness that moved up my throat. My internal response was unreasonable, but something told me it was normal. I really needed to get some help. This book had sold millions worldwide, so it wasn't too weird that a copy was here, in a cabin in Alaska. But the back flap being opened? Was that supposed to mean something?

"Beth?" Donner said.

I'd have to worry about it all later. "Sorry. Someone likes thrillers, but that doesn't mean much."

"Perhaps you could work on your personal library later," he said, his irritation thick.

"Sure." I closed the flap, hiding the me Donner probably wouldn't recognize anyway.

We looked everywhere but found nothing that told us where George and Willa might be. There was nothing personal in the house. It was an un-homey house. Somehow, they had made a cozy cabin in the woods sterile and unwelcoming. Probably a result of their identity changes.

"There's not much there at all," I said when we were back outside.

"I'd looked through it after Linda's body was removed, but it hasn't changed much. The bed wasn't made then, still isn't, but I can't tell if it's in the same state it was. I can't tell if George has slept here or not."

"Did he say anything else the day he woke up from that weird sleep?"

"No." There was emotion to that one word that seemed over the top.

"Hey," I said as I put my hand on his arm. I couldn't help asking.

"You don't have to answer if you don't want to, and I won't tell if you do, but *were* you and Linda involved?"

Donner bit his bottom lip and looked at me a long moment. "No, Beth, we weren't, but we might have been. If she hadn't been married."

"I see."

"We were friends, liked old movies and baseball, talked often about them both. She was a Detroit Tigers fan. We had a lot in common, but she was married. Nothing happened, and I didn't know her secrets. Gril knows everything about the two of us."

"Does Gril know about the Detroit Tigers part?"

Donner blinked. "Yes, I told him after I heard about the jacket."

"I'm sorry for your loss. Really," I said.

Donner nodded once, quickly. "I want to go around and search the woods. Do you want to come with me or wait in the truck? Your call, but you'll need to keep up."

"I can keep up."

"All right. Let's go."

I followed him and really, really hoped I could keep up.

Thirty-One

As we started out, the phone I carried buzzed in my pocket. I'd set it up for email notification. I took it out and tried to access the email. The notification had happened, so we must have hit a pocket of service, but we were out of that pocket quickly and I didn't even consider asking Donner to wait. As we trudged forward, I kept an eye on the phone, looking for a bar or two. Was Detective Majors writing with something important?

A bar popped up and I hurried to open the email. It was from my mother. It was short and it made no sense.

B. Girl—remem the fire note?

I was familiar with the format. She was drunk emailing, and I had no idea what she was trying to say. I was irritated by the distraction.

Except, there was something about it. I knew there was something there. But I'd have to figure it out later. I put the phone back in my pocket.

"Something important?" Donner asked.

"I don't know," I said. "I mean, no, not really." I looked toward the woods. "There's no visible path. Where would George have come from when he came around the cabin?" I asked as we peered into the woods.

"Good question. He didn't remember, and none of us pushed him too hard on it. Hang on a sec."

Donner looked at the ground along an uneven perimeter. No space was free of a vine or a weed. I saw a flower and had a moment of panic that I was seeing another daisy where there wasn't one, but it wasn't a daisy and it was a real flower.

"Here, this way looks somewhat worn." He high-stepped over a tangle of weeds and moved quickly into the thick woods.

I followed behind and did as I said I would do; I kept up, but it was hard work.

"I hear water," I said breathlessly. I'd been listening for everything—wildlife, voices, anything, but our footfalls and my breathing were the only noises that came through until the rushing sound hit my ears.

"We're close to the river." Donner sped up, presumably toward said river.

He stopped on the edge of a precipice and I stopped next to him, my calves and lungs relieved for the break.

"Now, that's a river," I said.

I'd seen my share of rivers, including two of the big ones in the lower forty-eight that bordered my home state, but I'd never seen anything up close like this one. From the plane, I'd seen rushing water, but in person, the ferocity of the foamy water was beyond intimidating.

"You have to be careful around them," Donner said, but even he knew that lesson wasn't necessary to vocalize. He smirked at himself.

"Good fishing though." His eyes scanned the river and then the woods across. "Shit. What's that?"

I followed his glance and soon saw the splash of blue that had garnered his attention.

"Could be anything. A piece of fabric, denim maybe," I said. "Doesn't look like it's attached to anyone."

"No, but that can be deceiving. I need to get over there."

"Is there a bridge?"

"Not anywhere near here." He started to search for something.

Was he going to ride a vine over or fell a tree? It wasn't a wide river, at least not compared to the mighty Missouri and the Mississippi, but surely it would be impossible to survive if you were swept away by it.

"Is there a way around to over there?" I asked.

"Yes." He stopped searching and looked at me. "I'm going to give you some gloves and my keys. Once I get over there, I want you to drive around and pick me up. It'll take you about ten minutes. I can cross in a couple."

"What?"

"Yes. From the cabin, take the first right, then right again, then left. You'll find me at the end of that dirt road. You'll see it. There will be no other options to take anyway, but it's important that you go right first." He took my hand and folded my fingers around his keys and then handed me some gloves from his pocket.

"How are you going to get over there?" Panic bubbled in my throat.

He unhooked something that looked like a thin, black rope from his utility belt and went to work tying it around himself. I watched in silent awe for a moment.

"Are you swinging over?"

"Not exactly."

"I really think we should drive over there," I said firmly.

"What if there's a person who needs help?"

"We'd still have to get them in the truck."

"I can administer first aid. I don't know if we have ten or fifteen more minutes to help them. I can't risk it."

"But. Well. I don't—"

"Beth, come on. Listen to what I say."

I nodded.

"I'm looping the rope around this tree. Here, you hold the end. You'll have plenty of leverage. If you don't let go of the rope, I'll be fine."

"Donner!"

"This will only take a few minutes, and then go, get to the truck."

I felt like I needed just one more minute, another instant to make my case. This wasn't a good idea at all. But I didn't have that minute; he was moving quickly. I glanced at my watch as I took hold of the rope and watched him hurry away, over the precipice, toward the rushing river water, toward, if not certain at least probable, death.

I'd never done anything like this before, but I must have seen the concept somewhere; in a movie or on television. I put the gloves on and braced myself. I could only barely see over the lip of the berm and into the river. I braced myself even more as I saw him step into the water.

His first step was followed immediately by a slip and he went down, falling into a sitting position on what had to be a hard, rocky floor. He stood quickly and waved up at me. "I'm fine."

"Right, whatever," I muttered to myself as I sent him a quick nod, all the while keeping both hands around the rope. It had grown tauter and harder to hold with his slip, but it was better now.

He moved through the water, but not easily. I hoped he'd be able to walk, but there was none of that. He moved with something like a swim but it was more a bob, and something that felt like an awfully lot to ask of my arms and legs. Wasn't this going to take at least ten minutes?

And then halfway across the not-that-wide river, he went under and the rope slipped through my gloved hands.

"No!" I yelled as I squeezed my fingers and gripped the rope with everything I never knew I had in me.

And somehow, it worked. Just before the end of it went through my hands, I got a hold of it again, tightly and surely. I gritted my teeth, leaned my body into the tree trunk I'd been propelled into, and held on. If it took Donner forever to cross that river, I would stand there forever. I wasn't letting go.

I couldn't see when he emerged on the other side, but I was thrown to the ground by the now slacked rope. I looked over. Donner was climbing up the other berm and loosening the rope from around his soaked body. He looked back at me and said, "Go!"

I smiled as a sensation I hadn't felt . . . maybe ever, came over me. Yes, I felt a distinct sense of satisfaction with each book I finished, even while writing their terrible first drafts. I loved what I did, and didn't want to do anything else. But this rush was new, and I liked it.

That crazy, stupid plan had worked. I'd helped. He couldn't have done it without me. I looked at my watch. The crossing of the river had not taken even two minutes. An eternity in two minutes.

I stood and ran to the truck.

Thirty-Two

'm pretty sure it's Willa's bag, backpack. No I.D. but I think I remember seeing it on her," Donner said as I crouched next to him.

I'd driven like a bat out of hell to get to him and it had taken the longest ten minutes of my life; longer than the two minutes he'd taken to cross the river, but seemingly by more than a measly eight minutes.

"Damn."

"I looked around and didn't find anyone, dead or alive. I could search deeper, but I think we need something more organized and more people. I need to get back with Gril, but there's zero signal out here."

I looked at the bag on the ground. Donner had gone through it and the contents were outside of it, spread out for inspection. A wallet, with bills still visible, a comb, some keys, a tube of Chap-Stick, and a small notebook. There was no identification inside the wallet, no credit or debit cards. Only eighty dollars in cash and a few coins. Even I still carried my identification, in the hidden bag around my waist. I'd thought about destroying it once I made it to

Benedict, but if my body ever needed to be identified, the driver's license would help.

"Did you look in the notebook?" I asked.

"Sure did. Nothing, but there were some pages torn from it. Maybe we can figure out what was written on those pages by looking at the top one that's left."

I nodded. "That's possible. There's a chemical. Does Gril have any sort of lab?"

"No, but we might try holding it up to a light or rubbing a pencil over it."

"Not as reliable, but it's been done successfully. Any letter? I saw her reading a letter. She was emotional."

"No letter," Donner said.

I wondered if Gril had searched or had someone search Willa's room yet. I didn't know if Viola had mentioned it to him yet.

We lifted the pack, contents still atop it, and carried it to the truck. Donner placed it on the bench seat in between us and we climbed in.

"You did good back there," he said, still soaking wet as he cranked up the heat. "Thanks for helping. I just couldn't risk the time it would have taken to go around. Someone might have been in imminent danger."

"I get that now."

I didn't want to tell him about the rush I'd felt. It didn't seem quite right. Much about me didn't seem quite right.

"I'm glad we didn't find a dead body," I said.

"Me too."

"Do you have any sense of what's going on? Does Gril?" I asked.

"No," he answered quickly. "It's bizarre and unexpected. Now that we know who she really is we looked her up. Willa isn't a criminal, or she wasn't. She doesn't even have a speeding ticket."

"There has to be a connection to the previous incarnations of George and Linda."

"Seems that way."

Donner pulled his truck to a stop in front of the Benedict House. "You're good to go, but I do thank you for your help."

"You're welcome." I was disappointed that he'd brought me home instead of back to the police cabin, but I didn't argue.

I hopped out, closed the truck door, and went inside. It was getting darker and the only thing I felt like doing in the dark was going inside.

No one was around so I made my way to my room, turned the lock, and put the chair under the doorknob. I wanted to think, I needed to sleep.

Anxiety tightened the muscles in my shoulders and arms. I tried to understand what I was so wound up about but there were so many options that it was impossible to pinpoint anything specific. So much, too much maybe. I thought about setting up my laptop and replying to my mother's email, but I didn't have much patience for her drunken communications. I'd talk to her tomorrow.

Maybe George and Willa would be found overnight, but it would be dark in the woods where we'd found Willa's backpack. I should have asked Donner if a search party would head out tonight. I thought about calling him, but I didn't.

I took some deep breaths and tried to relax all the muscles that were so tight. I needed some time by myself, in my locked room.

It was time to regroup.

Thirty-Three

did manage to relax and fall into a hard sleep. I woke up the next day ready to face whatever might come my way. But, again, I couldn't find anyone. If someone was supposed to be cooking breakfast, they were neglecting their duty. As far as I could tell I was the only person in the Benedict House. I even tried to open Willa's door. I wasn't sure if I would actually go inside and search, but since the door was locked, it wasn't a decision I was forced to make. I knocked on all the other doors but no one answered. I even looked out the window upstairs, but though the hook was still stuck into the side, there was no rope, no Loretta anywhere. No one.

I didn't receive any other emails, from my mother or anyone else. I thought about texting her for a call, but experience told me she might need a few hours to recover this morning.

I grabbed my backpack, wished for a McDonald's drive-thru, and headed to the *Petition*. I thought about taking the time for breakfast in the café, but I was in a hurry. I needed to purchase snacks for my room and the *Petition*, not to mention more whiskey, as soon as possible, but I wanted to get to work, or at least to the building with the good cell phone signal. I was as scattered as my thoughts.

When I turned the bolt on the *Petition*'s door, I realized how much time I spent locking doors.

I pulled out a phone and called Detective Majors.

"Beth?" she said as she answered. "That you?"

"It's me. Anything new?"

"Unfortunately, no. I'm sorry the sketch didn't help. Thanks for the information about the bite though. That might be important at some point."

"Good. I hope so. Can you tell me anything at all?"

She sighed. "We came upon another dead end yesterday, but it still might pan out to something. Any chance you remember a fire around Milton about ten years ago? A guy's barn was burned down by someone he let stay there. Livestock was killed."

"Uh. Yeah," I said, thinking about my mother's emails and feeling something in my gut shift, as if my intuition was telling me again to pay attention, that I should have been paying better attention all along.

"Okay," Detective Majors said. "Well, the guy that burned down the barn, his name was Levi Brooks."

"My mom emailed me," I said weakly. Pain tinged behind my eyes, but I wasn't going to let this happen again. "One of her messages wasn't clear though."

"Okay. We went out to talk to the guy who lives there, Harold Blankenship, but he has no idea where Levi went after the barn burned all those years ago."

"Not that one would help for sure, but is there a booking picture yet? There was an arrest, right?"

"There was an arrest, but no picture yet. Of course, no forwarding address, no real idea where he'd come from either. Probably Missouri, but we just can't be sure."

"Can you hang on a second?" I said.

"Uh. Sure."

I put the phone down and took a deep breath. If another spell or vision or whatever they were was upon me, I hoped to push it away. It was more than that though. Overlapped with foggy memories, that thing I was supposed to be paying attention to suddenly came clear. I remembered something that might be important to everything that had happened to me recently.

I picked up the phone a long moment later. "Detective Majors, where's my mom?"

"When I left Milton yesterday, she and the chief, Stellen Graystone, were going out for drinks. I went out there to talk to Mr. Blankenship with Stellen. Stellen's a good cop; he might be able to help us in our search, told me more than I think your mother wanted him to, but I'm sorry we didn't get anything from Blankenship regarding the barn fire."

"I just remembered something. We got a letter back when that fire happened. An anonymous note that said my dad had been seen at the scene of the fire. That's all it said. I remember Mom flying off the handle about it—but we were living with my grandfather by that time, so she went out to 'investigate' on her own. She couldn't find anything about my dad being there. You need to find her. She's got Levi's scent in her nose, or some scent. She's after someone or some information specifically. She'll get herself killed."

"You got a letter?" It was her turn to take a deep breath, let it out, but hers sounded more like a frustrated sigh. "Start over with that, Beth. Tell me the details again."

"There's not much more to tell."

"Where's that letter?"

"I have no idea, but if you find my mom, she might have it with her."

"Okay, Beth, let's spend a few minutes talking about your dad."

I nodded and we continued.

Thirty-Four

What if Levi Brooks had something to do with my dad? I didn't see how that worked together, but the coincidences kept piling up. Or it was just a small world after all. Battling memories and flashbacks, I told Detective Majors more about that time so long ago, when my mother first lost her mind, when she first became obsessed. I told her what I remembered about that note, just a quick handwritten thing that said someone saw "Eddy" there at the fire. That was it. It could have been a convenient prank, sent by someone who just liked to jerk people around.

Or someone could have seen my father at the scene of a crime that someone named Levi Brooks had committed.

It was unbelievable, and yet it had all actually happened. Nothing was unbelievable anymore.

We talked about the past, the letter, my mother, and that weird, obsessive time in our lives when I was saved by my grandfather. No one was going to be able to save my mother. She lived her obsessions. She would probably die because of them too.

The conversation with the detective also took me back again to when I moved in with and then eventually worked for my grandfather. I'd been so good with numbers. Gifted. Talented. Skills that helped solve crimes, or at least prepare reports. Grandpa had sometimes looked at me long moments and shook his head. I could see things—triangulations. I didn't even know it was something everyone else didn't have, didn't see the space in a room and where a bullet might have gone if shot off from different spots. Gramps knew though, he said I had a rare special intelligence.

Lord, girl, you are smart enough for two people, he'd say.

I didn't tell Detective Majors that part.

Since I'd started writing full-time, I hadn't had to use those gifts in any practical application for a long, long time. They weren't gone though; they'd simply become rusty. Until, during a moment in the conversation with Detective Majors when something occurred to me, something all about numbers.

Measurements. There was something wrong with the measurements.

No there wasn't, I told myself. But the voice was persistent.

After we disconnected the call and I thought more about it, it stuck there in my mind refusing to leave. The numbers came together in my head in a terrifying way.

Measurements at the Rafferty cabin. Something was off. I suddenly realized what was wrong. I had broken almost all of my grandfather's rules.

"Oh. . . . shiiit!" I grabbed my bag and hurried out of the *Petition,* forgetting to lock the door behind me. Forgetting everything but one small thing. Something that, in fact, was probably bigger than I'd originally thought.

The beauty of the Alaska morning was lost on me in my rush to get back to the police cabin. I ran up the steps and found the door locked.

I banged on it with my fist. "Anyone there?"

No one answered.

I pulled out the phone that was in my pocket, but it wasn't the same burner that I'd used to call the police before. The number wasn't in the recently called list and I'd left Gril's and Donner's cards at the *Petition*.

I hurried back to the truck and drove the short distance to the Benedict House.

No one was there either. Where was everyone?

I grabbed a piece of paper and wrote a note to Viola. *I'm running out to the Rafferty cabin to look at something. Come find me if I'm not back in a couple hours. I couldn't find Gril's number. Let him know too.* I signed off with my name and the time.

Viola was not going to be happy, but I wasn't sure exactly why. I just knew she wouldn't want me to do what I was going to do, but I couldn't wait another minute.

Finally, I jumped into my truck and headed out toward the Raffertys' cabin. I *had* done the math. I had even seen that entryway—Gril had made sure I went with Donner to see the space. But I had made what my grandfather would have called one of the biggest mistakes ever. No, two of them. 1) I didn't measure with a real ruler or measuring tape. 2) I didn't take the time to look at everything around me with doubt. Gramps used to tell us all: *Doubt everything, double-, triple-check everything, and for God's sake, measure at least twice.*

The numbers that had been written in the file and the ones I'd had in my head when I'd looked inside the Rafferty cabin were written down in centimeters. But that space where Linda had died was bigger than those centimeter measurements, I was *now* almost sure. It was something I would have noticed years ago—but that was a long time ago now. The ME had based her conclusion of suicide on a blood spatter measurement of thirty-two centimeters—I remembered the report Gril had shown me; I could still visualize it. If that measurement was actually thirty-two *inches,* either Linda would have had a harder time holding the gun to her own head or it simply wouldn't have been possible. I just needed to see that space again.

I should measure exactly, but I didn't have any way to do that. But now that I knew what I was looking for, I could peer inside briefly. Thirty-two centimeters was a little over twelve inches— twenty inches away from thirty-two inches—a long way. A glance inside, even without measuring, could probably tell me if everything was off by about twelve inches.

My truck rumbled over the dirt road, and I was again grateful for the new tires. I remembered what Donner had said about conducting a better search of the area where we'd found the backpack. Maybe that's where everyone had gone.

I'd get to the Rafferty cabin, but maybe everyone else was searching the woods behind it. That's where I'd look first. I turned and re-directed the truck toward the spot where we'd found the backpack, but I didn't see anyone else on the way.

Had this area already been searched? Where else might they be searching?

I parked next to the tracks I'd made the day before and hopped out of the truck. There was no one anywhere, but the woods weren't as thick here as they were in other areas and the sky was clear blue up above the tall treetops. I walked to where the pack had been.

Curiosity made me temporarily change gears. How did the pack get here? The only possibilities I could fathom were that it was thrown across the river, which someone with a good, strong arm could manage; or someone put it there after traveling the circu-itous route I'd taken, because I didn't think the other direction made sense. The other direction was the ocean. Finally, I wondered if there was another way across the river, a way that was farther down, that Donner didn't know about. I dismissed the possibility of him not knowing about it; he probably knew everything about these woods.

I took another moment or two of thought, but I looked in the direction where I thought the Raffertys' cabin was located. I set out that way. I hiked with some confidence, telling myself I would turn back if the path became too much to handle or if I felt like I was getting too far away from the truck. However, I didn't have to go much farther before I came upon a bridge, of sorts.

"Ah-ha!" I exclaimed, my voice pinging with a surprising echo, as I spotted a fallen trunk, wide and secure enough on each side of the river to serve as a bridge. Donner and I would have seen it if we'd moved down some, but if he knew about it, he hadn't wanted to take the time to get to it.

I didn't walk across it, but it wouldn't have been too difficult. Unless you fell in the river, it would be a short, easy trek.

I turned and looked back in the direction of the truck. I couldn't see it but since I'd traveled the path of the river, I'd be able to get back easily.

I looked over the bridge and tried to think if I knew where I was in relation to the Raffertys' cabin. Was I correct in thinking it was straight out from the bridge? I stepped closer and peered at the spot in the berm where the trunk had landed on this side of the river. The mud splayed around it had seen recent trauma. Grass or weeds covered the berm—except for that spot. This trunk had been turned into a bridge *recently*. And, that first day I'd come out with Donner, George had sprung from the woods in decent shape. He didn't look to have spent even one night out in the elements. Maybe he hadn't been away from his cabin; maybe he'd slept there and had lied to the police, or there was another place he'd gone.

I looked the other direction, toward the woods and toward where I thought the ocean would inevitably be found. Was there a shelter out there somewhere?

I stood and looked hard. My eyes zeroed in on a dark patch in the distance. It was far enough away that I couldn't be sure I was seeing anything more than shadowed leaves.

I didn't know what I was doing, really, but I had put extra socks into my jacket pockets. No one had told me to do it, but I'd walked through so much mud since arriving in Alaska that it seemed like a prudent idea. I took out one of the bright white socks and tied it to a high branch in a tree not far from the bridge. I would try to walk in a straight line and then put the other sock on a branch about half-way to the dark spot. Hopefully, my plan would help me get back to where I'd originally come from.

It wasn't until I'd passed well beyond the halfway mark where I'd tied the other sock, that I realized the dark spot was the tip of a hut-like structure. Someone *had* built a shelter out of tree branches and old blankets. It was almost as primitive as a kids' fort. If we hadn't noticed the backpack, Donner and I probably would have found it the day before.

Keeping a distance from the seemingly abandoned fort, I grabbed my phone and tried to call Gril. I knew there was no signal, but I had to try. It was a useless effort.

I needed to do two things: make sure there wasn't someone who needed help inside the hut, and get the hell out of there.

"Shit." I put the phone in my pocket. "Hey, anybody there? My name is Beth and I'm new in town. I'm a bit lost."

I sounded like a fool.

And, I received no response. I listened hard and heard absolutely nothing. Even *all the wildlife* was quiet, like when you knew no one was home.

I approached. "Hey. Anybody there?"

Still no answer. I didn't hesitate much longer before I pulled back one of the blanket walls. I was momentarily impressed. It was bigger than it seemed from the outside camouflage of branches.

About eight feet by eight feet, it was equipped with a cot, a small table, and an electric lantern. I recognized all the items as things be-ing sold in the Mercantile. Wrappers from cheese or peanut butter and cracker packets littered the blanket that had been thrown onto the ground. I looked up at the roof, a piece of aluminum. It was a good shelter, and would keep the rain away.

There was no indication who used it, but I smelled something that made me think of George Rafferty. I hadn't noticed that he smelled like Zest soap, but either I was smelling it now or I was making up my own imaginary story about where he'd been after his wife died.

I just couldn't understand why.

Since no one needed assistance, I wanted to get out of there and back to town. I left the shelter and set out for the first white sock. It was easy. I followed the path with no problem, but when I made it to the second sock, my confidence high and my sense of safety only growing, I heard a high-pitched scream.

I froze and listened hard. The longer I stood there, my hands up and reaching for the sock, something happened. That scream I wasn't sure I'd heard turned into my own screams, at least memories of them.

I was in Levi's van. I screamed and yelled. Begged and pleaded too, but mostly, I screamed. Someone was bound to hear me at some point.

Levi didn't try to stop me. He just laughed. I could see his blue eyes now, and hear his maniacal laugh.

"No!" I yelled in the here and now.

My gaze landed on my hands, still up and reaching for the sock. How long had I been standing there? Had I lost seconds or minutes?

During those long, frozen moments, my hands iced. I hadn't seen a glacier in Alaska yet, but I was suddenly cold to the bone. I was ice.

But I had to shake it off, get past whatever this was.

I'd almost forgotten about the real scream I thought I'd heard, but it was when another one rang through the forest that I came fully back to reality. Someone was screaming; someone needed help.

I stood and headed the direction I thought the scream was coming from. It wasn't an easy journey through the woods, which got thicker as I went, but my boots kept my feet dry, warm, and safe from sharp things as I trudged clumsily along. I couldn't break into a run, but I moved as quickly as I could. Long seconds passed and then as I came around some trees, I saw the Rafferty cabin.

I was breathing heavily as I stopped and tried to look in all directions. I bent over with my hands on my thighs, and waited to see something or hear another scream. Had I gone the right way?

It didn't take long to learn the answer, and for all hell to break loose. Again.

Thirty-Five

Two people came into view. Fists flying. Bodies being pummeled, falling, getting up again. They weren't skilled fighters, but they were both trying their physical hardest. I recognized them—Willa and George Rafferty. They were both holding their own, even though George was bigger.

I couldn't quite tell what was going on, and I was fully aware that I didn't know who the bad guy was in this scenario. Did one of them, or both of them, conspire to kill Linda? Or had she taken her own life and they were fighting for a reason I couldn't understand yet? Gril didn't think Linda had killed herself. No one I talked to seemed to think so.

But something was wrong, someone was in danger.

"Hey!" I yelled as I ran to them.

The battle stopped, and in an instant they both looked at me. It only took that instant for me to read the situation better. Willa was afraid. George was the angry, violent one. Murderous. And Willa was terrified, fighting for her life, defending her life.

I hoped I was right.

Levi's face wanted to crowd into my view, but with an effort that made me sick to my stomach, I pushed him away again.

"What's going on?" I asked. "Just . . . just you two just step away from each other."

"Who the fuck are you? What are you doing here?" George asked, but he didn't let go of his grip around Willa's wrist.

It was then that I realized George Rafferty and I had never shared a conversation. Actually, we'd never even seen each other, both of us with our eyes open. His voice was deep, and his eyes bright. He'd been the subject of my Internet searches, and my book with my picture rested on an end table in his cabin, but he must not have heard about the new girl in town.

"Is everything okay?" I said.

"No! Just get out of here!" Willa yelled, though her words were cut short as George grabbed her and swung his arm around her neck.

"No, no, come on now, whatever it is, let's just talk about it," I said, my hand up as I took steps toward them.

"Get out of here!" George said.

And then, with the arm that wasn't around Willa, he pulled out a gun. In pictures or in movies, people wielding guns didn't seem so out of proportion. Suddenly, the vision of George seemed to waver and his arm became too big for his body but not big enough for the giant gun.

I knew a memory of Levi was again trying to crowd its way in and set my vision funny.

"Get the fuck away!" I yelled as I balled my fists.

Either George loosened his grip some or Willa squirmed enough, or both. She got free from his arm. She pushed him to the ground, sending the gun flying toward some trees. I was back in the moment, and we all watched it. Time slowed as the gun twirled through the air and then landed with a sickening thud.

In the next heartbeat time whirred back up to speed and Willa set off in a run—though I didn't know where she was going—and George speed-crawled toward the gun.

Just as Willa almost made it behind a tree, the gun fired. I hadn't moved, but my body reacted to the noise; my eyes shut and my hands went up to my ears. When my eyes were closed, more memories of Levi threatened to make their way in. I opened my eyes and looked at Willa.

She was upright and hiding behind a tree.

"Run!" I told her.

I knew George was there somewhere in the background, with the gun, but I couldn't focus on him, even though I knew I should. I should find cover. I was out in the open, exposed. He could shoot me dead even if he didn't have good aim.

Finally, though it might have only been a second later, I lifted a foot. The other one followed behind and I ran to my own tree. With my back against the trunk, another shot fired. I heard a whistle that I thought happened only in movies, but I didn't know where the bullet had gone.

I looked over to see Willa, still hiding behind a tree. She was holding her arm and blood oozed through her fingers. She'd been hit but I didn't know when—that bullet or an earlier one?

"Just run!" I yelled. I didn't know if that was a good plan, but it was the only idea that came to me.

"He did it!" she yelled. "He's the one who was driving. I saw him. Linda wanted to go home, tell the police the truth. She wanted both of them to be forgiven. I'm sure he killed her."

"Okay, we'll get it worked out," I said. She wanted me to know what had actually happened. She wanted someone to know. I could put the pieces together, but now wasn't the time. I muttered quietly, "Don't die," and yelled again, "Run!"

Why wouldn't she move?

She shook her head. "I'm not going to make it."

"Yes, you are! It's just your arm."

But I noticed that the gun hadn't fired again, and after two beats and more silence from Willa, I had an urge peek around the tree. I took a deep breath and held it as I leaned around.

It was what George had been waiting for—someone to look, a target he could aim for. He pulled the trigger again and a bullet came in my direction. It ricocheted off the tree but scared me so much that it sent me to the place I'd been trying so hard to avoid. The van and Levi's voice filled my head so completely that I didn't know if I was ever going to get out of there again.

Even running to Alaska wasn't going to save me this time.

Thirty-Six

"You are mine!" Levi said as he pushed back on my shoulders.

My back hit a lump in the floor of the van. I cringed and tears squeezed through my eyes. I wondered if I'd cracked a rib.

"Open your eyes. Look at me."

I did as he commanded, but his face was still a blur; I couldn't even see the blue of his eyes now. He moved on top of me and kneed himself in between my legs. No matter how much I tried to keep them together, he got them apart. Tears started to fall out of my eyes and down the sides of my face.

"You will never be anybody else's."

"No!" I tried kicking, elbowing, biting at the air, but he was stronger than anything I did.

Bile moved up my throat, but I couldn't throw up. I wanted to. I tried. If I could throw up on him, maybe he wouldn't do what I knew he was going to do.

He stuck one of his dirty socks into my mouth. "Shut the fuck up."

The humiliation was worse than the pain and it fueled me. I squirmed, I kicked, I spit out the sock. I did whatever I could.

For long beats, he did nothing, just sat still atop me.

"Why? Why don't you love me?" he finally said.

"I will never love you." My voice was oddly quiet, maybe sinister, I'm not sure. But it did what it needed to do. Or something did.

He propelled himself off me and out of the van, slamming the sliding door shut. He was furious, yelling, screaming. I tried to get up, wriggle my way out of the van too. I would fight him, with my fists, with whatever it took. If I could just get out.

But I couldn't. He'd zip-tied one of my ankles to one of the seat braces. I hadn't even noticed until I sat up and saw the tie. Once I did, I noticed the pain as the plastic tie dug into my skin.

But I had won, even if it was a small victory. He hadn't raped me. I don't know if he didn't really want to, couldn't, or if I wasn't behaving as he wished I would.

But I wasn't naïve enough to think it would last. He was broken, and he'd either break or kill me at some point, probably not long from now.

I had to get out of that van. And I would, I just had to come up with a plan.

As tears of victory and frustration and fear continued to roll down my cheeks, I turned my head to the side and saw something. There, if I focused on that envelope, a piece of junk mail he'd thrown in the back, atop that bright, pink blanket, I could think. I could come up with a plan.

"I don't want to do this. I don't want this. I don't want to die," I muttered.

"What? Nope, you're not dying!" A voice said before someone slapped me hard.

"Ouch," I said as my hand went up to my cheek and my eyes opened and moved out of the past. "Viola?"

"There you are," she said. "You're going to be okay. Come on now. I don't like slapping folks who've had brain surgery, but you gotta do what you gotta do."

I was still in the spot behind the tree, but I was sitting on the ground. "What? What happened?"

"You saved Willa's life, probably," Viola said. "We all got here just as George was trying to reload the gun. Gril grabbed him—it's something to behold when that big man can run faster than who he's chasing. I'll never forget it." Viola smiled.

"You all?"

"Yeah, we all met at the lodge and got our search party instructions. We caravanned out here, planned to start with the woods behind George's cabin and then head over to where you and Donner found Willa's backpack. Imagine our surprise when we came upon this scene."

"I was pretty surprised too," I managed to say.

"I bet. What the hell were you doing here?"

"I . . . I was also searching the woods. There's a shelter out there. I found it."

"You did? I'll be."

"Who killed Linda?"

"Still don't know, but we're working on it. We know this though, George was shooting at you and Willa. Come on, let's get you up and looked at by Powder. You were in a weird daze. All the shooting probably put you into shock."

"Probably," I said.

"Come on."

Viola helped me stand and led me around the tree. I was surprised by the crowd. It looked like the entire town was there, all five hundred of them. But some were leaving, packing into vehicles and driving back down the road toward the civilization that was made up of only a corner.

"We tried to let you know about the search party. I knocked on your door, but didn't want to bother you too much. Now, I wish I would have," Viola said as she led me toward a truck. "You shouldn't have been out here alone."

I nodded but my mouth was dry and I was trying to stave off some tunnel vision. I didn't want to faint, or whatever I'd done, again. There were no ambulances in sight, no paramedics, but Dr.

Powder was looking at Willa's arm as she sat on the open tailgate of the truck we were walking toward.

"Get her up here," Powder said to Viola. "I'll look at her next."

As if I was a child, Viola hoisted me up to the tailgate and then walked away.

Willa didn't look at me at first, but kept her gaze on the ground.

"You coming along saved me, I'm sure," she said quietly.

"I don't know. You were holding your own during that fight." I still didn't understand what had happened, but I saw that George was handcuffed to the door handle of Gril's truck. I didn't know if Willa would be handcuffed too, after her wound was attended to.

She might not tell me, but I asked, "What the hell happened, Willa? Did you kill Linda Rafferty?"

Dr. Powder sent me a quick frown but kept working on Willa's gunshot wound.

"Of course not," Willa said. She sucked in a breath as Dr. Powder wrapped her arm with gauze. "I saw the accident, in Detroit, the one where the boy was killed."

"You weren't in it? You weren't related to the boy?"

"No, I was just a witness. I saw it happen and I saw George and Linda switch seats after it happened. I was the only witness, the only reliable one anyway."

"You didn't tell the police you saw them switch?"

She shook her head. "No, I saw . . . an opportunity. You know."

"Blackmail?"

"Yeah."

"And they paid you?"

"Until they disappeared." She paused as if she wasn't going to continue. She looked at the doctor and then over at me. "I missed the money, still needed it. I found them here. I was pretty smart how I did it too, smarter than I'd ever been. Then Linda and I talked some. She wasn't going to pay me any money anymore. She decided to tell the Detroit police what had actually happened. I tried to talk her out of it, but instead she talked me out of it. Told me how important the truth was and all that bullshit, wrote me a letter all about it. I fell for it. I believed her. But then he," she nodded toward George, "figured out what was going on. He killed her. He wanted to kill me too. Jesus, why didn't I just tell the police?"

"Why couldn't he take the rap?" I said.

"He's a piece of shit. Used to sell drugs. Would have been his third strike. He'd have probably gone away for a long time. It was Linda's first strike. I didn't find this out until later though. I knew something was up when they switched seats, was smart enough to keep it to myself until I approached them later." She sounded proud of herself.

"Good grief." I paused. "Did he have you out at that shelter in the woods?"

"Yeah, but he didn't hurt me out there. He said he was just trying to figure out what to do. He thought he'd be able to get out of here without being noticed, but the police started watching everything more closely. The guys at the ferry and the airport were taking names and IDs and shit. George was trying to figure out a way to sneak onto the ferry. He just wanted me out of circulation until he got away. I ran away instead. You found us not long after he caught up with me. He was going to kill me, I'm sure."

"You didn't think he would kill you out there?" I looked toward the woods.

"I did at first, but I think killing his wife messed him up pretty bad. I think he thought he could get away with everything. He knew I was lying too; he didn't think I'd risk running, risk everyone knowing what I was really up to." She laughed once. "If he'd figured out a way to sneak onto the ferry, we both might have gotten away, but he was getting crazier by the minute. I got scared, and I just didn't want to be around him."

I hoped Dr. Powder wasn't being easy with her. I wanted to shake her and tell her she was an idiot, but her ruse to get to Benedict *had* been clever. However, I wasn't in the mood to even pretend to be friendly. "You're not the best at blackmail, Willa. You might want to consider a new line of work. Once you're out of prison and all."

"All right, all right." Gril approached. "That's enough, Willa." He looked at Dr. Powder. "She ready to go?"

"She needs to get to Juneau. She's going to be fine, but I'm not fully equipped to care for her wound. They'll do better."

Gril sighed. "Donner will take her and George to Juneau. Hank's getting the plane ready."

Gril helped Willa off the back of the tailgate and handed her to Donner before he turned back to me as Dr. Powder put a stethoscope up to my heart.

"You okay?" Gril asked.

"I was on my way to the Rafferty's cabin. I think the ME used centimeters instead of inches. That would have thrown off the bullet trajectory. If so, Linda couldn't have been holding the gun that killed her," I said. "That's what I was going to do, see if it was supposed to have been inches instead of centimeters. That would change everything."

Gril rubbed his chin. "Dammit. I can't believe I missed that, but you're probably right."

"I can't believe I missed it either. I told you I was good at that sort of thing, but I didn't take my time. I didn't measure for myself. I didn't doubt what I was seeing." Gramps would be so disappointed.

"She okay?" Gril asked the doctor.

"Fine. Heart rate's up a bit, but she'll be okay."

"Come on, Beth, let's go measure together," Gril said. "If you're up for it."

"I am." I slid off the tailgate carefully, testing my legs. They were fine, and no more tunnel vision. I looked around to see if anyone was listening. No one was. "Gril, there's a copy of my book inside the cabin, it was open to my author bio and picture."

"Oh, shit, Beth. That was me. I'm sorry. I didn't even . . . When I was searching the cabin, I saw the book and opened it. You don't look a thing like that picture, by the way. You've disguised yourself well. I'm so sorry."

Relief swept through me. "Willa said George killed Linda. I think I got the story."

"Yeah, something about Linda telling the police he was the driver who'd killed that kid, his third strike. I'll work on getting him to tell me all the details. Son of a bitch that he is. Juneau police and I will get the answers, Beth, I promise."

"I believe you will."

"Come on, let's go take some measurements."

I followed Gril, but stopped at the Rafferty's doorway and looked back. Lots of people were still milling around. Donner, George, and Willa were gone, but Viola and Loretta were still there. So was Trinity; she stood at the edge of the crowd and bit at her fingernail.

Benny and Serena and the woman I'd met at the visitor's center, Maper, were gathered together discussing something.

Orin was there too, talking to a man I hadn't met yet. He caught me looking at him and smiled, and, of course, sent me a peace sign. I had something I wanted to talk to him about.

Most important, and even though he was still in my head, Levi Brooks wasn't there. He wasn't in Alaska. He couldn't be. I was safe for now. But for how long?

My hands iced again with remaining fear or some sort of premonition. I wiped them on my stiff jeans and they thawed some. I followed Gril inside.

Thirty-Seven

opened the email.

Hi, Baby Girl. How be ya? I hope you are doing okay. Sure
do miss you. Glad you're safe.

I know it's not the best news, but I wanted to let you know
that we've all hit dead ends. Stellen can't find the Levi
Brooks that burned down the barn. He and his girl Friday
will keep working on it, but I get a weird sense that it's
not the same Levi we're looking for. I could be wrong, but
I sense that we will hit another dead end there. Really,
there might be two bad-guy Levi Brooks. Shit, I don't
know.

BUT, I'm not giving up. None of us are.

Detective Majors told me she told you they got DNA off
that blanket. Yours, and two unknowns. Hard for me to

believe Levi hadn't done anything before to get put in the system yet, but any-fucking-thing is possible. Right?

That old Jesus-loving woman, Geneva, and I have a plan. Fingers crossed it works out. That's all I'm going to tell you for now. Don't tell Majors, though. Don't worry about it. I got this.

I haven't given up. Neither have the police, but I'll get this taken care of long before they do, you can count on that.

Love you more than sauce on my tacos. Talk soon.

Me.

"Oh, Mom," I said with a sigh.

She would hunt him like she'd hunted my father. She would probably never find either of them. Or at least I hoped not. The police would find Brooks. Eventually. I hoped.

I'd sent emails to my agent and editor already this morning. I was going to get back to work. I was sure they'd be happy to hear I was ready to try. I planned on calling Dr. Genero to talk about some sort of therapy, even virtual therapy if it wasn't like a sitcom I'd heard about.

Detective Majors had emailed me about the blanket, but even though her words were positive, I sensed she felt the same way my mother did: frustrated by the dead ends.

The parolees were all gone. It was just me and Viola this morning. Viola had bought me breakfast at the café. I'd eaten the best pancakes I'd ever tasted. I was already excited to eat them again tomorrow.

Loretta and Trinity had gone back to Anchorage. I didn't know what would happen to them, and we made no plans to keep in touch. I really didn't think Trinity's hometown of Washington, Missouri, had anything to do with me, but I would keep that fact filed away for a while.

George and Willa were taken to Juneau with plans to get them back to Detroit. Willa had at least told the truth, in the end. She *had* come to Benedict to let George and Linda know she still wanted money from them. Linda told her she was tired of living a lie—that really was the letter I'd seen Willa reading.

Time to come clean. Time to live an honest life. You should live honestly too, Willa. It's the only way to live.

In fact, it had been Willa who Linda had been arguing with next to the lodge, but that argument hadn't been about Willa wanting more money. It had been about the fact that Willa thought Linda shouldn't have told George that she wanted to come clean, go back to Detroit. Willa thought Linda was in danger, that George wasn't going to go back without a fight. It had been much worse than a mere fight.

Gril had gone over to Juneau to question George with the Juneau police. Apparently, George had broken quickly, admitted to killing Linda and making it look like a suicide. The ME and I, and every-damn-one else, according to Gril, had the measurements wrong. If inches had been used instead of centimeters, the police would never have thought Linda killed herself. My grandfather would be mighty impressed by Gril's tenacity. But he'd be pretty darn angry we'd all missed the obvious. Gramps didn't like it when the obvious was missed.

I smiled sadly to myself.

That was the thing I didn't see coming, how much all of what had happened to me, in Missouri and here in Alaska, would make me miss my grandfather. Or miss him more than I already did.

George would face murder charges in two states—Michigan and Alaska. His three strikes would now be four, and the murder of his wife would trump everything. To satisfy everyone's curiosity, Gril found the baby in Detroit. The expectant mother was, in fact, Linda's niece. She hadn't heard from her aunt for a few years and was happy to hear that the baby had given Linda some happy news, but desperately sad about the turn of events.

Willa was in trouble too, but I didn't know how much. I was still impressed by her ability to hide in plain sight. I was doing the same, though I hoped with better intentions.

It was a new day, and I really wanted to begin a new life. I was safe from my captor. I was far away. More than that, I'd gotten away from him. I still didn't remember the exact way I got out of that van, but I hoped it was something good, something that might have hurt that evil man even more than my rejection had. Maybe it would come to me.

However, there *was* something trying to edge its way into my thoughts.

What was it? Was it those moments I'd escaped?

I was going to have to close my eyes and think hard about it. I didn't really want to, but I was compelled to.

I took a deep breath and closed my eyes as my thoughts went back to the visions I'd seen yesterday when all hell had broken loose at the Rafferty cabin. This time, it was as if my memory could skim over things. I didn't *feel* them quite so much. It seemed too fast, though; I was going to miss something important.

But, no, the subconscious doesn't work that way. If it wants you to remember something, it won't skim over it. It will stop right where it needs to stop and show you what it wants to show you. Well, that's what it did this time.

And there it was.

I was in the van again, looking at the pink blanket and the envelope. Those things had let me focus on something other than Levi. That envelope was one he'd picked up from someone's tardy mail run, when he'd been looking for money or credit cards he knew how to activate and use.

That envelope had been addressed to Levi Brooks.

My eyes popped open in the here and now. Oh, no, my kidnapper's name wasn't Levi Brooks. I'd been so sure it was because that was the name that had stuck with me, the only thing that had been so clear. But, Levi Brooks hadn't kidnapped me. In a way, he'd saved me.

Oh no. Oh, fucking no, Mill would say.

I picked up the phone again, this time with shaky fingers to call Detective Majors, but it started vibrating in my hand before I could hit send. I recognized the number as Gril's.

"Gril?" I answered.

"Beth, I need your help. We've had . . . there's no way to talk around this, but we've had a body come ashore. I need you to come as soon as possible and help me with . . . some things. I'm sorry. Donner is on his way to pick you up."

I nodded, but didn't say anything as I hung up the phone.

I'd have to call Detective Majors later.